Georgina studied creative writing and film at university and has since pursued a career in videogames journalism, covering some of the most popular games in the world. Her psychological thrillers are inspired by her surroundings, from the congested London streets to the raw English countryside. She can be found playing games, writing stories, and reading anything from fantasy to crime fiction.

 twitter.com/glees_author

# THE GIRL UPSTAIRS

## GEORGINA LEES

One More Chapter
a division of HarperCollins*Publishers*
1 London Bridge Street
London SE1 9GF

www.harpercollins.co.uk

HarperCollins*Publishers*
1st Floor, Watermarque Building, Ringsend Road
Dublin 4, Ireland

This paperback edition 2021

6

First published in Great Britain in ebook format
by HarperCollins*Publishers* 2021
Copyright © Georgina Lees 2021
Georgina Lees asserts the moral right to be identified
as the author of this work

A catalogue record of this book is available from the British Library

ISBN: 978-0-00-848542-9

You said I don't understand love
Gated by worlds I cannot reach
Inexperienced and incredulous
Love is something you cannot teach
I tried, though, in many ways
To untangle and construct
Build it from a simple base
Plant a seed that buds
But seasons have come and gone
And I am left untouched
My soil spoiled from recklessness
My roots shattered to dust
You said I don't understand love
And even though you're right
In the dark, barren undergrowth
There's a small sliver of light.

## Chapter One

I heard Emily before I met her. The harsh smack of heels against cheap wooden floorboards. The gentle buzz of a phone followed by a surge of high-pitched notes, sometimes angry, sometimes excited, rarely sad. The sadness came through the slim pipes in the bathroom, the soft gurgles that slipped down the plumbing and escaped through my extractor fan. The incessant music thrumming through the ceiling, invading my space. Emily has terrible taste, mostly new tracks, screeching pop singers holding long, high notes, the same beat in every song.

I knew Emily before I met her. Italian food on Mondays, meatballs rich and smothered in tomato sauce. Tuesdays, something eggy. Wednesdays, something meaty. Thursdays and Fridays, mostly wine. A takeaway on Saturdays, usually Chinese, the sticky leftover noodles escaping through the shared food waste bin like silky worms breaking through soil. Sometimes I could smell the food and other times I knew from a discarded receipt in our communal hallway.

On Sunday the shake of bottles being emptied into the recycling bin outside from her weekly wine shop. A crate of six, always. They sound lovely from the tasting notes I found clinging to the letter box. A Malbec, blackberry and vanilla notes with a finish of chocolate and nutmeg, soft and warm.

I've been in London for over ten years now and I haven't found a quiet place. I live in Angel, Islington. The nice part, with the grand white townhouses, the ones advertised as being on tree-lined streets. I can't see any trees, just blunt shavings in the ground, weeds rising and arching over the stubs like gravestones. I'm on the ground floor of a two-storey house and Emily is above me. She moved in over six months ago and I thought she might leave, as people do here. People Emily's age, early twenties, they come and go like the seasons and it's spring now. Time for new life. Time for Emily to leave.

How do you afford to live there? It slips off everyone's tongue so easily. Why is everyone so concerned – so intrusive? I'm in marketing, I say, and I can see the forced smile at the broad term, the mouth widening and the gentle nod. Meeting new people has become tiresome, so now I prefer to stay inside with my books. Things that can't judge, objects without expression. Thirty-five, living alone, in marketing. I stare out onto the street as the rain sluices through my open windows and down raspberry-coloured curtains, like fingers through hair. The black streetlamp glows faintly in the ghostly evening haze, a cat is whisked into a bush and cars fight through the wall of rain. There is always noise.

I pick up a cup of coffee from the table wedged into the bay window and take a sip. I let the bitterness tear through my mouth, down my throat and into the warmth of my belly. It grumbles. I'll cook dinner soon, a lasagne tonight. Mondays are Italian night after all.

Work was long today, monotonous, and I think how much I don't care. Do people know? They must. I exist at work, quietly and unimposingly, but that's threatening, isn't it? It threatens the nature of those who swap stories on what they cooked for dinner, the film they saw at the weekend, the latest true-crime documentary. I work at a design agency, in the copywriting department. I close my eyes. A stepping stone, I always used to say, but there is nowhere left to step. The specks of rain ricochet onto my face and I smile. An ambulance roars in the distance and a man's coarse voice rises in the street outside. I take a deep breath and taste nothing but the expelled fumes from a passing car; I open my eyes and lean forward to close the window.

I see Emily walking up the street, her slight frame shielded by a large umbrella, her incongruous red wellies flicking dirt into her path. She has her tanned legs exposed in a short denim dress, a charming brown coat skims her figure and long brown hair emerges, clutching her face like a web. I sink back behind the curtain. The familiar jingle of Emily's heavy keychain and the rattle of the key. A sharp slam of the door and a fuss to get her wet wellies off. She'll leave them in our shared hallway, as she always does when it rains. I've laid paper out for her before, but she misses, leaving them inches from the edge. I choose not to think it's deliberate, but I know people like her, entitled and uncompromising.

She trudges up the stairs and I risk a peek around the corner of my door. The red wellies lie on their side, mud mixing into the shabby carpet and flicked up the small table we use for our post. I put my door on the latch and tread carefully into the hallway, stand up the wellies and place them on a spread newspaper. Emily won't know, she won't care. I glance at the post on the table; she didn't take hers up. I can see a letter in a slim white envelope with her name and address scrawled in curly handwriting. Not important to her, nothing is. I take the letter, walk up the staircase quietly and place it on her tattered doormat where she won't be able to miss it.

I stoop carefully back into my flat and close the door. I walk across the small lounge and into the kitchen area. I bend down and pluck a lasagne from the freezer and turn the oven on. Emily flicks on her TV and the noise drones down as if escaping her. She is heavy-footed, and

4

I can hear her move from room to room, the various sounds that she is home. The snap of the fridge door, the flush of the toilet, the phone calls. Noises designed to cover her loneliness. Well, it won't work, I say aloud. She won't hear me.

The smell of tomato and basil sifts through the ceiling and settles on my taste buds. She plonks down in front of the TV and the sofa shifts forward, the TV turned up. She's placed her phone on the floor and I can hear the dense vibrations directly above me, taunting me. I look up and catch myself in the lounge mirror, my face scrunched and deep frown lines clawing my forehead, my pale complexion a host to dark purple circles under my eyes. My sandy blonde hair is knotted into two plaits resting on bony shoulders. I sob, but I can't hear myself above the deep static tones of Emily's television; as with her, noise is more important right now and I let the tears drift away and place my lasagne in the oven.

I slip my phone out of my bag and see the familiar missed calls, my mum and my sister. They'll be worried. I text the group family chat saying I'm fine. My mum sends a hug emoji back, followed by:

*Shall we call later?*

I wince at the thought and type back,

*No I've got some work to do, maybe tomorrow.*

She won't take it personally, but she'll worry. I look up. I need for her not to come here. It will break me if she does, noise I don't need, can't fit in right now. I type again,

*We'll video chat, it'll be nice.*

I look around again. I won't video chat with her here – it can't be here.

Emily gets up and moves to the kitchen, I hear the movement of cutlery, plates clattering in the sink, the pots edged up to the kitchen tiles. I wonder if she is messy. I think of the wellies in the hallway and smirk; of course she is.

I grab my new version of a Joe Hill novel, the spine sharp and fresh, the front cover smooth and unmarked. There are no memories in this, I think, and I revel in that for a moment.

My timer chimes to get the lasagne out of the oven, just as Emily strides over to the TV and switches it off. Her phone is vibrating aggressively and then it stops. Her voice, shrill and keen, laughs, laughs again. I wish I knew what was so funny. The high voice, the giggles, the long, drawn-out sentences can only mean she's talking to a guy. I've heard men up there. I'm never sure if it's the same man, or different men that flit in and out of her life. I've heard Emily before, the creaking of the bed as it rocks back and forth. I've turned my music on then, so loud, to let her know that I hear her, that I hear everything. She'll never stop though, because she's twisted in it, selfishly enjoying the feel of a man. I gulp, looking down at the wet lasagne as I slide it onto a plate. I push it away, no longer hungry.

Emily ends her call and shuffles to the bathroom. I hear her piss sink in the toilet bowl and then the flurry of water down the pipes. Maybe she's getting ready, maybe the man from the phone will be around soon and she needs to prepare. The shower starts and dinner is forgotten. I smile, remembering when I used to forget dinner, the excitement of the evening too overwhelming, too thrilling to bother. Now, it is a regime, a signifier of time.

I slump on the leather chair and coil the blanket around me. I pull in the Joe Hill book and cradle my chin between my knees. A man is yelling over the road into his phone and motorbikes full of food deliveries pace the streets as water sloshes to the side of the pavement. I curl further into the blanket as the night descends and the streets grow more vicious. I bury myself in the chapters of my book, occasionally glancing between the cracks in my curtain, watching shapes move past, each more threatening than the last.

The sound of music revives me, sending my book toppling from my lap onto the floor. I lean up and glance at the book sprawled across the rug at my feet and can smell the lasagne going stale on the kitchen counter. My head thumps to the music. Emily. The sound of laughter, hers, and a man's low, enticing voice. I can make out the words to the song. I mime them as I clutch my head, 'I'm a sucker for you.'

I curl my fists into small balls and fight back the tears. Without thinking, I fly towards the door and flick it on the latch. I storm up the stairs and come face to face with Emily's front door, Flat 2, the 2 crooked and rusty. I bang on the door, hard. I feel the weight of the movement vibrate through my clutched fist.

The voices stop, I hear movement off the sofa and Emily whisper, 'I don't know, shall I answer it?' I slam my fist into the door again. *Yes, you should answer it.* The door opens slowly and Emily's small face peers around. She sees me and a flash of recognition and concern crosses her features. She furrows her eyebrows and opens the door wider.

'It's my neighbour,' she says, looking at me.

I hear a body shift in the background. Emily looks up at me, her brown eyes glistening and confused. There's a harshness to her features; she's frustrated at my presence, bored almost.

'It's your music,' I say finally.

Her expression doesn't shift. She doesn't go to defend

herself. It's like she's heard it a million times – other neighbours, her parents, other people.

'I'll turn it down,' she says, already shutting the door.

'Okay, thanks,' I say quietly, but the door is already closed on me and I can hear Emily stride across the room, irritation circling her words, 'Turn the music off. Let's go to the bedroom.'

I'm left alone in the hallway, all my anger evaporated and all that's left is a longing to speak more, to say something. To scream into Emily's closed door. Instead I pad downstairs and stare at her red wellies. I yell, thrashing towards them, and I kick as hard as I can, but they just flop to the floor. How they were when she left them.

## Chapter Two

I've just finished work, but instead of heading back home, I walk out of Angel tube station and turn the other way. I push through the crowds towards the small green patch separating the rows of townhouses with colourful doors and expensive cars parked outside. The sky is grey and bleak, reflecting the stale faces of those that fly past me. Since I moved to London, I never quite adjusted to the rudeness, the selfishness, the 'me' mentality. I'm from a small seaside town called Hove, where the morning dog walkers greet everyone with a grin and a small wave. Every bartender knows your name, your drink order and your favourite baguette. The air tastes thin and sweet, like damp bark and sea salt. You can walk a metre without intrusion, but now as I evade oncoming Londoners, the air is heavy and tastes thick like diluted tar.

I push into a crowded coffee shop, the noise plaguing me as I find any available seat. The windows are steamed up and the incessant chattering from other tables echoes through the shop. A lady wipes my table, but ignores me. I lay my coat across the chair and walk to the till; someone dives in front of me and doesn't look back. I order a black coffee and hold my card out, recoiling at the cost. I carry the coffee back to my table and look around. I can feel eyes on me and I try to swat them away like pesky flies, but they continue to look.

I retrieve my phone from my small backpack and video call my mum, pushing back wisps of my hair behind my ear. I force a smile. I plug in my headset and do my best to look together, pulling the coffee closer to the edge of the table in focus.

My mum's pixelated face appears on screen and so does mine. I catch myself and smile more, wider, until I don't recognise myself. My mum is waving into the camera, her white teeth shooting across the screen and her soft red hair falling elegantly to each side.

'Mum,' I cheer.

'Suzie.' She grins back and fidgets to the side. 'Your dad is just pouring me a glass of wine.' She jumps up and swivels the camera onto my dad, who stands waving in the background. His thick grey eyebrows high on his forehead and red lips stretched wide.

'Hi, Dad.'

'All right, love, how's it going?'

My mum leaves him in the background and walks out of the room.

'Are you not going to let me reply to Dad?' I say, half laughing.

'No,' she giggles, waving her hand. She grins more. 'Where are you?' she says.

'I'm just in a coffee shop, having a quick coffee before I head out for dinner.'

My mum looks surprised. 'Who are you going for dinner with?'

'Just some London friends,' I reply, my face fixed in a permanent smile.

'That's nice. It's good to do things like that, even if you don't want to.' Her lips quiver.

I nod. 'I think we're going to The Breakfast Club – you know, that place we went with you and Dad.'

Tuesday, something eggy.

'Oh, that's nice. How's work?' she continues.

'Fine, slow at the moment, but fine.'

She nods slowly.

'You're looking thin,' she says finally.

I lean back and take a long sip from my mug, letting the powdery coffee rest on my tongue, wishing I had prepared. I let the chatter of the coffee shop consume me and I turn slightly to the crowd, looking at them differently now; they are my ticket.

'Sorry, Mum, it's busy in here.'

She ignores me. 'Shall Dad and I come up soon? Or do you want to come home for a bit?' she says, rushed.

I feel my eyes glistening, the familiar warmth in my chest and the words caught and distraught in the roof of my mouth.

'We can make up your old room and look after you for a bit? Lunch down the pub and coastal walks, doesn't that sound nice?'

'I am home,' I say quietly and so hesitantly that even I don't believe it.

'I want to look after you.'

Anger floods me and I fight back the tears. I feel so hot, frustrated and anxious. My chest is tight and I can feel the heat in my cheeks rising.

'I can look after myself.'

'Don't push us away,' my mum says, her expression passive.

'Mum, I have to go.'

She doesn't fight me; a weak smile slips across her face and she brushes back her long hair.

'Call your sister, let her know you're okay.'

'Yeah.' I hold up my hand and wave. My mum waves back; her long fingers, limp and pale, scrunch in front of me.

'Bye,' I say, my hand already on the red *hang-up* button.

I place the phone on the table, the screen face-down. I take a deep breath and push away the remainder of my coffee. I let the tears slide down my face and cool the warmth in my cheeks. I swipe at stray hairs circling my face and gather my belongings.

When I moved to London, my cousin had told me that 'everyone in London is invisible', but as I turn I see the unapologetic faces staring at my blotchy face. I drop my bag and the contents spill onto the shop floor. No one moves to help, they just watch. I don't feel invisible at all.

The stuffy street air clings to me as I move through the small strip of green towards my flat. My shoulder bangs against other commuters as we move fiercely in our own direction, all driven by a different purpose. I glimpse the familiar yellow glow of my local off-licence in the distance, with its large fruit and veg stand jutting out onto the pavement and the group of local kids piled on bikes, eyes searching for a distraction. I think how horrible it would be to grow up in London, nowhere to explore, no trees to climb or woods to get lost in. I think about sweet ice-cream cones down the beach in Hove, lemon sorbet sliding down my chin as a child and my mum zipping up my white puffer coat as we waddled with our deck chairs to the beach. My sister Clara always a step ahead, bounding in silver jelly sandals towards the sea, her sun-kissed hair flowing innocently in the gentle breeze.

Home, I think. I pass the kids on the bikes and enter the shop, shielding my face from the guy behind the counter. He knows my name, but I don't know his and I think, I'm part of the problem. I grab a couple of microwave meals and a pack of chocolate biscuits. I press my hand over the freezer and stare at the tubs of lemon sorbet, my mind lost in a distant memory.

'Suzie.'

The shopkeeper is standing beside me, giving me a flash of white teeth. A small basket clings to his outstretched hand.

'For your things,' he says, shaking it.

I let my purchases clatter into the basket and take it from his hand, smiling as I do. I mutter thanks and bow my head away towards the toiletries. I can feel him hovering behind me, questions edging towards the tip of his tongue. Instead he clears his throat and moves away, back behind the counter. Good, because I couldn't answer him.

I pay for my things and take the thin blue plastic carrier bag from him, never once making eye contact. I leave the shop and see the kids cycling away towards the canal, shouting into the evening air, one or two arms raised into the sky, as if they were waiting for night to fall.

I check my phone and see a message from my mum telling me to have fun tonight. I scan the rest of my messages and see all the group chats I've left recently, the friends that have slowly fallen away. Maybe I should go back to Hove, but as I round the corner and see my flat perched there, I know I could never make the journey; it would be too painful to leave. I quickly text Clara saying we should catch up soon, and think about her in her small terraced house in Brighton, cuddled up to my niece and nephew, her husband, Ian, crashing through the door and bundling his family into his large, strong arms.

---

When I enter my flat, I see Emily's letter right back where I found it, sitting on the communal table. She doesn't want to deal with the responsibility of whatever's in it, I think, entering my flat. I pick at the pack of biscuits as I read and slurp flat Diet Coke from a mug from the comfort of my leather chair. I hear Emily bustle through the front door, plastic bags brushing against the wall as she makes her way upstairs. Company tonight?

Emily walks into her flat and suddenly my evening is over and hers begins. The TV soars into action, the kettle flicks on and howls in her kitchen. She's wearing heels today; thick chunky soles smack onto her floor and she doesn't take them off. She's on the phone, but she's not flirty today, she's angry. Her voice is raised and fast, I can't make out the words, but her tone is curt and wooden. Short sentences are barked out like orders. Maybe someone cancelled on her? The man from yesterday? The phone hits the floor and I jump, sending my mug tipping to the ground, and black bubbles slosh onto my piles of books. I unfurl myself and collapse to the floor, pulling the books from the small puddle forming.

Emily is crashing across her lounge and towards the bathroom. I leap up and follow her into my bathroom and hear her tears echoing in the room above. 'Fuck,' she says over and over. I hear a tile shift and the sobs quieten. For a moment there is just the gentle whirl of her extractor fan. I stand staring at the ceiling, unsure of what to do. I reach up and let the tips of my fingers trace the pattern on the ceiling and, as if in response, Emily rises, but this time without shoes on, and slams the door of the bathroom behind her. I stand, feeling shut out, like a mother scolding her daughter and being told it's none of her business and to leave. I wrap my arms around my ribcage and start to cry.

Pop music floods the flat and I wipe my tears away and go into the lounge. I hear every word explode into my home, the harsh beat raining onto me. I don't think before racing to the kitchen cupboard and pulling out a broom. I place myself directly under the worst of the noise, where the sofa is, where I know she's sitting, wallowing in it. Holding up the broom, I smack it as hard as I can over and over until I see a small dent appear in the ceiling. The TV halts and the music softens. I throw the broom to the floor in triumph.

For a moment the only noise is the soft drumming from the music, until I hear Emily's bare feet against the floorboards trampling towards her front door. The sudden charge of her feet on the staircase in the hallway and the hollow rap of her fist on my front door. I freeze, embarrassed, and look around. I try to mask my flat, throwing sheets and throws in every direction, but it just makes it worse. I creep towards the door and this time it's my turn to peel open the door and peer around. Emily's face is stained with mascara; she is bright red and her dark auburn-brown hair sits in a high bun like a bird's nest atop her head.

'Just a sec,' I whisper, before glancing back. I open the door a little further and edge my body into the gap in the door between Emily and my home.

'Was that a broom?' she says callously.

'Yes, I—' The anger has fizzled and has been replaced by shame. I go to speak, but Emily is there first.

'This is my home,' she says, a statement I can't contend.

'I know, but the music is so loud. Can you turn it down?'

'This is my home,' she repeats, petulantly.

'This is also mine,' I whisper.

'I am not making too much noise.' Another statement, not a question, no argument or debate to be had. 'My speaker is tiny, tiny,' she says, holding up slim fingers to demonstrate the size of a small square box. She holds her palm out and points at it.

'I don't'—I hesitate—'think it matters about the size of the speaker.'

Emily leans back onto her heels and tries to look behind me.

'You shouldn't live in a flat if you don't like noise,' she says finally.

I can't argue with her; she has me pinned. I start smiling and break into a laugh, remembering other similar conversations. Emily stares bewildered and then she looks me up and down, and a new emotion laps over her features – pity.

'I'll try and keep it down,' she says, before turning and walking away upstairs.

I rest in the doorway and my smile fades to a frown. I look at Emily's unread letter bunched on the communal table in the hallway. I reach forward and grab it viciously. Pity this, I think, slamming the door. I throw the letter on my floor, but I don't feel victorious, just self-conscious and ashamed.

I scoop my laptop up from the kitchen counter and pick up the letter. Emily Williams. I open the laptop and scramble back on the chair. I type in 'Emily Williams, London' and *search*. I don't have Facebook or Instagram, I never saw the point, and it might make this more difficult, but I'm good at research, I'll find her. I frantically search through results pages and images trying to find Emily's face. An Instagram account appears on the first search page and when I click on it, I'm faced with rows and rows of pictures of her. I click on the first one of Emily in a pale pink jumpsuit clutching a slim glass. The caption reads 'The Fence with work chums', posted recently. I go back to her main account and pore over each image. Emily blowing on a hot chocolate in a cosy café. Emily pawing at her scarf as she giggles, against the backdrop of what looks like Hampstead Heath. Then older ones from the summer – Emily playfully chewing a straw and clutching an iced coffee. Emily staring down at a large fishbowl cocktail, her hair in loose waves cascading down her delicate face. Emily rolling her eyes at the camera as she sits cross-legged in a park. I scroll down the page, consuming every image of her, until a pop-up asks me to sign in. I exit the page and feel my stomach tighten. How much she wants to be seen, to be heard. *Well, I hear you, Emily.* I have LinkedIn though. I swat the Emily Williams profiles and scan the page. I pause to think why I'm doing this and let the thought simmer quietly – because I want to know what she's doing here. Because I need to know how she affords to live here by herself. Because I must know if she'll leave soon.

My finger slides across the touchpad and Emily's small face comes into view, her long golden-brown hair in a neat ponytail, trailing down her small frame. She's in a grey dress and a creased black blazer, and red lipstick lines her pouting mouth. Deep brown eyes stare back, buried under dark eyebrows. She's more tanned in the picture; she looks stoic, a contrast to her Instagram. Underneath her picture I see her name, Emily Williams, and just the job title 'Sales Executive'.

My phone starts to vibrate, and I scramble to find it tangled in a throw on the floor. I see Clara's name appear on the screen and remember I'm supposed to be at dinner with friends from London. The call screen fades and I pull up her messages, typing,

*Just at dinner and drinks with friends, will call you tomorrow, send my love to Ian and the kids.*

I stop to think about my sister, sitting on her hideous green sofa she picked out from the DFS sale. Cat sick. That's what Ian had said when she got it home, adding, 'Don't blame it on Bruno,' their old affectionate tabby that Clara had had since she was nineteen. I had laughed and Clara had this stubborn smile on her face, holding her swollen stomach as the delivery men carried it in.

I suddenly long to speak to her and hear her whimsical voice tell me that it's okay to feel sad, that it's normal. I look around my own empty flat and feel the familiar pang of sorrow ooze from my puffy eyes. I clutch the phone and press the sides so hard that the small buttons make dents in the palm of my hand. I settle the phone to the side and say to myself that I'll speak to her tomorrow. Emily's TV blares into the night and I gently close the laptop and sink down under the bundles of covers into the chair. A car horn roars relentlessly outside, a motorbike speeds up only to slow down for the speed bump, and a siren whines a few streets away. I pull the blanket over my head and take a deep breath, praying for the noise to stop.

## Chapter Three

The next day, after work, I decide to call the landlord upstairs about Emily. I've got to know him well since I bought the ground-floor flat five years ago. I asked the estate agent on the second viewing, 'Who owns upstairs?' The reply: Mike, a nice guy, sensible, described as a bit older. I remember nodding enthusiastically; it all sounded so perfect. A few days after I'd moved in, I wandered upstairs to introduce myself to Mike and give him my details in case he ever needed them. I hadn't seen him coming or going from the flat and apart from the little movement I heard upstairs, I hadn't heard much from him at all. But Mike didn't open the door when I knocked. Instead a young guy did and when I asked if Mike was home, he told me that was his landlord and fetched me Mike's number. I stood for a while outside Flat 2, confused.

It turned out Mike did own the property, but he let it out after he and his girlfriend needed a bigger place, and over the years I've seen people come and go, some worse than others, but none quite as bad as Emily. When the tenants have been bad, I've called Mike and he's apologised and told me that it's only a six-month lease, they'll be out of my hair soon. Emily has been living in the flat upstairs for just over six months and I waited for the moving boxes that never came.

Mike answers. 'Suzie, everything okay?'

'Hey, Mike, you know…' I let my words trail off.

I can hear him nod, his grey stubble brushing against the collar of his jacket.

'Is this about Emily?' he asks, straight to it.

'I'm afraid so. I'm sorry to call you, but it's just—' I bite my bottom lip and struggle for the words. I can hear Mike shift and the light tread of his feet as he walks. 'Have I caught you at a bad time?' I ask.

'No, don't be silly,' he says briskly. 'What's she been doing?'

'I don't want you to think—' I stutter. 'I know to expect noise.'

I feel like those words have left my lips so many times that they sound odd to me now. Expecting noise, like it's a part of living, as seamless as breathing, as existing. I think spitefully about the people crammed into the city, the daily herd moving for the tube or the bus, and what it's all for. To live. I should expect music between the hours of 8am and 11pm. I should expect that someone should wear the shoes they want around their own flat. I should expect to hear my neighbour.

'It's the music,' I say finally.

'Okay, is it past 11pm?'

I smile, rolling my eyes. 'Yes, most nights.'

'I'll give her a call, sort this out.'

'Is she staying in the flat, do you know?'

Mike is silent for a while before saying, 'She's got a year's tenancy.'

'Oh, okay, I just didn't know as people usually stay for six months.'

'Sorry, Suzie,' he says, but he sounds distant and like apologising is the right thing to do, not because he means it. 'I had to let it out again because the last girl cut the tenancy short. I'm not doing any six month lets anymore. How you holding up?' Mike adds.

I cross my legs across my leather chair and stroke the arms gently as I gaze around my flat.

'Fine,' I lie.

The wind whistles into the phone as if it were mocking me.

'Okay, I better be off,' Mike says and before I can reply, he is gone.

The pungent smell of lemon chicken fills the air and I sit reminiscing about Sunday roasts at home, always pork with apple stuffing. I think about Mum's sly smile at me, when Clara would moan at the repetition; Mum knew it was my favourite. I've always been like that, comforted by familiarity and routine. Meanwhile Clara, so boisterous and flighty, had travelled the world and seen so many places I longed to see. She spent most of her teens and twenties in France, South America and India. She'd send masses of colourful, beautiful photos and I'd send back sarcastic emojis and pictures of the same pub in Hove, a twinge of jealously poking me, but the weight of home more real and exciting than any photo she sent.

It's funny how we swapped places along the way, and now she's settled in her own home, a house in Brighton, married to a lovely guy and with two beautiful children. Now the jealousy is real because I have none of that and she sends me the pictures I always wanted to send her. I stare at the emptiness of my flat, and can't imagine filling it with anything, but I can't move either. I can't leave.

I check Emily's Instagram account for an update and she has been out a lot, frequenting bars, mainly The Fence, different coloured cocktails perched in her hands as she pouts for the camera. Who's on the other side, taking the picture? People she works with – 'work chums'. Even her Instagram is selfish, adorned with pictures of her, a smile plastered across her face.

Emily shifts upstairs and the oven clangs as she checks on the cooking chicken. I hear her stabbing at a timer and I soak in the soft citrusy juices as they float down. Wednesday, something meaty.

Emily's phone rings. She has it on loud today – maybe she's expecting an important call. She's quick to the phone, expectant. The ringing stops but I can't hear her speaking; whoever is on the other end is doing all the talking. After a few minutes, Emily says yes. I can only just make it out, but it's short and clipped. Yes. The phone call is over.

The second call I make tonight will be to Clara, but it won't be a video call because I can't look at her right now. Her face is more expressive and her features run deeper than Mum's. I know she'll try and convince me to go back to Hove or to visit her. I know she'll offer to come and stay, and if I waver, if I give her anything, then she'll be in her car and on the way. This will be the hardest test, calling my sister and telling her I'm okay. The person I shared a room with growing up, who I swapped clothes with and went for lazy bike rides with on Sunday mornings. Who I let cut my hair and dye my hair and plait my hair. Who I could tell anything, but I can't say that I'm not okay, I can't do that.

I pick up the phone and call her. I'm already close to tears at the thought of hearing her and I go to hang up after three rings, but then she's there and all the pain brims to the surface like an over-boiled pot.

'Sorry, just clearing up after dinner,' she says.

'Sorry,' I gulp, 'I can call back later.'

'Don't be silly, you're my chance to escape.' I hear her say something to Ian and then blow kisses to her kids, then the sliding of her conservatory door. I can still hear the commotion in the background, the clatter of dishes and cutlery sliding of plates, Ian saying to be quiet and my niece's high-pitched squealing. A different kind of noise, I think.

'How's it going, Zee?'

'Yeah, not bad, how's you?'

'Oh, you know, busy,' she says breathlessly. 'How's smog city?'

'Smoggy.' I laugh.

'I bet. And that neighbour upstairs, is she still giving you hell?'

'Yes, but I called Mike earlier though, so hopefully it'll get better now.'

'You could come stay here, you know? Or with Mum and Dad? Clear your lungs.'

I wince. 'And miss all this? Plus I'm not sure I'd be able to get the time off work.'

I can feel her swat the air. 'Time off work, fuck that, Zee. If you need time, you take it.'

I smile.

'What do I always say?' she adds.

'Hustle or be hustled.' I laugh.

'Exactly.'

We're silent for a moment.

'I need to be here,' I whisper.

'I know,' she says quietly. 'I'm not saying it's unhealthy.'

'I think that's exactly what you're saying,' I say jokingly.

'Well, maybe it is, but I just want you to be happy.'

I bite my lip, digging my front teeth into the dry skin.

'London never made you happy.'

'No, but he did.'

We don't say anything. I know Clara doesn't know what to say next and I want to let her off the hook. She's not sure how to tread and I'm not sure where I want her to go.

'How's Ian and the kids?' I say finally.

I think she's crying, but I can't be sure. Her voice croaks, 'They're good. Ian got a new contract managing the electrics for the Co-op that's going up down the road.'

'That's great news.'

'I miss you,' she says suddenly. The conservatory door slides open and I can hear Ian whisper to her and my sister reply that she's coming.

'You go,' I say

She ignores me. 'I can come stay.'

'No, sounds like you've got a lot on.' I muster a laugh. 'I'll visit soon,' I lie.

'No, you won't,' she says, her upbeat tone laced with cynicism. 'Love you, Zee,' she says.

'You too, Cee.'

I hear her speaking to Ian before she's hung up the phone, and smile thinking of the evening she'll have, tucking the kids into bed and kissing their foreheads. Her and Ian settling down to watch Netflix on their ugly green sofa with a couple of cheap, warm ales. Bruno the cat squashing himself into the dip of the sofa seats between them.

I lay a flat hand over the arm of the leather chair and dream of old evenings spent here. Us curled up under a cream fleece, our personalised tumblers sweet with the smell of Highland whisky and orange peels. The room dark and the TV flickering tirelessly. You are watching intently, and I am lost in thought, my head planted on the groove of your chest, your heartbeat solid and firm.

## Chapter Four

I fell asleep on the sofa early Friday evening. I drifted off reading Stephen King's *Cujo*. I always wanted a dog, a big dog like Cujo. It felt cruel in this flat though, and you always said I'd never get up in time to walk it. You were probably right. It's my second time reading *Cujo*, but I bought a fresh copy. I always buy a new book, even if I already have it. There's something about the fibres of books, traces of old life and marks of vivid memories – no, I need the new.

When I wake up, the streetlamp shines through a dent in the curtains masking my face and I hold up a hand to shield the brightness – but that's not what woke me. I hear yelling right outside my front door. It's more distorted here, but I know the voice is Emily's, shrieking into the small hallway, but I don't know what at. I glance at the time and see it's only midnight, early for her. Maybe she's just arrived home drunk, but I've heard that tone before when she's been upstairs on the phone. I can't make out another voice, just hers, and she seems to be repeating something, the sentence so high-pitched, so panicked, that now I feel worried.

I clamber up off the sofa, pulling the blanket with me to wrap around myself. I place *Cujo* softly back onto the sofa and tiptoe between the stacks of books towards the door. Then I hear it, a low gravelly voice, almost inaudible between Emily's sharp cries. I tread carefully towards the door, aware of the thin carpet and creaky floorboards underneath.

'Make up your mind,' she says.

He replies, but I can't make out the words. It's a short murmur, barely even a word, just a noise back at Emily. I take another step towards the door and carefully reach for the peephole latch, sliding it up until I can see out into the corridor.

'Make up your mind,' Emily says again, her voice thick this time, as if she's choking and trying to force out the words.

I take a deep breath and look through the peephole and see Emily swatting her arms from side to side as if she's trying to visualise something, as if she's trying to magic something from thin air. Standing opposite her is a man, who is just in view. I can't see his features as his head slumps against his chest and he holds up a hand to grasp his head.

'Please just make up your mind,' she says again. It's quieter now, more like a plea than a demand.

Should I open the door? I think. Or would Emily hate me for that? I imagine swinging it open and her head twisting towards me, her eyes slanting in frustration and annoyance. No, I remain quiet, holding my breath. I try to crane my neck to see the man, but he treads backwards mostly out of view. There's a smell though, strong, sickly sweet aftershave and metallic beer. Not any I recognise as Emily's smells: she leaves a trail of mango shower gel and spicy peppercorn perfume in the hallway, but this man's smell is wrong, and I wonder if she smells it too.

Emily goes to speak, but the man takes another step back until he is completely out of view. Now I'm just left looking at Emily, her mouth hung open and her arms extended as if she's trying to grasp something that isn't there. Then the main door opens and closes firmly, releasing a roar of traffic then stamping it out again.

Emily is frozen in the same pose and I let my breath slowly ease out. She turns expectantly towards my door and I wonder if she knows. I place a flat palm next to my head against the door and we stand like that for just a few seconds, until she turns to leave, her footsteps soft on the stairs. I repress the urge to fling open the door and ask if she's okay, maybe invite her in for a cup of tea and then she'll understand me and I can understand her. But I don't want to embarrass her. She shouldn't be embarrassed though. We all say things we don't mean. We all get caught up in conversations that are painful, don't we?

## Chapter Five

The next day she was up early and cleaning the flat. Something I rarely heard. Therapeutic, my mum would say. Maybe that's what Emily's doing, scrubbing the flat to try to remove the taste of the argument from last night. The hoover scraped over uneven floorboards and hit sideboards, and furniture shifted as she whisked from room to room. I don't remember the last time I cleaned the flat, and the shame clings to me. I used to get up early on Saturdays and put some jazz playlist on, and bob along to the gentle rhythms as I cleaned my way around the small one-bed flat. I left the bedroom till last, piling clothes onto the bed to put away, whilst trying to decide what was dirty and clean, putting my nose to the armpits of T-shirts and examining the bottoms of socks.

I trail to the bedroom doorway and hover a hand over the handle. I almost open it, but pull myself away. I haven't been in the bedroom since you left; it harbours the most memories and they fall around the room like lustrous beacons calling me in. I leave the door closed and walk away before I get the longing to look.

Am I being cruel to myself? The thought is sucked into the hoover upstairs as it pounds overhead. I know I must venture out to the shops today, but I want to go to a big supermarket, somewhere I won't be recognised, where I can't feel eyes on me. I collect a few large shopping bags from the kitchen and ready myself for the journey. I add far too many layers, like a padding against the outside world, and zip my grey raincoat up so high, I can barely see over the top.

The gentle whirl of the hoover circles above me as I close the front door to my flat and head down the communal hallway and out the shared main door. The front garden has become overgrown and my ankles fight their way through the dense grass and stooping weeds on the awkward concrete paving. At the end of the path there used to be a black wooden gate attached to the low brick walls, but I asked for it to be removed when no one would close it properly and the wind would knock it tirelessly at night. I pause in the hollow of the wall and long for the gate to be there to seal me in.

London is not as busy on Saturdays, but there is a different crowd. The weekend crowd walks slower and with less purpose. They hold their heads higher and spread across the pavement so there's no way around.

They are louder and more abrasive, making things personal – not business. In some ways it's worse. So many people vying for London's attention. It's hard to distinguish between visitors and Londoners on the weekend; the movement is fluid and the excitement is palpable.

I stand observing for a while, readying myself for the fifteen-minute walk to the large Sainsbury's in central Angel. I see an opening and dart onto the pavement, adjusting my pace to suit those around me. There's a couple in front of me holding hands and swinging their arms slowly. The woman is holding a bunch of yellow flowers and her dress is too summery for this time of year. I wonder where they are going: to a party, a family gathering? I chew my lips thinking of the possibilities.

I round the corner. The day is crisp yet sunny and I am wearing too many layers. The sweat bubbles to the bottom of my back and sticks to my T-shirt as I take rapid breaths and walk faster towards town. The crowd is thicker now and it's difficult to weave between people. Someone is shouting, and no one will let me pass. The sirens pass along the main road like a parade of bad news. I can feel the space closing in on me and it's suffocating. The heat in my chest rises until my heartbeat is uneven and terrified. I fall into the shop and let the air-con blast my clammy face. The security guard is staring at me intently, but he stares at everyone that way, like we're all guilty somehow.

I collect a basket slowly and compose myself, desperately trying to move out of the way for people to get their own basket. I think I hear someone mutter under their breath, but I ignore it and unlock my phone and scan the notes section for all the things I need.

I pile things into the basket, straying from my shopping list. After gathering the essentials, I ignore the dinner options I wrote down and hit the sweetie aisle instead for biscuits and large sharing packs of chocolate. I stride past the spirits and into the wine aisle. I see Emily. She's running a finger along a row of pink sparkling wines. She plucks out a bottle and drops it into her basket. I swivel away and duck into the spirit aisle to conceal myself. She walks down the main aisle slowly with her shopping basket full of bottles of wine and gin weighing her down on one side. I hope she's going out, but realise now why she's been cleaning the flat. She's having a party. My face scrunches into a tight pinch and I turn my head, coming face to face with the whisky. The memory winds me and I double over to be sick, but instead I gag and splutter into the floor.

'Are you okay?' A woman has her hand hovering above my back and she's bent down to hang her face next to mine.

'Yes,' I choke, evading her. I straighten myself up and hold up a hand. 'I'm okay, thanks.' I grip my basket tighter and dive at the whisky, grabbing a bottle of Talisker and scuttling away down the aisle.

## Chapter Six

Y ou didn't like peaty whisky. I'm sat staring at the bottle of whisky placed on the coffee table in front of me. I need to be selfish tonight if I'm going to get through Emily's party.

'And I like peaty whisky,' I say out loud. I reach forward and peel open the seal and pull out the cork. I let the smokiness waft into the lounge and pour myself a large measure into a mug. I can't use the tumbler, not yet.

It's 5pm and Emily has spent the afternoon rearranging her flat for tonight. She's had the radio playing on a low volume as she shuffles to each room. The bottles clink together as she moves the bag of booze around and I wonder who's coming to drink them. I swig the whisky until a small dent has been made in the top, and I grab a bag of chocolate biscuits and a new Jeffery Deaver book. I consider turning my music up high as well, but I can't compete with her and I don't want her to know she's won.

By 8pm I'm dizzy on whisky and my mouth is dry. No one has arrived at Emily's yet and I hope I'm wrong about the party. Maybe she's sitting upstairs alone in the middle of an empty room, all the furniture pushed to the side and just her, with the bottle of sparkling rosé wine and a straw sticking out. Then her buzzer sounds, sharp and precise, signalling the arrival of her guests. Emily whines into the intercom, her voice high and excited. The front door swings open and I can hear other young women squeeze into the hallway, making cooing noises like a flock of hens. I hear more bottles jingle and sway against my wall and from nowhere I lash out and smack the wall myself. It makes a disappointing thud that I know they haven't heard. I swing my head back to reading my book and swig more whisky.

By 11pm the party is in full swing. I can't hear any male voices; this is a girls-only party. The music has been turned up and Emily must be playing one of those awful girls'-night-in playlists from Spotify as all the worst pop hits rotate throughout the evening. I can't read anymore; the words dance and jump off the page and my head sways to the shit music blasting from upstairs. I drink more whisky directly from the bottle and feel the heat burning the back of my tongue. I smile and jump up as 'Girls Just Wanna Have Fun' comes on, the second time this evening. They are singing along to it upstairs, cackling, glasses clinking. None of them have taken their shoes off, but instead of block heels, slim stilettos prick into my ceiling. I start to dance, and sing along out loud, twirling around my lounge and bopping my head, until it feels as if it might burst. I sink into the leather chair, feeling delirious and sick. I drift off, the room spinning like a record track.

At 3.45am I wake to the sound of screaming girls and the clacking of shoes above my head. I stand up and carefully find my way across the crowded floor to the bathroom and sit lazily on the toilet, clutching my head. Above me one of the girls is pissing and laughing. I think they're all gathered in the bathroom. I dry myself and make my way back to the lounge and crash onto the sofa, pulling a cushion over my face. The girls shriek and start to sing, but I can't help noticing as I drift back to sleep that I don't hear Emily's voice, the one I've grown to know so well over the last seven months.

When I wake on the Sunday, my head is throbbing, and I spend the morning shovelling water, tea and tablets into my mouth as I lie sprawled across the chair. I don't know if the other girls stayed or left, but Emily's flat is quiet for the moment. I keep the curtains closed today, but I can hear the Sunday brunch crowd spilling across the street and their voices are perky and bright. I want to let some fresh air into the flat, but the windows remain closed against the sound of motors churning and the occasional child's cry.

I pull my laptop over to rest on the arm of the chair and bring up the council website. Rubbing my temples, I find the neighbour noise complaint section and hastily write an email, outlining everything I know and have witnessed from my neighbour Emily Williams in Flat 2. After I'm finished, I'm rewarded with the slightest satisfaction and I let that feeling fester away in the rawness of my hangover.

I click *send* and lean back into the sofa, where I feel something dig into the bottom of my back. I bend an arm and reach back for it, feeling between the spaces in the seats. Something sharp pricks my finger and I grasp it with my hand, clawing it out. I yank it with force and a small glass photo frame emerges, face-down. I chew my lip and look around and down at the back of the photo frame. I slide it back into the crevasses of the sofa where it came from and cover the space with a cushion. Emily pads slowly into the lounge, her small feet beating gently on the floor, and the sofa moves as she slumps down. A long night for the both of us.

I fetch my laptop and make a large mug of tea, wincing guiltily as I close my empty fridge and move aside dirty plates and mugs from the kitchen counter. I used to love spending time in the kitchen, our kitchen. I was never much of a drinker, but a cook, yes. I used to be a talented cook, conjuring up incredible meals and bakes without needing a recipe. I just kind of knew what worked with what. You learned that about me in our first year together, how much I adored cooking. Especially at Christmas, you found out how big my family and I went at that time of year. The house always full of sweet aromas, a gigantic gingerbread house, warm cinnamon buns for breakfast and an abundance of homemade panettone.

You gained a stone in our first year together, and I remember how seriously you'd said it at first and then how hard you'd laughed afterwards. I sit with my laptop staring at the black screen. Mornings spent sitting right here watching *Masterchef* and *Saturday Morning Kitchen*. You announcing which recipes you wanted me to try. Now our fridge is empty and our kitchen is cast aside.

I check Emily's Instagram and there it is, a picture of her leaning on a red velvet booth with the caption 'What a lovely surprise'. She's glammed up to the eyeballs, every part of her looks coated in something, long eyelashes and tight curls. It doesn't look like Emily. I close the laptop and stare up at the ceiling; she won't want to be seen today.

---

The following week the council emails me asking for my number so they can follow up on my noise complaint and for a moment I'd forgotten I made it. Emily had been quiet for several nights, and I've not seen her come or go. I think she's spending most of the time in the bedroom, but that is the place I do not go. I wonder if she's eating, but the buzzer never sounds for deliveries and I can't hear the whirl of the extractor fan in the kitchen.

I email back my number and lean into my leather chair. Typical, I think. I stare at the ceiling, tracing the pattern and grooves until my eyes rest on the dent I made the other night with the broom handle. A three-day hangover maybe? I sigh. Not at that age. I can't handle my drink now, not I like used to when I'd spend all day and night in the pub guzzling pints of beers and shots of tequila, only to hit the gym and eat chip butties the next day. Now I can still taste the whisky lingering on my breath from Saturday night and my eyes are heavy and my body aches. I turn my nose up at the greasy food, opting for plain biscuits and cups of milky tea. I'm not muscular and lean anymore. My collarbone sticks out and my arms drape next to me like loose wires. I make a mental note to quit the gym, so I don't have to watch the money dissolve from my bank account each month.

The floorboards creak slightly as Emily wanders into the kitchen. I hear her scoop a saucepan from the cupboard and the gentle clang as its rests on the hob. She switches the TV on and a woman's voice whirs into my flat. Emily is on the phone, her voice upbeat and assertive as she paces her flat. I hear a different side to her without making out the words, like she's in control somehow. Yes. The word clear and final.

My phone rings and I stare at the London call ID, hesitating before I lift the phone to my ear.

'Hello.'

'Hi, this is Matthew calling from Islington Council, am I speaking with Mrs Suzie Arlington?' The man is professional, his tone precise yet tempered.

'Speaking, yes,' I say in a rush.

'Good evening, Mrs Arlington, I'm following up on a noise complaint you made regarding your neighbour at the same address, is that correct?'

'She lives in the flat upstairs, yes,' I murmur.

'Great, okay. I just need a few more details from you before we can take any necessary action.'

'Okay, no problem.'

'Have you spoken to your neighbour regarding the level of noise?' He speaks as if he has a pen at the ready to check a box.

'Yes, I asked her to keep her music turned down. It was after 11pm,' I add.

'Okay, and is the occupant a tenant or does she own the property, do you know?'

'She's a tenant. She's been in the flat for the last seven months.' He goes to reply, but I cut in, 'I've spoken to her landlord, I can give you the details if you like, but her behaviour is still anti-social. She's playing music after 11pm, she had a party just this Saturday and there's no speaking to her,' I say, exasperated. 'I've asked her to just keep it down and she won't.'

'I understand, Mrs Arlington, this can be very frustrating. I would really appreciate if you could send me her landlord's details and I will contact him directly. Let me give you my email address and you can send the details through at your earliest convenience.'

I scribble down the address onto a piece of kitchen roll and thank him. He's in the middle of asking me if anyone else lives in the flat upstairs, when the music fires up, forceful drumming into the ceiling and the screech of a pop-rock band. I hold up my phone high in the air.

'Do you hear that?' I cry desperately. I bring the phone back to my ear and I know he is on the other side of the phone feeling awkward and unsure.

I climb up onto the leather chair and stand haphazardly on the arm and spread my legs to balance myself. I stick the phone to the ceiling and the contemptuous music howls back, its derisive, incessant pounding mocking me.

'That's what I have to deal with,' I say, sinking back down into the chair.

He is quiet. I hear soft breaths until he says, 'Please send me those details, Mrs Arlington, and I'll follow up with the landlord.'

'Okay,' I muster, thrown off by his composure. I hang up the phone and feel childish.

'Sorry,' I say into the emptiness of my flat.

## Chapter Seven

A flurry of people surge past me as I exit Angel tube station. It's Friday night and already my mum has been in touch asking what my plans are for the weekend. She's offered to come up tomorrow and asked me to visit Hove for a long weekend, but I've declined both. Just hop on a train, she said, as if it's that easy. I reply saying I'll visit them soon, but I don't know how much longer I can keep up the pretence.

When I get back to the flat, I make myself a cup of tea and this time I sit at my small wooden dining table in the corner of the lounge. I have a notepad and pen in front of me, because I need to ask myself a question.

'What next?' I say aloud.

I start to make a list, like a contingency plan to the life I was supposed to have, and already the pen is shaking in my hand at the prospect of accepting this reality. The pen has barely hit the paper when there is a knock on my front door.

I go to speak, startled by the interruption. I hurry towards the door, confused about how someone got through the main entrance. My hand rests on the door handle, but I hesitate.

'Who is it?' I call, thinking it might be Mike.

'It's Emily.'

I recoil. What does she want?

I slip the door open gradually until I'm wedged in the doorway. Emily has her hair drawn into a high French plait, and she's wearing a baggy black leather jacket and skinny jeans. She's holding a piece of paper high to her face and her eyes are enveloped in a dense frown. She licks her lips and glances at the letter.

'Anti-social behaviour,' she says vehemently.

I go to speak, but the heat of her presence silences me.

'Suzie, right?' she says, dark eyes blazing at me.

'Yeah, I'm just... it was the other night.' I gulp, my throat dry and coarse.

'It was my birthday,' she says determinedly.

'I didn't know.' I go to wish her a happy birthday, but stop and feel stupid.

'This is my home and I don't like feeling like this in my home.' Her nostrils flare with anger and suddenly I want to hug her and apologise. I understand not wanting to leave your home, better than anyone.

'If you could just keep down the music after 11pm I'd be really grateful,' I say, edging my door closed.

'This is a letter from the council,' she says, thrusting the letter in the space between us.

I look at the letter, the small council logo positioned in the top right corner. Memories of Saturday night trickle back, the loud music, the shifting of furniture and the raucous giggles. The heels protesting against the floorboards at 4am and the sound of alcohol-induced piss hitting the toilet bowl.

'This has been my home a lot longer than it's been yours and I'm not putting up with your drunken parties and awful music any longer. I know what your contract says. It says you can't play loud music after 11pm.' My voice is getting higher. 'So don't play loud music after 11pm.' I slam the door shut on Emily and bury my heavy breaths in the palms of my hands.

## Chapter Eight

The buildings cocoon me as I stride away from work. I fight through the crowd of hapless faces and swing my arms deliberately to propel myself forward.

My mum has been asking for dates for my visit. I didn't reply all weekend, but it's Monday now and I use work as a steady excuse for being busy. 'I've got a lot on at work, let me check.' She's read my text and not responded, and I imagine her poised against the kitchen counter, a mug of green tea clasped in her hands. She'll ask my dad what he thinks whilst he's cooking dinner. I can almost smell the sweet chilli, but it drifts away into the stream of clammy London air. I push the thought away for later.

I haven't heard Emily all weekend and I think she must have gone to stay at a friend's or back to her parents', wherever that is. Her absence has been a welcome break, like there's now room for other thoughts that I've been suppressing for a while. I've been consumed by Emily's noise and I selfishly hope she won't return soon.

I bask in the temporary silence in the flat. My eyes wander to the lounge mirror and I remember myself fuller, with rosy cheeks and thick legs from afternoon runs down the canal and pints of beer in the small courtyard at the back of the house. I turn to face the kitchen and watch grey drizzle slick the windows. Beyond, the dull concrete courtyard lies vacant and drained of life. The rusty grill sits in the corner, next to our small patio table and your bike storage. I slip off my shoes and work clothes and pull on loose joggers and a baggy top.

I slump in the leather chair, my legs wide and my feet splayed on the floor. I reach for the remote and switch on the TV. I overheard two girls in my department discussing a new Netflix show and I vowed to give it a go, to try and integrate myself into the conversation. All these new promises I've made to myself lift my spirits ever so slightly and I want to celebrate somehow. I look at the kitchen – could I make a cake? I never finished my list, but I'm satisfied with the small steps I'm taking as I brave switching on the TV so as to make small talk at work.

The black screen dissipates, and the familiar red logo

slips off the screen, leaving the user selection page. I drop the mug I'm holding and stop breathing. Frozen, I want to speak, I need to move, but I can't. The cursor circles your name in a luminous frame and I choke, trying to will myself to look away. I stab uncontrollably at the remote, until my shaking fingers find the round power button and the image fades.

I throw the remote as hard as I can at the TV, screaming, my lungs expelling the tension prying at my insides. The remote reacts with a sharp thud and slides down to the floor. All that's left is a slim crack spiked across the top of the TV screen. I try to pat down the spilt tea but the pressure exerted on my head and the slow acidic bile rising in my stomach stop me. I gasp and start to cry. A motorbike charges past my window and a woman cackles loudly on the phone outside. *Shut up, shut up, shut up.* I scrunch my hands over my ears and double over until my head dangles between my thighs.

'Shut up!' I shout.

## Chapter Nine

It's been a week now and I still haven't heard anything from Emily. I think she must be on holiday, maybe somewhere hot and exotic, her already tanned skin growing more sun-kissed by the day. I think about the heat on my skin and brush my arm as if erasing the memory of the sun touching me. Lost days spent with salty water skimming my ankles and my pale skin shining with milky sunscreen. The taste of sugary poolside cocktails and fresh seafood. I open my eyes and stare out my lounge window onto the crowd-soaked London pavements and the menacing sky shrouded by overbearing grey towers.

I checked Emily's Instagram a few times, but only the picture from her birthday night out stares back. It's uncharacteristic for her and I feel irritated by her sudden evasion. She's flighty as well as selfish.

I hear Emily's buzzer shriek into the space of my flat and I peel back the curtains carefully to look at who is at the front door. A delivery man wearing a hi-vis vest and holding a small brown parcel sways impatiently and swats at the buzzer again. I dart into the hallway and open the front door just as he is about to walk away.

'Emily Williams?' he says, gazing at the package then back up to face me.

'I'm her neighbour,' I say. 'I can take that for her?'

He says nothing but extends his arm with a small black machine to sign.

'Thanks,' I say as he is walking away.

I close the front door and go to place the package next to Emily's red wellies in the hallway, but I stop, looking up the stairway instead. I grasp the box and carefully tread upstairs, one hand clasped around the thin wooden rail. As I face Emily's flat, I place an ear to the door, but hear nothing. I make a fist and knock gently and as I do, the door flickers open.

I stand back, startled, and grip the package tighter as if threatened. I lean forward and push the door wider, slotting my head into the gap.

'Hello, Emily?'

The flat is silent apart from the churning of the fridge in the kitchen.

'Are you there?' I push the door open a little further until I can get a full view of the flat. My body turns cold. The flat feels wrong, and I gaze around without being able to place why. The lounge is dishevelled, with clothes sprawled across the floor. The strip of kitchen counter is piled high with dishes and discarded cereal boxes. The smell is rancid, like old bins and stale food. I run my fingers along the door lock and see it's on the latch. Has she been in and popped out somewhere? I would have heard her.

I venture further into the flat and take in the stacks of pizza boxes and piles of empty gin bottles dripping from the overfilled recycling bin. Emily's lounge is bigger than mine and is filled with a giant cream leather sofa, two small coffee tables and a large TV. The kitchen is made up of four counters lined against the back wall with a small fridge and two large black bins. I wander carefully past the kitchen and poke my head into the bedroom. The double bed is unmade and the covers stream onto the floor, joining the mountain of clothes. I'm unsure if they're clean or dirty. She has a large double wardrobe with a mirror stuck on one side; I can make out the smear marks from the doorway. A small chest of drawers obscures some of the doorway as every drawer sticks out, empty.

I move back into the narrow hallway and turn to the bathroom. I tug on the cord and the light flickers on with the familiar noise of the extractor fan. The medicine cabinet is open, revealing Emily's toiletries including tubs of lotion, hair products and a toothbrush propped in a metallic cup next to a half-full tube of toothpaste.

Towels line the floor and drape over the bath. I slowly push back the shower curtain to reveal an excess of toiletries circling the bath. I switch off the bathroom light and quickly retreat from the flat, leaving the door on the latch, the way I found it. I stand outside Emily's door, wondering what I should do. Surely if something had happened, someone would know by now, her friends, work, her family? They would have come to the flat and asked questions. I'm still holding the package and I slowly release it onto the floor next to Emily's front door.

I stumble back downstairs to my flat and search for my phone in my coat pocket. I see a message from Clara asking for a phone call tonight, but I swipe it away for later. I bring up Mike's number and press *call*.

'Suzie?' Mike says, breathlessly. I can hear a crowd chanting in the background and the waning cries of a football match.

'Sorry, Mike, if you're busy.'

The crowd grows fainter and a door creaks open.

'What's up?'

'Well, I haven't heard Emily for a while.'

Mike interrupts, laughing, 'Isn't that a good thing?'

Speaking to Mike now, I feel silly. I shift awkwardly and walk back into the communal hallway, staring up at Emily's flat. The feeling I had when I entered there chews at me and I realise what it is – the lack of noise. It felt, unnatural, forced silence.

'She's not been there for a week and she had a

package delivered, I went upstairs to give it to her and her door was open, but she's not there.'

Mike is silent. 'Wide open?' he says finally.

'Well no, on the latch, but she's not there, Mike.'

Mike's tone adjusts. 'Suzie, she's probably popped out or forgotten.'

'I don't think so.'

'Did you go in there?' he says, surprised.

'I went to see if she was in. I thought it was odd.'

He says nothing.

'It just didn't feel right. Can you call her?'

Mike sighs. 'Sure, I'll ask her not to leave the door on the latch.'

'Thanks, Mike. Will you let me know when she responds?'

He sounds frustrated. 'Sure,' he says.

I hang up the phone and switch it onto loud. I hover in the hallway, uncertain whether to close Emily's door or not. I leave it on the latch and go back into the flat, locking myself in for the evening. I nestle into the grooves of my leather chair and curl up into a ball feeling restless. Why would Emily leave the door on the latch? I try to remember getting a glimpse into her flat when I'd confronted her about the music. A man was there. I could hear him, but I couldn't see him in the gap of the doorway. The flat hadn't looked like that though, had it? So unorganised, as if someone had rifled through it. I think about the toothbrush in the bathroom cabinet and the empty chest of drawers. I look around at my own flat and think about what it says about me. If someone walked in when my door was on the latch, what would their thoughts be? The idea softens me as I burrow down further into the safety of my chair.

The sound of a siren wailing past my flat wakes me. I quickly search for my phone and see another message from Clara and one from Mike. I click Mike's name first and read the disappointing message:

*I've left Emily a voicemail asking her to not leave the door on the latch. Sorry you've had trouble.*

I think about the last part of his message, 'sorry you've had trouble,' and wonder what he means by it. Emily? Or is he referring to something else? His tone had been patient, but only just, as if I was almost out of cards to play. I shouldn't push it with Mike, he's dangerously close to not caring.

I reply,

*Thanks for letting me know.*

But I'm not satisfied with his message.

I wonder if I should go back into Emily's flat and hunt down a number to call, family or a friend. I try to ease myself into the thought that someone would have turned up by now if something had happened. I feel the need to call in sick to work tomorrow, like a protective instinct. I must be here if Emily's door is open. What if there is a break-in? I know that's not the reason though. It's the uncertainty that clung to me as I pushed Emily's door open; it was so immediate, and the grasp hasn't let go since.

I decide to call Clara. She picks up after the second ring, sounding exhausted and confused.

'Were you asleep?' I ask.

'I drifted off on the sofa,' she says drowsily. She sucks saliva in through her mouth and yawns.

'So did I.'

'Long day?'

'Hmmm yeah, something like that.'

'What's up?' She knows, of course she knows.

'I don't know, it's just—' I pause.

'Out with it, Zee, has something happened?' She sounds concerned now.

'No, not to me, no. I got home and the upstairs neighbour, you know who I mean…'

'The cow, yes, go on.'

'Well, she had a package delivered and I took it up to her and her door was open, so I knocked and went in and she wasn't there. She hasn't been home all week either.'

'Oh,' Clara says. 'So you just went in?'

'Well, yeah, I was worried.'

'I guess that's odd. Was it just wide open?'

'No, on the latch.'

'I wouldn't worry, she probably just forgot to close it.'

'Why does everyone keep saying that? I wouldn't be calling if she just forgot to close it, would I?' My voice is curt.

Clara is silent. 'Why did you call then?' she says quietly.

'Clara, I… it's the way the flat looks. It's the feeling.'

'Did you contact her landlord?'

'Yes, he's been useless.'

'What was it about the flat in particular that you thought wasn't right?'

I pause. 'It just had a feeling. It was messy, things looked out of place.'

'You can't call the police over a feeling.'

'So you do think I should call the police?'

'I don't know, Zee, it seems extreme, but if it will make you feel better…'

I nod, biting my lip. 'Don't you think her parents or someone would have shown up though, if something was wrong?'

Clara sighs. 'I don't know. A young woman, living by herself in the city, who knows?'

I realise that Clara's right. I don't know Emily at all, who her family is, who her friends are, where she goes during the day. All I know is that she's a sales executive, she goes to The Fence, and she hasn't posted on her

Instagram in a week. My irritation is replaced by worry. Emily loves to be seen, so where is she?

'Are you okay, Zee?'

I realise I haven't spoken for a while. I stutter, before realising that I am not okay. I bite my lip harder and squeeze my eyes shut.

'If it makes you feel better, you should call the police,' my sister says gently.

I consider this and open my eyes, releasing my lip from my teeth. 'Yes, I think it would,' I say.

## Chapter Ten

I waited up most of the night to see if Emily came home, but she didn't. I went through mixed emotions as I lay on the sofa, my mind racing. Just a day ago I was happy that she had gone away. I was enjoying the peace. But now it feels bitter and I wonder if I did have the same feeling that something wasn't right the whole week. Maybe it's why I chose to walk upstairs and knock on her door instead of place the parcel next to her wellies in the hallway. Something even more sinister bites at me. Was it the council letter that drove her out? Did she really feel so uncomfortable here that she couldn't stay a moment longer and she whisked around her flat stuffing what she could into a bag and leaving the rest? Did she forget to close the door properly as she stormed out? Is that the reason I feel so responsible?

I didn't go to work today and settled on calling the

police non-emergency number. I waited until 9am and called Mike, but it went straight to voicemail. 'Hey, it's Suzie, I just wanted to let you know I'm going to call the police and alert them about Emily. I'll leave it until midday in case she responds to you. Let me know.' I hang up the phone and wait patiently for midday to arrive.

Mike calls back around half ten, his voice gravelly from a night of drinking. 'I've not heard from her,' he says bluntly. 'I'm going to come round and take a look this afternoon. Will you be in?'

'Yes,' I reply hastily.

'Okay, I'll be round about half twelve, so hold off calling the police for now.'

I end the call with Mike and gaze around my flat. I think about tidying up and feel instantly guilty.

'This is my home,' I say aloud.

---

I perch by the window waiting for Mike. I nurse a cup of coffee in one hand while the other hovers next to the curtain. He's half an hour late and I try to be patient, but there's a sense of alarm welling up in me. Mike rounds the corner and I see his stocky frame come into full view. He's wearing a blue polo shirt and a tight suede jacket with a mound of stomach peeking out the bottom. He rubs his shaven head as he approaches and produces the keys from his baggy denim jeans.

I dart to the front door and step out into the hallway, closing my door, masking the inside of my flat. Mike turns to me, his face drawn and pale with red blotches prickling his cheeks.

He doesn't smile, and instead points in the direction of upstairs. 'She's still not home?'

I shake my head and follow him up the stairs. He treads slowly and glances at the parcel I've left next to the front of the flat door. He gets out his keys.

'It's still open,' I say in a rush.

He frowns at me before pushing open the door. He stands momentarily in the doorway and then staggers slowly in, as if returning home after a night of drinking. He looks around and I can see his frown lines deepen as he takes it in.

He rubs his head again. 'Well, it's messy, yeah, but I guess she tidies whenever I've been here. Maybe this is what it's usually like?'

I nod slowly. I can tell he's not convinced. I stay in the lounge as he walks slowly through the flat inspecting each room. He halts in the doorway to the bedroom and I can see his large frame withdraw slightly into the hallway.

'Is something wrong?'

He swings around and takes in the lounge again, before looking at me.

'What made you call me?' he says slowly.

I shrug, suddenly unsure. When I look at the flat now it just looks untidy, unclean, as if a messy young student lives here who's just left home and doesn't care.

'Her drawers are empty in the bedroom and all the cabinets are open in the bathroom.' Mike is nodding as I say this.

He licks his lips and sighs, before staring at me intently. 'I'm going to call her parents,' he says, and I see the fear in his eyes as he says it.

He walks past me and goes to place a hand on my shoulder, before dropping it to his side. 'Thanks for calling me, Suzie. I'll let you know.'

Mike waits for me to follow him out of the flat and this time flicks the door off the latch and closes it firmly behind us. I trail after him down the stairs, but he doesn't pause to say goodbye and instead lets himself straight out of the front door, joining the crowd of passers-by. I stand motionless in the hallway, half expecting him to come back and say something, but as I pry open the front door and see Mike disappear around the corner, I have only the image of his fearful expression left to think about.

When I'm back in the confines of my flat, I dig under the leather chair and fish out the remains of Talisker from the night of Emily's party. I release the cork and sip slowly from the bottle, savouring every mouthful. Did Mike get the same feeling I did when he entered the flat –

that something was off? Did he see something I didn't? He knows that flat, and he must know Emily to some extent, what she does for a living, how she pays the rent and where she used to live before. You need them all for references, I remember from the first year living in London.

I call in sick to work the next day as my head feels swollen and my body aches from the whisky. I traipse to the window and slick back the curtain revealing London's baleful gaze. Not today, I think, relishing the sanctuary of my small flat. Work haven't responded to my emails saying I'm unwell, but I think there is an acceptance on their part. My line manager told me to take more time if I needed it and although Clara said I should distract myself, it wasn't the distraction I needed or wanted.

I wince, thinking that Emily is now playing a part in this, like a pawn I've moved to block a checkmate. There is an impending notion that something is coming for me, but I can't place what it is.

My phone chimes and I delay in retrieving it from the mound of covers sprawled across me. Dad flashes across the screen. I imagine him leaning back in his big leather study chair and my mum perched in the doorway biting her nails. I answer reluctantly, but it's not because I don't want to speak to him.

'Hey, Suzie,' he says as I pick up.

'Hey, Dad, you all right?'

'Yeah, yeah, just got back from the garden centre. Picked up some hydrangeas for the back.'

'Nice, how's it looking?'

'Yeah, good actually, coming along, more time now I'm retired.'

'How's the olive tree?'

He laughs. 'Slow, but getting there. You should come see it.'

I pause. 'Is Mum there?'

I can hear him fidgeting and the telltale squeaking of the chair as he rocks back and forth. I feel cheated.

'So that's a yes,' I say bluntly.

'We just worry. You're being very stubborn, Suzie.'

'Stubborn?' I cry. 'This is my home and you're adamant that I leave it. I'm not the one being stubborn.'

'You're shutting us out,' he says, unmoved.

He was always a lot better at this than Mum. When Clara and I were young and we'd misbehave, or when we were teenagers and something upset us, our mum would feel every part of it as if it were happening to her. Dad, though, he was the anchor in this, the unyielding force that held us together. I chew my lip and want to cry, thinking of his strong, all-consuming hugs and the peace and wisdom in his knowing smile.

'I don't mean to,' I whisper.

'Come home.'

I'm nodding into the phone and tears are spilling down my cheeks.

'You're not in this alone.'

And it's not much to bear. I sob into the phone and my dad waits patiently for me to reply.

'Next week.'

'Looking forward to it,' he says, and I hang up.

---

In the early evening, I wake to the noise of keys in the front door. I must have drifted off and I lazily wipe saliva from my warm chin, as I prop myself upright.

Voices ring in the hallway and I can make out Mike's low East London accent. He's leading people down the hallway and up the stairs. I peel myself off the sofa and swing to the front door, pulling it back.

'Mike?'

Mike is halfway up the stairs and trailing behind him are a man and woman. They all stare down at me, before Mike slips down a step and introduces me.

'This is Suzie, who lives in the flat below. She alerted me about Emily's door. Suzie, these are Emily's parents. We'll be down in a minute. I just want to show them the flat,' he says, turning away.

'Is everything okay?' I ask, glancing at the woman. She has full, thick blonde hair bunched into large curls and her skin is tanned like Emily's. Light blue eyeshadow skims large doe-like eyes and her lips are painted a deep brown. She's beautiful. She turns to follow Mike and her long cream coat trails up the stairs like a ball gown.

'We'll be down in a minute,' Mike repeats.

The man smiles sympathetically, revealing uniform white teeth. He's more tanned than the woman, but naturally, his olive skin complimenting smooth golden-brown hair speckled with grey. He's wearing a light blue sweater and dark suede jacket. He takes the woman's hand and cups it gently in his as they ascend the stairs.

I retreat to my flat and press myself against the closed door. I can't let them in here. I stoop in front of the bay window and watch as slivers of sun pry through small cracks in the clouds. I lift my jacket from the table and wrap it tightly around my body, and pull my Converses over thick pink socks. I rifle through the kitchen cabinets trying to find what I desperately need. Wedged right at the back is a half-empty pack of cigarettes and an emerald green lighter. Not mine, left here from one of the many summer courtyard BBQs. I grip them gloriously in my fist and panic at the realisation. Do I remember how to smoke?

I shut the door to my flat gently behind me and wander into the front garden. It's colder than it looks and I do my best to stop my teeth chattering as I pluck a cigarette from the packet and fiddle with it awkwardly. I position it in my mouth and ready myself with the lighter. Just look natural, I think.

Five minutes later the front door opens, and Mike

emerges with Emily's parents. I immediately light the cigarette and take a long drag. The smoke escapes down the wrong windpipe and I splutter slightly, composing myself as they approach.

'I knocked, but saw you out here. I didn't know you smoked, sorry. This is Christie and Stuart,' Mike says, as Emily's parents step out the front door.

'Sorry,' I apologise, waving the cigarette and looking around wildly to find some way of putting it out. I clumsily lean over to the wall and stamp it out on a brick. 'I don't usually smoke,' I say.

'Hi, Suzie, thanks for letting Mike know about Emily's door,' Stuart says in a raspy, refined voice. He extends an arm to pull in Emily's mum, who burrows her full curls into his neck. She twists away from me, a pained expression sloping from her blue eyes.

'We haven't heard from Emily for over a week,' Stuart continues, 'so you did the right thing to call Mike.'

'Of course, I'm sorry,' I say, stepping forward.

'She's done this before, ghosted us for weeks, but this'—he points towards the front door—'it's not like her.'

'Do you think something's wrong?'

'We've rung around her friends that we know of, but most of them live in Cambridge, near us.' He shakes his head. 'They haven't heard from her.'

Emily's mum pulls her head away from Stuart's neck, and drapes back her hair with long preened fingers. 'She only moved to London seven months ago for a job,' she says with effort. 'She left a week ago and—' She looks up at Stuart. 'We said she should stick with it. She's not very'—she turns to me—'resilient.'

'Oh,' I murmur.

'She got angry with us over that. We haven't spoken to her since,' continues Stuart.

'We don't know who her friends are in London. She never mentioned anyone by name.' Emily's mum reaches into her small black purse and pulls out a tissue and stands with it clasped in her hands.

I shuffle on the spot and pull my coat tighter around my waist. 'She had a party, about two weeks ago,' I say, gazing awkwardly at Mike.

Emily's parents exchange glances. 'It was her birthday,' Stuart says. 'Do you know who came?'

'I didn't see anyone, I just—' I scuff my foot against the pathway. 'I heard girls arrive and music and that.'

I'm still holding the half-used cigarette in my hands and slide it into my coat pocket. Emily's parents are staring up at Emily's window with a vacant expression.

'We're going to call the police,' Stuart says defiantly. He turns to his wife. 'I'm sure she's fine, Chris, we know her, we know what she's like, but we need to make sure she's okay.'

Christie nods. 'She has her bag with her – I couldn't see that anywhere – and some clothes at least.'

Stuart smiles reassuringly. 'Exactly, she's probably

just at a friend's house for the week sulking after losing her job, that's all. We'll contact her work this afternoon as well,' he adds. 'Just to check if they've seen her.' He leads Christie up the path and past me. They smile sheepishly, and Stuart extends a hand to Mike. 'Thank you for calling us. We're going to stay in London for the night. I'm guessing the police will be in touch to arrange to collect keys.'

'Of course,' Mike says. He looks so scruffy standing next to Emily's parents, and pats his jeans in an awkward gesture. 'You've got my number, yes?'

Stuart nods as he squeezes past Mike. 'Thanks, Suzie,' he says, holding up a palm. Christie coils a slim arm around him and he leads her down the street. I see them stop next to a silver Mercedes and Stuart open the door for Christie, as if it's too heavy for her. Christie slides into the seat gracefully and stares back at me with glassy blue eyes. I can make out the small lines of her pursed lips and the indent between arched eyebrows as she raises her head slightly and looks away.

## Chapter Eleven

The police turn up the next day with Mike in tow. I'm waiting at the window with a grey fleece wrapped around my shoulders. I've had the windows open to try and get rid of the smell in my flat. At first I think it could be the state of Emily's flat seeping down, the sticky smell of kung po and stringy stale cheese hanging reluctantly in the air, but I glance back at my flat and realise the true reason.

I crane my neck but remain hidden to get a better look as they round the corner. There are two male police officers; one is hidden under a black cap in uniform and the other is wearing black trousers and a white shirt. They tail Mike up the pathway. The keys slide into the lock and the deep voices penetrate the hollow corridor.

'Just upstairs,' Mike says, and I hear the solid tread of heavy police boots ascend the stairs. I follow them around the flat, noting where they are. There isn't much talking, just soft movements as they inspect Emily's home. What do they expect to find?

I've been feeling calmer about Emily's disappearance since her parents visited. They were concerned parents, yes, but not worried, not afraid for Emily. They'd offered several explanations and now I felt like the police were here to teach Emily a lesson more than anything. So, her selfishness ran deeper than loud music in the early hours. It wasn't just reserved for strangers, it extended to her family too.

I follow the steps of the police officers through the kitchen and pause at the bedroom door, my hand resting gently on the handle.

'Just go in,' I repeat to myself. 'Just go in.'

I put a little more pressure on the handle, but flit away at the last second. My heart races and I steady myself against the lounge door. Blood rushes to my head and my knees and calves start to give way. There is a gentle rap against my front door and I blink lazily, willing myself to stand properly.

'Just a sec,' I call. I tilt my head down to the floor and take long breaths. My mum taught me how to do this when I'd had anxiety attacks before: stick your head between your knees and take deep breaths. In through the nose, out through the mouth. There is another knock.

I rise slowly and wade towards the front door, the blood trickling through me like rainwater down a gutter.

I take another long breath before I open the door slightly. The two police officers are standing there with Mike hovering behind them.

'Hi, sorry, I'm off work sick,' I say, looking at the floor.

'We're sorry to bother you, but it would be really helpful if you could answer some questions for us,' says the officer in shirtsleeves. I notice he's gripping a notepad and pen in one hand, 'regarding a reported missing person, Emily Williams, from Flat 2.'

I nod.

'Would you feel up to that?' he says again, his voice soothing.

I nod again.

'Could we come in?' he says. 'It's a little cramped out here.' He laughs slightly.

Panic rises in my throat and I glance back into my flat.

'I'm going to get off, Suzie,' Mike says. 'I've provided a set of keys for the officers and Emily's parents. Will you be okay?' he adds.

Mike is barely visible over the towering shoulders of both police officers. The uniformed one masks most of his face, but I can see the top of his shaved head and his concerned brown eyes.

'Yeah,' I say. 'I'll be fine.'

Mike squeezes past and calls back, 'Let me know if you need me,' before closing the front door behind him.

I risk looking up at the officer with the notepad and pen. He is tall, with broad shoulders and a sharp jawline. Scruffy sandy-blonde hair vines down his face towards dark stubble. He smiles at me and lines ripple from the corners of his grey eyes.

'I'm the inspecting officer. My name is Detective Sergeant Noah Peters, and this is Police Constable Martin Gallows.' He gestures to the uniformed officer next to him, who nods politely at me.

He stands expectantly in the hallway and flickers his eyes above my head to the inside of my flat.

'Come in,' I say, biting my bottom lip.

'Thank you.'

I pull back the door and the officers loom past me into the confines of my flat. I suddenly feel vulnerable and exposed as I pull the fleece tighter over my shoulders.

I close the door steadily and watch them rotate on the spot, eyes drifting across my home. I follow their eyeline and then see what they see.

The lounge floor is barely visible beneath the piles of books, the Talisker balancing on the top like a trophy. The small dining table in the corner is covered in empty glasses and stacks of pictures I've removed from the walls. The kitchen area is lined in grease, with different-coloured sauces icing their way down the cabinets. The sink is overflowing with used mugs and glasses that I've failed to clean.

My cheeks flush crimson and I go to apologise but Detective Peters speaks first.

'We won't be long.' He slides a few books across the sofa and sits down, leaving a small space for the other officer, who joins him.

'Can I get you a drink?' I ask meekly, staring back at the kitchen.

Detective Peters smiles. 'That would be lovely, a cuppa tea for me please.'

'A black coffee if you don't mind,' the other officer adds.

I bumble into the kitchen and flick the kettle on and wash two mugs out with cold water, shielding the sight with my body. I carefully make the hot drinks and find a spot on the small coffee table, pushing over a stack of books onto the floor as I do. Detective Peters bends down to pick them up, but I wave frantically.

'It's okay, just leave it.'

'This is a great collection, Mrs...?' he says, holding up two of the books and stacking them neatly next to his feet.

'You can call me Suzie,' I say quietly, as I perch on my leather chair opposite them.

'Great, thanks, Suzie. Are you happy if we ask you some questions?' His voice is composed as he readies his notepad and pen.

'Of course,' I say.

'When did you first notice Emily was missing?'

'I didn't know she was missing.'

'Let me rephrase that,' he says. 'When was the last time you heard Emily?'

I think about this. 'Over a week ago, I think. She had a parcel delivered and I went to give it to her but she wasn't there.'

'Did you think Emily was home when you went upstairs to give her the parcel?'

'I didn't know, but her door was open so I went in.'

'What made you go in?'

I gulp slowly. 'Her door was open, but I didn't think she was in.'

The officer scribbles in his notepad and looks up at me. His features are relaxed and he smiles.

'I'm just trying to get a sense of a timeline,' he says reassuringly.

I nod, signalling for him to continue.

'When you entered Emily's flat, did you notice anything out of the ordinary?'

'I'd never been in her flat before, so it's hard to say, but something felt off.'

'So you called the landlord, Mike.'

I nod.

'And he came over to check it out?'

I nod again. 'Then he rang her parents and they came yesterday to look at the flat and decided to call the police.'

'Okay, so when was the last date you saw Emily?'

I flash back to Emily standing in my doorway waving the council letter in my face, her nostrils flaring. It was a week after the party.

'I think the twelfth of April,' I say.

'You saw her on that day?'

I nod slowly.

'Did she seem upset?'

I think about how I slammed the door in her face, the bewildered expression plastered across her features.

'I don't know,' I say, clasping one hand in the other.

Detective Peters's eyes rest on my hands and he smiles.

'Thanks, Suzie.' He rises from the sofa with the other officer and does his best to tread carefully between the piles of books on the floor.

'There'll be officers in and out in the next couple of days. They shouldn't bother you, but may have some other questions,' he says. 'Also, would it be possible for me to come back and speak to you again, maybe with your husband?'

I turn numb and stare up at Detective Peters, speechless.

'Would that be okay?' he asks again.

'I don't have a husband,' I say slowly, and the words burn my throat as I do.

'Oh, my mistake, sorry,' he says and pulls the door closed behind him.

I turn around slowly and start to cry, pacing back to

the warmth of the leather chair. In between shallow sobs, I glimpse something on the sofa where Detective Peters sat moments ago. I fall to my knees and crawl over, propping myself on my heels. I swat at the object and pull it towards me until I come face to face with the photo frame I'd buried weeks ago. A picture of two newlyweds. They smile back.

## Chapter Twelve

I spent Sunday at the table again, with the empty notepad and untouched pen laid in front of me. When I looked up it seemed glaringly obvious as the grimy flat stared back. I feel ashamed looking at it now and remembering the expression on the officers' faces. The sink full of unwashed cutlery and pans, the cabinets growing a sheen of dust and the plants languishing along the windowsill. The kitchen had once been full of the sweet smell of chocolate cake and rich, pungent aromas of your favourite coconut curry. Extra spicy, you'd request as I plucked chilli from the plant by the window. Now, shrivelled remains hang from wilted branches and smears of leftover microwave meals line the sink. I spend Sunday cleaning the kitchen, moving through the small space to the sound of kids playing in the garden and low bass escaping from a nearby flat. I open the fridge and discard the old cartons of milk and forgotten pots of yogurt, wiping each shelf methodically. I open the back door to the courtyard to let fresh air in, but I don't go out there – baby steps.

Maybe I'll cook something tonight, something proper. I feel a pang of guilt that almost winds me as I consider it and tears brim in the corners of my eyes. Cooking used to be therapeutic, relaxing, but more than that – it was our thing. I don't see the point of it now, without the ceremony of a Saturday night spent preparing you a meal and sitting down together at our small wooden table. Now it feels pointless without you here to make cooing noises. You never once said you didn't like something I made. I smile through the tears, although I bet you didn't really mean that.

As Monday rolled around, I hadn't seen anyone come or go from Emily's flat and I started to wonder if everyone had forgotten about her. I scoured the internet over the weekend for news or social posts about Emily but found nothing and her Instagram still hadn't been updated. I'd hovered over the image of Emily's mum when I'd looked for her Facebook profile, but couldn't view any of the information without an account.

I texted Mike and left a voicemail asking if there was any news, but no response. Maybe Emily had been found safe and well and now she was curled up in a large wing-backed chair at her parents' home as they fetched her cups of tea and finger sandwiches. The thought washes away as I walk down the familiar street on my way back from work, my handbag slapping at my leg and the stale breeze enveloping my face. I see a police car parked outside and a uniformed officer staring up at the window. I rush forward as a man in a suit exits the front door, talking to someone I can't make out behind him.

Mike is perched on the low brick wall and turns expectantly towards me as I arrive at the front of the building.

'Sorry I didn't get back to you, Suzie, there wasn't any news,' he says, turning away. The police officer staring up at the window jots down some notes in a pad and saunters towards the car.

'What are they doing?' I ask, releasing my bag onto the ground.

'No one's heard from Emily, so they're searching the place more thoroughly,' Mike says, dejectedly.

The man in the suit emerges from the doorway and is followed by Detective Peters. His large frame fills the space and he smiles at me and holds his hand up awkwardly.

'Suzie, this is Detective Inspector James Freeman,' he says, as the two men approach Mike and me. 'Would it be possible to speak to you privately?' he adds, smiling.

I crouch down and swipe at my bag, pulling it back on to my shoulder. 'Yes, of course.' I smile warily.

'I'll talk to you soon, Mike,' I say, leaving him leaning on the wall as I follow the officers through the front door.

They squeeze to one side as I search for my keys and release the door, letting them into my flat. The inspector enters first. He is shorter than Detective Peters and I see now, in the close quarters of the flat, that he is older, with denser lines filling a broad face, and a thick moustache climbing across unshaven cheeks. Detective Peters stands aside for me and gestures that he'll follow. I smile politely and wait for them to arrange themselves in my lounge, before I close the door. There are still books everywhere, but I don't look at them as an obstruction; they are a staple of this flat, a piece of furniture, you used to say, placing a mug on top of a steep pile, pointing and saying, 'See, a table.' I didn't get mad at the coffee marks, I liked the memories – a stained book with rings of mornings spent with you.

'Sorry about this,' the inspector says, sucking in large flat cheeks. 'I know my colleague asked you some questions the other day, but this has been escalated to a missing persons case and we're doing our best to track the movements of Emily prior to her disappearance and establish a time and date she was last seen.'

I nod. 'Of course, do you want to sit down?' I gesture towards the sofa.

Detective Peters is looking around my flat quizzically, his grey eyes bright and assertive and his tongue between his lips as if he is about to speak. The inspector notices this as well.

'Do you have anything to add?' he says to Detective Peters.

The officer blushes, shaking his head, and looks at me guiltily. They both lower themselves onto the sofa and produce a notepad and pen. The inspector retrieves something else from his pocket, a torn envelope he keeps face down on his lap.

They shake their heads at my offer of drinks as I fill up a pint glass with tap water and join them in the lounge.

'We were searching Emily's flat when we came across this...' The inspector turns over the envelope and I see the council logo sitting in the top right corner. My body stiffens as my mouth falls open.

'A noise complaint,' he says. But I already know what it is.

'Yes,' is all I can manage.

'She was a noisy neighbour?' the inspector says, eyeing me suspiciously. Detective Peters fidgets next to him and I see sympathy flash across his face.

'Yes,' I repeat.

The inspector nods and looks at me patiently as I dissolve into tears. I wipe viciously with the back of my hands at my soaked cheeks and through blurred vision I see Detective Peters's outstretched hand holding a tissue. I slowly reach for it and shake my head.

'Do you think she left because of me?' I choke. 'Maybe something bad happened because of me.'

Detective Peters turns to the inspector who leans forward towards me.

'No, we don't think that,' the inspector says reassuringly.

'We're here because we think you might be able to help us with her movements,' Detective Peters adds. I straighten myself in my chair and finish drying my eyes, before nodding for them to continue.

'So,' says the inspector , readying his notepad. 'We know it was Emily's birthday on Friday the 5th of April and she had a party to celebrate on Saturday the 6th of April. Do you remember this event?'

I glance at the letter. 'Yes, I remember.'

'Was that the last time you heard Emily?' the inspector asks.

'No.' I shake my head and bite down on my lip. I point to the letter. 'She came downstairs to confront me about that.'

'Okay, had you spoken to her much before this interaction?'

I shake my head.

'And was Emily upset about this letter?'

I squeeze my eyes shut and remember the anger rising in her voice as Emily held up the letter.

'Yes, she was.'

The inspector nods. 'What noise issues had you experienced?'

I think about this carefully. 'She wasn't very considerate,' I say slowly.

'Parties, loud music, things like that?' the inspector suggests.

'Yes, I suppose. I know she only has wooden floors and they are very thin, so I hear a lot of noise anyway, but yes, loud music, the TV, people round.'

The inspector is nodding. 'When did Emily confront you regarding the noise complaint letter she received from the council?'

I think for a moment. 'It was the Friday, a week after that party, the 12th of April. It was when I got back from work, it would have been around 6pm.'

'Okay, and think carefully about this, Suzie,' the inspector says, his tone intensifying. 'Did you see Emily after that Friday?'

I lean back in my leather chair and bite my lip. I glance up at Detective Peters, but he remains impassive. I feel small and complicit, like a child, and I purposefully pull myself forward on the chair until my feet hit the floor.

'No,' I say with certainty. 'I heard her, but barely. She wasn't as loud as she usually was, the weeks after the party. Maybe it was the letter.' I glance at the council letter gripped in Inspector Freeman's hands. Or maybe it was something else.

'I overheard an argument the night before the party, a bad one between her and a man,' I say, pointing to the hallway. 'It was quite late, but I heard a commotion in the hallway.' I remember the smell of booze and sweet aftershave penetrating my front door and the distorted faces of Emily and a man facing each other.

'Did you know what the argument was about?' asks Freeman.

'I couldn't hear much, but it sounded…' I pause, adding, 'heated.'

'Had you heard this man before?'

'Maybe. There was a man upstairs a week before her birthday. I don't know if it was the same man, or someone else. I'm sorry.'

'That's okay,' Peters says soothingly.

I dip my head into my hands and try desperately to remember what I'd heard in the hallway. 'She asked him to make up his mind,' I say. 'Over and over again, and then he left and she went back upstairs.'

The detectives eye each other and Freeman nods. 'Anything else?'

'She did most of the talking, I didn't really hear him, just deep noises. Maybe he was saying no, I'm not sure.' I look up. 'I went to my front door and looked through my peephole and I saw Emily and a man, but—' I can't remember his features and I start to grab the tips of my hair in frustration and gnaw on the bottom of my lip.

'It's okay,' Freeman says. 'That's really helpful.'

I want to remember the man's face but I can't, just the musty scent of stale beer, but I wasn't looking at him, was I? I was focused on Emily, I didn't take my eyes off her until he left. I stayed with her in the silence when he shut the door on her and she was left in the hallway alone.

'And these girls at the party – we're having trouble locating any close friends she had in London. Did you see any faces?'

I shake my head.

Detective Peters smiles at me, letting me know the questions are over.

'That's been really helpful,' the inspector says, scribbling in his notepad. 'If you think of anything else…?' he continues, looking up at me.

I frown, almost annoyed that they don't understand. I heard everything that went on in that flat and if Emily's in trouble, or in danger, shouldn't there be more to it than that? Officially a missing person now, and with that there is a responsibility to the girl upstairs. Don't I know her better than they do? Her movements, her poor choice in music, what she eats during the week, the wine she drinks and when she goes to sleep. I know the tone of her voice when she's happy and the sounds echoing her flat when she's not. I know she cries in the bathroom when she's sad and that her wellies are red, and her eyes are brown. I know something is wrong.

## Chapter Thirteen

Inspector Freeman is wandering around Emily's flat and I'm left standing in my lounge with Detective Peters. He focuses on the ceiling, his eyes squinting and hands resting on his hips.

The inspector is speaking, and we can hear the shallow dips in his voice as he tests the pitch and levels of noise. He moves in and out of rooms and I mutter which ones they are under my breath as he pulls open cupboards in the kitchen and scrapes the bedroom door open.

Detective Peters catches me doing this and smiles. 'It's loud,' he says.

'I didn't know when I bought the place,' I say, shrugging. 'He's just gone in the bathroom,' I add, following the inspector's footsteps into my bathroom. Detective Peters hangs in the doorway with his eyebrows raised as I turn to him. The sound is more effective here, and the inspector's voice echoes through the pipes and invades the space between the detective and me.

I point towards the ceiling. 'You can really hear everything in here.' I don't mean to be funny, but the he stifles a laugh and nods slowly before turning away. I follow him into the lounge as the inspector clambers back down to join us in my front doorway.

'I couldn't make out any words, but the voices are clear,' Peters says to the inspector. They exchange a look of concern, before Inspector Freeman turns to me.

'The man you heard, had he visited before when you'd been in or that you knew of apart from the two times you told us about?'

'I'm not sure.'

'Her parents didn't mention a boyfriend,' Peters says to the inspector.

I fidget awkwardly with my fingers. 'It wasn't just friendly the first time,' I say looking at the inspector.

'Friendly? So, they argued?' the inspector asks, shifting his weight onto one foot.

Detective Peters holds up a hand. 'I don't think that's what Suzie means.'

Recognition flits across the inspector's face and his mouth forms an O. 'We'll ask the parents again and see if she mentioned a boyfriend to anyone she used to work with.'

'This might be a little unorthodox,' Peters says. 'But

we could let Suzie have a look around Emily's flat, and see if there's any noises that mean something to her? It might help us understand the noises Suzie heard Saturday morning.'

The inspector considers this before glancing sideways at me. He squares himself to face me and leans forward slightly. 'Her parents seem worried,' he says slowly, adding gravity to the situation. 'We want to find her safe. Would you mind taking a look for us?'

I look up at Detective Peters and feel oddly comforted by his presence, like he wouldn't let anything bad happen to me up there, he wouldn't let me disappear like Emily.

'Yes, okay, any way I can help,' I whisper.

I follow closely behind the two officers as we climb the narrow staircase to Emily's flat. Inspector Freeman pushes open the door and gestures for me to enter.

The flat still looks the same as when I was last here, the pizza boxes piled to the height of the sofa arm and plates swamping the kitchen counter. The whole flat has a feeling of disarray and the same unusual feeling nudges me further inside.

I wander through the lounge trying to conjure images of what could have caused the noises, but it was all a blur that Saturday morning. I swallow the guilt as I wade through a stray pile of clothes and enter the kitchen area.

'Anything?' the inspector asks.

I shake my head. 'I'm sorry I can't be more useful.'

'Well, just take a look, but be careful not to touch anything,' the inspector says, pacing back to the doorway.

I stand awkwardly in the kitchen and look over at Detective Peters. He is staring at me intently and glances away when I look over. I consider the photo he found and what he must think of me. *I don't have a husband...* I flinch.

He pulls out a phone and I think he pretends to check it, but I can't be sure. I leave them both in the lounge and walk into Emily's small hallway. The bathroom light is on and the extractor fan whirrs gently as if inviting me in. I had heard Emily in the bathroom that morning. I walk in and look around, taking in the same open cabinets and masses of toiletries. I twist my body and position myself just in front of the toilet and close my eyes.

I always heard Emily in the bathroom, slow sobs when she sloshed around in the bath. The tug of the shower curtain. The clink of a tile. I open my eyes and peel back the shower curtain carefully and scan the outside of the bath. Had she grabbed something, and it knocked a tile? But I'd heard that noise before, hadn't I. I heard it when she cried.

I stare at the blue and white tiles lining the length of the bath and notice something off, one of the tiles jutting out slightly. I lean forward and gently skim my fingers over it, prying it loose until it comes away and falls into my hand. I hold it by the edges in a claw-like grip, staring at the grey empty slate where it came from. I sigh, about to slide it back into place until I feel something sharp tickle the top of my finger. I turn the tile over and gaze down at it. There are small white pieces of paper taped to the back. I peel the open edge of the tape and pull loose the bits of paper, slightly damp from the moisture in the bathroom. I can hear the officers talking in the lounge and I almost let the tile slip from my hands. The pieces of paper rain onto the bathroom floor and I bend quietly to collect them. I place the tile gently on the bathroom mat and shuffle the pieces into a neat stack. I glance towards the door and can't resist looking. I open the first piece and stare down at a day and time, a small message underneath:

*Thursday, 8pm, Casse-Croûte, don't be late.*

Inspector Freeman's voice grows louder as he moves towards the kitchen.

'Suzie?' the inspector calls, as I collect the papers and place them under the tape on the tile. He pushes the door slowly to reveal me standing bewildered and the papered tile perched in my hand. He glances up to meet my eyes.

'It's the noise I heard,' I say, offering the tile to him.

The inspector leans forward and takes the tile from

my hand and waves it in front of my eyes. He looks around the bathroom. 'Where did you get this?'

I point towards the bath. I see Detective Peters hovering in the hallway, craning his neck to see what's going on.

'Have you found something?'

The inspector says nothing, but reaches forward to skim his fingers over the empty space where the tile came from.

'It was loose.'

Inspector Freeman flips the tile over in his palm and stares down at the bunch of creased papers strapped to the back.

'The tile shifting, I've heard it a couple of times,' I say, nodding.

His eyes flicker up to meet mine. 'You shouldn't have touched this,' he says sternly.

I shake my head. 'I'm sorry, I know.'

Detective Peters shifts into the doorway and the inspector turns to him with the tile. They both exchange a quizzical look.

'We better see you out, Suzie. Thanks for helping us,' the inspector says.

I go to speak, but see Detective Peters shake his head slightly. 'Of course, if there's anything else you need, just let me know,' I say.

The inspector musters a smile as I edge around him and out of the bathroom. Detective Peters leads me to the front door in silence and I turn to speak but lose the words in the constricted hallway. We stare at each other for a moment, before we hear Inspector Freeman's heavy footsteps approaching. I feel like there's something he wants to say, but he stops himself before disappearing behind the closed door.

## Chapter Fourteen

**B**ack in the safety of my flat, I think about the message, and what it means, hidden away behind a tile in Emily's bathroom. I search for Casse-Croûte and a French restaurant pops up on Google maps in South London, Bermondsey. I think fondly about the Bermondsey beer mile a group of us conquered three summers ago and try desperately to remember the area, but all I conjure is the sticky taste of caramel stouts and pork loin burgers.

I can still hear Detective Peters and Inspector Freeman upstairs, but their voices are deliberately low. For my benefit, I think. I wonder what they will make of the note, and all the other small pieces of paper stashed away in Emily's bathroom, and then my mind flits to another thought. Would I get in trouble for looking? I know the answer is yes.

They both tread heavily down the stairs and I hear them pause for just a moment outside my door, then a decisive breath and they leave. I risk peeking around the curtains to see their backs as they stride down the narrow pavement.

Detective Peters had shaken his head. Why? It was a hidden gesture, something he didn't want his boss to see. Does he know I looked? I turn my attention to pictures of Casse-Croûte, the large plates of steak frites and bowls of moules marinière. I look at Street View: Bermondsey Street, lined with colourful cafés and expectant faces gazing into shop windows. I don't recognise this place from Emily's Instagram and it bothers me. If she were here, wouldn't she take pictures of the food, of her fawning over a cocktail in one of her tight dresses?

Emily had hidden the pieces of paper somewhere they were not supposed to be discovered. I'd heard the noise before – the clatter of the tile on the slate. She had hidden something in her own home. Did she not trust her visitors? My mind swims with possibilities.

Clara's name flashes up on my phone and I sigh wearily at the screen, reluctantly answering.

'Hey.'

'How's it going?' she asks.

'It's actually been quite a manic few days,' I tell her, adjusting my position on the leather chair.

'Oh yeah, with work?'

'Not exactly. I didn't actually go to work for the whole of last week.'

'Really? And they were okay with that?'

I shrug. 'I had a lot on.' I correct myself. 'I have a lot on.'

'Mum says you're visiting Hove soon, that's good,' she says, a statement.

'Yeah, I don't know how soon it will be though,' I say, licking my lips.

'She says soon.' Clara's tone changes, and I hear a note of anger.

'There's just a lot going on,' I say bluntly.

Clara pauses. 'I'm coming up.'

'No!' I blurt. 'Please don't.'

'Honestly, this is ridiculous now. I feel like the shittiest sister ever, just accepting that you're fine and you don't need me.'

'I don't need you,' I whisper.

Clara says nothing.

'I don't need you,' I hiss.

'No, of course you don't, Suzie, you don't need anyone,' she says, before hanging up.

I immediately feel rotten inside, like a bruised apple, fragile and soft and no good. A siren blasts past the window and I can hear an argument a couple of houses away. I scream as loudly as I can into the emptiness of my flat, before trudging to the kitchen and forcing open the fridge. The emptiness stares back.

I grab my jacket and head out into the foggy April evening. There is a chill in the air and the moist wind beats against my body as I walk in the direction of Angel tube station.

Emerging from Bermondsey station, I turn right and head in the direction of the beer mile. The familiar archways come into view and, as the night descends, small bleary lights gleam from the low brickwork. A large group is gathered outside one of the breweries and, as I pass the sea of suits, I watch as beer sloshes out of pint glasses and the conversation grows louder. The after-work crowd in this area revel in the lighter evenings. I push my way through, out onto the main street. I never go for drinks after work anymore. I used to be invited to the pub down the road and I'd sit nursing a gin and tonic and laugh at jokes I didn't find funny. I'd try too hard to be funny myself – I cringe remembering. We'd huddle by the door in winter and laze out onto the streets in summer. Now, I see them leave early on Fridays without me and I flash a solitary smile, letting them know not to ask anymore.

I round the corner onto Bermondsey High Street and push through the blanket of noise until I reach the other side. Sitting on the corner is Casse-Croûte, a small French bistro. There are tables each side of the doorway and a couple of wicker chairs sprawled across the narrow pavement. I think about going in, but what would I say?

The restaurant looks romantic and quaint, somewhere

a couple would share a bottle of wine and chorizo croquettes. Is that what Emily was doing here? Meeting someone?

I wander up the street, passing a bus stop and a group of girls in their early twenties swigging cans of lager. As I glance up, I see Detective Peters standing with Inspector Freeman; he's pointing over the road at the restaurant and jotting down notes. I slip under the bus stop shelter, my heart pounding.

Night settles on the bright street and as I peer around the bus stop I can see the officers hovering in the restaurant's doorway. I settle back on the thin red plastic seat and peek through the slim gap in the bus shelter. Inspector Freeman is shaking his head as Peters talks to a waiter, twisting slightly to look my way. I slide away from the gap, nudging into someone the other side, one of the girls sipping a Camden Hells lager. Golden liquid spills from the can and makes a satisfying slap on the pavement in front of us as she sighs deliberately at me. I apologise to her and her friends, holding up a hand in forgiveness, before I stumble to my feet and make a last glance to make sure the officers haven't seen me.

The sky starts to spit as I walk through the thinning Monday night crowd and head in the direction of London Bridge tube station. All the way home I feel drunk on my actions, and tiredness surges through me, but the brazen cackles of a group of drunk women and the loud music escaping nearby headphones keep me awake for the four-stop journey to Angel station. The thick London tube air penetrates me as I try to stand and I fall onto one of the tube poles, knocking my head slightly. I walk home slowly through the hazy night, feeling the musky April air push back at me, like a warning – don't go home, don't bury yourself in it.

As I round the corner, I catch the darkness of the upstairs flat above the emptiness of mine. A house standing in solitude, it feels like an entity, a place that has secrets and has rejected its inhabitants. I don't feel safe anymore and I suddenly feel desperate to be at home in Hove, to feel the salty breeze sting my face and smell the doughy warmth from the kitchen as my mum bakes apple and walnut cake. I want Clara to fling herself over my shoulders and to feel the weight of her lean into me, like an anchor holding me in place. I start to cry as I get nearer to my home, and I realise it's not home anymore, it's a crater of hatred that I've festered in for too long. Is this me acknowledging I need to move on? I'm not ready to move on, even if my body, my mind, is telling me I am. My heart is saying no.

## Chapter Fifteen

The next day I call in to work sick again, and this time my boss's voice is clipped; she just says the word 'fine' before hanging up. I know I've exhausted my options, but I struggle to care. Slouching forward, I pull out my phone from my dressing-gown pocket and call Clara, but she doesn't pick up. I send her a text:

*I'm sorry C.*

As much as I want to, I can't tell her I need her, because she'll come, and that same feeling from yesterday rises in my stomach, the fear of moving on. I lay my head back in the soft groove of the padded chair.

I wake to the sound of my phone buzzing lazily on the top of my thigh. It's Clara.

'Hey.' My voice is deep and croaky.

'You sound like shit. Late night?'

'No, I'm not well.'

'Oh, so you're off work again?'

'I guess.'

'You know, if things get tough, we can help out with your mortgage? And, before you say anything, it's not fucking pity. It's what sisters do.'

I smile. 'Thanks, but I'm okay.'

'Or would you think about selling it?'

'Maybe,' I say quietly, knowing I never could as I grip my hand around a crease of the leather chair.

'Something to think about,' she says casually. 'So what have you been doing?'

'My upstairs neighbour, she's still missing.'

Clara is silent.

'Did you call the police?'

'No, I called her landlord. I guess he let her parents know and now the police are involved.'

'So no one else knew she was missing?'

'I guess not.'

'Are you okay?' Clara whispers.

'Yeah I'm okay, it's just...' I trail off.

'Tell me,' Clara says gently.

'It just brings up old emotions.'

'Of course,' Clara says. 'That's only normal. Let me come and get you,' she says. 'Mum and Dad are expecting you.'

'I can't yet,' I gulp. 'What if Emily comes back?'

'Zee, this isn't something you have to worry about anymore. The police will do their job, she must have family.' Clara sighs. 'You need to think about yourself.'

'You don't understand.'

'What don't I understand?' Clara says, exasperated.

'No one knew she was missing, for a week.'

'There's nothing you can do. Just come home.'

I pause, thinking about roving the streets in South London, the small pieces of paper stashed away behind a loose tile in Emily's bathroom. A girl with secrets and no one to tell. I think about when it happened before, and how I just let it, but I can't this time, I have to be in control.

'Zee?' Clara interrupts.

'I have to help,' I say.

'It's not your job to help,' she says forcefully. 'Don't get involved in this.'

But I am involved. I think about Emily sitting in that little French bistro, the empty flat upstairs, and Emily's face as she waved the council letter in my face.

'I'm sorry, Clara.'

She sighs. 'Am I a bad sister?'

I frown. 'No, why do you say that?'

She is quiet, and then I hear my niece scream in the background and the swift screech of tears.

'I have to go,' Clara says.

'Yes, of course.'

'I'll call you later in the week, yeah?'

'Love you,' I say.

'You too,' she replies, before hanging up.

I pull my laptop onto my thighs and drape my legs over the padded leather arms. I reach for my cold cup of coffee. A silk film dances across the surface. I take long sips before my headache eases and I press my hands around my temples, squinting.

Detective Peters and Inspector Freeman would be asking questions at the restaurant, something I had planned to do, but it would have been reckless, even more irresponsible than going there in the first place. What would Clara think? Don't get involved.

I bring up the restaurant on my phone, cycling through the Google images again, when an email pops from work to my personal emails asking for a meeting when I'm next in the office. I swipe fiercely at my phone and think about what Clara had said. Selling my home. Was that even an option? It feels like a force is tightening around me, closing in and propelling me forward, and I desperately want to cling onto what I have now. I look around my home. I can't lose this. I need to do better at work, prove I'm okay, so I can return home and not be. The façade is slipping quickly and I'm scrabbling to keep up the pretence that I can do this.

'I can't do this,' I admit, out loud for myself to hear.

I'm running out of time, out of lifelines. I flick faster through the images of oily prawns, flutes of champagne and smiling faces.

Who did Emily know in London? She didn't have any friends, according to her parents. What had they said? She moved here for a job. I bring up Emily's LinkedIn page and this time, with my account set to private, I click on the small image of her staring back at me.

The page isn't detailed, with the little experience she has sparsely covering the page. Just her education, 'University of Cambridge', and then her first and only job, in London, 'Sales Executive' at PBL Associates. She was only there for six months. Maybe she didn't pass her probation? Too many late nights… I always left for work before her in the morning, although I'd hear her feet hit the floorboards and the heavy tread of her thick slippers slap against my ceiling. Did she ever make it to work, or was she fired for always being late?

I punch PBL Associates into *search* and arch my eyebrows as the results appear down the side of the page. London-based financial services firm. Address, Butlers Wharf Pier, Shad Thames. I click on the small map next to the large deep purple logo hoarding the screen. I furrow my eyebrows in confusion; the restaurant is only a short walk away. I think about the crowd of suits congregated on the edge of the dimly lit bar, swilling glasses of dark amber liquid.

London, with its secrets and seedy edges. I'd grinned through it, I'd tolerated it, for you – hadn't I? But you're not here anymore and suddenly I feel dirty and imprisoned. I want to leave, I want to go home, but I can't. I don't belong to myself anymore, I belong to London. I'm breathing to survive, to get by, but I can't breathe at all now.

The buzzer rings and I think it's for Emily, until I realise the sound is coming from my own buzzer, someone ringing for me. The curtains are drawn and I think it would be so easy to pretend. Maybe it's my boss and the meeting couldn't wait; they've come to fire me, to tell me, 'It's just not working out,' but they'll be sympathetic at the same time. Maybe it's my parents and they've come to drag me away from it all. I sink deeper into the sofa as the buzzer sounds again. I cover my ears and want to scream.

I relent and rise from the comfort of my leather chair. Stabbing at the intercom button, I ask curtly who it is.

'It's Detective Peters.'

I frown. 'Is everything okay?'

'Yes, I just need to talk to you, if that's okay?'

I pause. 'Okay, I'll come to the door.'

I slip on my trainers and pull a woolly jumper from behind the bathroom door. Scooping my hair up into a tight bun, I pull my front door closed on the latch and open the main door.

Detective Peters holds up a hand in a small wave. 'Hi, Suzie, sorry for dropping by.'

I nod, casting my gaze over him towards the streets heaving with the lunch work crowd. Groups of workers flocking along the street grasping uniform white plastic bags. I turn my attention back to the detective, who waits patiently for me to focus.

'What is it?' I ask, and it comes out blunter than I intend. He seems to ignore it, as he follows my gaze back towards the road and comments about the weather, before turning to me.

'Suzie, I just want to be as upfront as possible, because—' He shifts awkwardly. 'You're obviously a concerned neighbour.'

I dart my attention back to him. He isn't as composed as normal; his tie is loosened around his neck and his blazer is hanging open.

'I saw you at a bus stop in Bermondsey Street, at a location we were looking at it in regards to Emily's disappearance.' He pauses. 'Were you following us?'

I shake my head, but he doesn't believe me.

'Okay, well, my colleague doesn't know and'—he wrestles to find the words—'I'm happy to keep it that way, as you seem to have a lot going on right now, and —' His jaw twitches. 'Just so you don't get into any more trouble, as this is very serious.'

I stare at him; he seems genuinely concerned. I remember the way he handed me a tissue, the way he reacted when I told him I didn't have a husband and the subtle shake of the head when I was holding the tile in Emily's bathroom. Does he know what I've been through? He saw the state of my kitchen before I cleaned it. He saw the way I reacted when he asked to speak to my husband.

'I understand,' I say quietly.

He nods. 'Good, okay then.' He raises a hand, extending his thumb towards the road. 'I better go, but let me give you my card,' he says. 'That way, if you think of anything else you may have heard or seen, you can reach me.' He dives into his trouser pocket, slips a card out of his wallet and hands it to me, before extending another static wave and then walking away down the path. I look down at the card:

*Detective Sergeant Noah Peters*

'Thank you,' I say into the noise of my busy street.

## Chapter Sixteen

Three days had passed since that afternoon Detective Peters gave me his card and I patiently waited for updates. I called into work sick for the rest of the week and waited by the window, occasionally peeling back the curtain to see if anyone was coming.

I decided to wash my clothes, which had been lying between the piles of books and lining the bathroom floor. I wanted to change out of my tatty jogging bottoms and feel a different material around my hips. I noticed I'd been picking at the bobbles forming on my pyjamas as I read stretched out on the sofa, and the habit started to grate on me. My favourite green hoodie was stained with sauces and had darker sleeves from a build-up of dirt. It was comforting before, but it started bothering me, and as I rooted through the unwashed clothes, I found outfits I'd forgotten about – clothes that used to make me feel good. I usually wear the same jeans and a plain T-shirt to work, clothes I won't be noticed in, blending in with muted colours, beiges and blacks.

I pulled out a jumpsuit and some silky blouses and stuffed them into the washing machine. It wasn't much, but I know my mum would notice the difference on one of our video chats, and she'd think I'm getting better. I can imagine her saying it: *You look more like yourself.*

With the weekend approaching, I decide to call Mike to see if he's heard anything or if he knows if Emily's parents were still in London.

He answers the phone in the same rushed, exhausted tone he always uses.

'Suzie,' he states.

'Hey, Mike, how's it going?'

He sighs and I feel deflated. No news.

'Nothing?'

'No,' he confirms.

'Have you spoken to the police anymore?'

'Just to provide documents, tenancy agreements, things like that, but no, I'm not really involved anymore.'

'Do you think—'

'I hope she's okay,' he finishes.

I nod. 'And her parents? Do you know if they're still about?'

'No idea. I've had no contact with them.' He goes quiet. 'When I spoke to them I felt pretty reassured, like she does this kind of thing all the time.'

'Well, if you hear anything.'

'Same,' he says. 'Speak soon, Suzie.'

He hangs up and I clutch my phone in my hand. I search for my small black handbag and fish out Detective Peters's card. He gave me it for a reason, I reassure myself.

I decide to text him, something informal. I write out the message several times until I settle on:

*Hey, it's Suzie Arlington, just wanted to see if there were any updates you were allowed to share with me?*

I hit *send*.

I spend the rest of the day staring at my phone, willing, each time it lights up, that it's a message from the officer, and quickly disregarding any emails or messages from my parents or Clara. I trudge to the kitchen and flick the kettle on, opting for a cup of ginger and lemon tea. I flick my head to the mirror and notice the smoothness of my combed hair, the pale pink lipstick I applied this morning and the baggy blue jumpsuit that hangs on my shoulders.

My phone vibrates in the deep pockets of my jumpsuit and I fetch it, expecting to see my work calling, but instead it's Detective Peters.

'Hello,' I answer.

'Hi, Suzie, it's DS Peters.'

'Hi,' I reply, unsure of myself.

'I just wanted to get back to you about your message. We're still working to find Emily, so I don't have any updates for you right now, but I will let you know.'

He knows it's important to me, I can tell through the concern in his voice. I can hear a busy atmosphere in the background from where he's calling, maybe the office. I suddenly feel very silly, but it's the familiarity, isn't it? I clutch the phone and bite my lip. I've been here before, haven't I?

'Did her work not know anything?' I try to breathe steadily.

'No,' he replies firmly, then softens. 'I will let you know.'

'The girls I heard, or the man, nothing?'

He doesn't reply. I see how I look to him, mad probably, with my messy flat and photo of my husband stuffed down the sofa, piles of books and an empty bottle of whisky. I want to tell him I'm getting better, I want to say to him that it's not personal, I'm just a concerned neighbour. But it is personal, of course it is. I wonder if he knows.

'I wanted to ask you if everything's okay.' He says it so formally, but there's a friendliness in his tone, an understanding underpinning the question. I realise it's not a question; he knows I'm not okay, he's asking why, he's asking me to tell him. For a small moment I want to, I could tell him all about you and I'm sure he'd listen and he'd say the right thing. This is more than duty of care, he is a good person, but I can't tell him, because I can't say it out loud.

'I'm fine,' I reply, my voice sounding coarse and small.

'Well.' He pauses. 'That's good then.' He stops before changing his tone and saying, 'I've got to go, but if there are any updates, we'll be sure to let you know.'

He doesn't wait for me to reply before putting down the phone. I stand in the middle of my lounge and let tears dry and stain my cheeks. I rub the lipstick off with the back of my hand, feeling stupid and futile. I unzip the back of my jumpsuit and step out, like a snake shedding old skin, and pull my blanket from the leather chair around me. I sink into the chair thinking about you. I've never had to tell the story, everyone I've been around just... knew, like a noise I couldn't silence. They were told by my family, most probably. Everyone always asks if I'm okay, when they know that I'm not. I wish people would stop asking. I wish the noise would stop.

When I wake up, it's dark outside, apart from the burnt-orange glow from the street lights and low white beams from passing cars. Still wrapped in my blanket, I settle by the window, watching the London night guzzle the peace I scour the streets for. I see two scraggly foxes by a car and I see myself in them, worn down to the bones. They start to cry into the night, sharp painful screams that make me wince. A window slides open and a man's deep voice shouts, 'Shut up.' I look back at the foxes, agitated and distressed. Then something flies at them and they scamper away, like me, in search of peace. I stare at the fallen object, a piece of scrunched-up cardboard, and I let out a small cry.

---

I struggle to go back to sleep in the middle of the night. Suddenly all the London noises are amplified and I hear every car horn, front-door slam and drunk argument until the sun peeks through the crack of curtains into my lounge and the Saturday morning crowd slithers onto the street.

I stand in the shower for over twenty minutes and listen to the steady stream of water cascade down my body and into the drain. I dip my head backwards and take several gulps and feel the lukewarm water soften the dryness of my mouth and dampen my throat. I close my eyes. I've always used the shower to drown my thoughts, but instead they bubble to the surface and my eyes prick with guilt, rage and shame.

'I'm sorry,' I whisper.

I used to hear Emily above me when I showered, the clang of the toilet seat, gush of water, the medicine cabinet close. Now there's nothing, just an empty tile where she kept her secrets. Do I miss her noise? The terrible music and the smell of her cooking – there was something so hopeful about it, every sound charged with anticipation and promise.

Detective Peters had told me that Emily's work didn't know anything, but I couldn't squash the feeling that they did. The girls I heard upstairs, all squealing happy birthday to Emily, they are somewhere, they exist. I don't think I'd recognise their voices if I heard them again, but I know London offices, the pressure to socialise, to conform to Friday drinks and make friends at work. Did they all meet at that restaurant nearby? The officers didn't push this, but I will.

I make a plan to visit Emily's old workplace, the PBL Associates offices, on Monday, but I'll need to be careful. I've already been caught once and if Detective Peters or, worse, Inspector Freeman finds out I've been asking questions then it's serious. I wonder if I care, or if this is my redemption.

## Chapter Seventeen

I try to hold onto some of the feelings that made me slip on that jumpsuit and coat my lips pink, because it's the same feeling that took me to the doorway of our bedroom on Saturday evening. I stood there, gazing over the room, letting myself be sad, giving in to some of the pain until it became too hot and I started to burn.

Now I'm striding along the bank of the Thames and the day is relentlessly grey as the river churns and swallows the sky. People bump into me and sigh impatiently as I keep my shoulders steady and unmoved. The bars are full of laptops and notepads and meetings over bottles of Barolo. Tapas plates covered in padron peppers and salted squid scatter the tables, and tourists fawn over their small glasses of expensive Prosecco.

I reach a bleak brown-bricked building with black painted bars lining the windows and scan the list of companies on clear plaques next to the door. PBL Associates, floor six. I press the small silver button next to the logo and after several rings, a woman's clipped voice says, 'PBL Associates.'

'Hi, I'm Emily Williams's sister. I'm here to collect her things.'

The woman says nothing for a moment, before replying, 'Floor six.' The buzzer sounds and the door releases.

I walk into the small lobby and head towards the barriers, watching people tap in and out. The receptionist catches my eye and shouts to me, 'What company?'

'PBL Associates,' I reply.

'You'll need to sign in if you haven't got a pass,' she says.

'Oh no, I'm just visiting.'

She frowns. 'Okay, well, you'll need to sign the visitors' logbook and I'll get you a pass.'

I reluctantly walk over to the reception as she places a logbook and a pen on the counter.

'Can I ask who you're here to see?'

'Interview,' I reply.

She nods. 'Okay, that's fine, you can go up.'

I take a pass from her. She doesn't smile as she watches me walk to the barriers and presses something to let me in. People are waiting by the two lifts and as I reach forward to press the '6' button, I see a few eyes glance sideways at me.

I'm wearing a smart black dress, with tights and small kitten heels and my green blazer. I think I look the part, but the doubt presses into the small of my back and I start to sweat. I blow upwards at my fringe and stare straight forward.

The lift doors open and I wait for someone to let me go, but everyone scrambles quickly for a space and I squeeze in last, awkwardly. As we reach the sixth floor, most the people exit and push past me. There are two men in dark suits and three made-up women wearing tight skirts and high heels. They move in unison and I tail slightly behind towards the reception as they branch off in all directions. The office is larger than I expected, with glass walls exposing the open-plan floor and rows of desks full of stacks of papers and people hunched over computer monitors.

I approach the reception, where the purple PBL Associates logo is fixed on the front of a curved white desk. A young woman with a slick black ponytail swivels to face me.

'Emily's sister?' she says, her young features hanging in an expression of uncertainty.

'Yes, I just came for her things.'

'I called her department and Emily took her things when she left two weeks ago,' she says, standing up.

'Oh, I think she must have forgotten something,' I say, trying to compose myself. 'My parents wanted me to double-check.'

The woman nods, picking up the phone. 'Okay, well, I'll call through again and ask someone to check.'

'I'd much rather do it myself. It's quite sensitive, as you can imagine.'

The woman nods and gestures for me to take a seat. She watches me walk over to the purple tub chairs before glancing away. She speaks into the phone in short bursts and hangs up, before calling over to me, 'Someone's on their way.'

'Thanks,' I reply.

'I'm sorry to hear about Emily,' she says in an even tone.

I say nothing, but nod slowly.

A few moments later, I hear the clicking of heels against the hard floor and a woman appears, about mid-twenties with honey-blonde hair and thick, dark arched eyebrows. Her sweet perfume wafts in my direction as she stops abruptly at reception and points at me with long manicured nails.

'Emily's sister?' she asks.

I nod.

'Okay, right, do you want to follow me?'

I pick up my bag. The woman has already swivelled in the opposite direction and is strutting down the narrow aisle towards the back of the room. I struggle to catch up, as she bends her neck towards me.

'I didn't know Emily had a sister.'

'Yeah, half-sister,' I say awkwardly.

'Right, that explains it.'

I smile.

'What side?' she says.

I think about Emily's parents, her mum's small frame, wispy blonde hair and paler complexion.

'Mum's side.'

The woman arches an eyebrow. 'I'm sorry to hear about Emily,' she says, stopping at the end of a row of desks. I look around, but the area is mostly empty.

'Everyone's in a meeting at the moment, so you'll have some privacy. Her desk is in the corner, at the end.' She points. 'I thought she cleared it out, but if you want to double-check.'

'Thanks,' I mumble.

She smiles and turns to leave.

'Sorry,' I say, reaching out a hand. 'I didn't catch your name?'

'Brittany,' she says, staring me up and down.

'I'm Suzie.'

She grimaces. 'Emily never mentioned you,' she states.

'We weren't close,' I say, looking away.

'She was pretty reserved, like I told the police,' she says. 'She didn't say much about anything.'

I bite my lip. 'She called me sometimes, spoke about these friends she had.' I look up at Brittany. 'Work friends, and a place she liked to hang out – The Fence, I think it's called?'

She recoils slightly and folds her arms. 'I can't imagine that,' she says forcefully. 'Anyway, you can look in her desk. I'll be over there, let me know when you're done.'

I nod and squeeze down the row, pushing desk chairs out of the way. I sit at Emily's old desk. It's completely bare apart from a computer monitor and a couple of wads of Post-it notes.

I lean down under the desk and pull open the drawers of a white pedestal, but they are all empty. I drum my fingers on the table and look over at Brittany, who is facing the other way. An office door opens at the back of the room and people pile out into the aisle holding their laptops open. They charge in separate directions and disperse back to their desks around me. They eye me suspiciously and instead of sitting down, place their laptops down and walk in the direction of reception.

I swivel back to the meeting room to see a man exit. He halts in the doorway, staring down at a phone that he thumbs with one hand. He looks up at Brittany and I can't see her expression, but he quickly turns to face me. His broad face is lined with grey stubble and his eyebrows are thick. Smart, gelled black hair is combed to one side. He smiles, revealing a row of white teeth. He is extremely handsome, and as he steps towards me, I see his slim figure is dressed in a tailored waistcoat and pinstriped trousers. He strides towards me and hovers at the end of the aisle, waiting for me to join him. I clumsily manoeuvre between the chairs until I reach the end.

'Emily's sister,' he asks.

'Suzie, yes,' I say.

He smiles, and small creases splay from the corner of his deep brown eyes. 'Did you find what you needed?'

'No, but it's fine. My mum wanted me to check.' I smile warily.

'Of course, I think the police did a sweep of the desk when they came in as well.' He looks at me impassively.

'Brittany, would you show Suzie out?' Maybe it's more forceful than he intends it to be, but the conversation is over. He smiles at me.

'I hope Emily is okay. If you need anything else, you know where we are.'

I nod. 'Thanks.' I collect my bag and Brittany brushes past me, beckoning me to follow.

'Sorry, she never mentioned you. Were you her boss?' I say, turning back.

He looks surprised, then smiles. 'Darren,' he says. 'I'm the head of sales.'

'Of course, thanks,' I say.

He turns away and continues back towards the glass rooms. I go to leave, but pause. The smell of sickly sweet, citrusy aftershave lingers, the scent of bitter orange mingled with smoke permeating the air. I know this smell. I think about the fight in the hallway between Emily and a man, the figure just out of view. Could it be?

'This way,' Brittany snaps.

I can feel him watching me as I follow Brittany as she bounds back towards reception. She leads me past the front desk and taps a green button at the office door.

'Sorry, could I use the loo before I leave?'

Brittany narrows her eyes, before curling her lips. 'Of course, just down the corridor on the left.'

'Thanks.'

She nods and walks back towards reception. I scuttle to the doorway and edge past two women leaving the toilets. I lock myself in a stall and lean my back against the door, taking short breaths. I try to force my breathing under control and wipe my face gently with both hands. Gathering my belongings, I pull open the door and standing in front of me is the receptionist I saw on the way in.

The rest of the bathroom is empty as I gaze around. The young girl's eyes remain fixed on me as I edge forward to the sink to wash my hands. She reaches out for a paper towel and hands it to me. I look up at her.

'You're not Emily's sister,' she says.

'Half-sister.'

She shakes her head. 'Emily doesn't have a sister.'

'She just didn't talk about me,' I say, drying my shaking hands.

She bends her neck so her thick black ponytail hangs next to my face.

'Who are you?'

I can't reply. I turn to face her. She stares back at me, eyes glazed over.

'Were you really a part of it?'

'Of what?'

She leans back and heads towards the door. She hesitates, as if trying to make a decision.

'That family,' she says, before leaving.

I stand at the sink, terrified and frozen. The door swings open and two women ease past me, giggling. I smile at them in the mirror, then collect my things and head out through the open door and along the corridor. I risk looking at reception, which is empty. I stab the green button and rush into the lift and out onto the crowded street. The people push me away from the office and I'm thankful, for a moment, to be carried effortlessly away in a sea of faces.

## Chapter Eighteen

'That family.' So Emily did have friends, or at least people she confided in. What did she tell them? The truth? A dramatised version? I remember hating my own family when I was younger, thinking at times I'd never speak to Clara again, that I'd cut off my parents and for what? Nothing, just a passing phase, just the people who could take it and would remain.

Emily had sometimes gone weeks without speaking to her parents, that's what they'd said. They had seemed overbearing, detached, but concerned. I can imagine they were hard to deal with, but then again I knew Emily could be too. Was it that kind of relationship where they spoiled her when she was young and then adulthood hit and the cushy lifestyle Emily knew came crashing down and she'd gone to work, and told her co-workers awful stories about a family that had cast her out?

I didn't know if Emily's parents were still in London. I wonder if Brittany or the receptionist rang the police after I left and told them I'd been there. They'd describe me and the two officers would know who I was.

I think about ringing Mike, but he seemed so dismissive when I last spoke to him. Not involved anymore. I want to reach Emily's parents and understand what the receptionist meant by 'that family', because Emily's hiding something. Or they are.

I take my laptop to the dining table and search for Stuart Williams, Emily's dad. Nothing. I try Emily's mum, Christie Williams, and to my surprise, on the right-hand side of the page, a business pops up, Christie Williams Art Studio. I click the web link to their site and I'm taken to a page full of abstract paintings. I've always hated art. A sweeping statement, Clara would say.

I feel more than ever, after meeting Emily's parents, that there's something off about them. The way they shifted the blame onto Emily, trying to normalise that she's missing. I stare at the pictures of some of the abstract paintings they have on sale, each going for at least three thousand. Broad, empty strokes and an empty price tag to match. I think about them sliding into the leather seats of their Mercedes and move my cursor over to the 'about' section.

A family-run business, I read. Bespoke original paintings as seen in... and an endless list of galleries to follow. I search the site for an address and find they have a shop not far from Cambridge, in a village called Saffron Walden. I take a look at how long it will take me to get there, and see a direct train runs from London to Audley End station. On Street View, the road is lined with trees and picturesque houses and the art gallery sits between them all, framed in cream with a red painted sign.

I need to speak to Emily's parents, to understand what the receptionist at PBL Associates meant by 'that family'. I think about what I'll say to them, but I settle on being honest. I'm her neighbour, I want to help.

This is riskier; Emily's parents have met me before and they'll tell the police I've visited. I look down at my phone and think about calling Detective Peters. He'd sounded understanding and patient when I'd spoken to him before. I search and find his business card wedged under an open book.

'Hello,' he says when he picks up.

'Hi, it's Suzie Arlington again. Sorry to bother you.'

I hear a car horn and then the sound of an indicator. 'It's no problem,' he says.

'I actually needed to talk to you about something, about Emily. I think it's important.'

He doesn't reply straightaway. I hear another indicator, then he says, 'I can stop by if that's easier. I was just driving back from our offices by Liverpool Street.'

'Oh,' I say. 'Yes, if that's not too much trouble.'

'No, it's fine, I'll be there in about ten minutes.'

I hang up the call and look around my flat. It's tidier

now, more respectable than the last couple of times the officers visited. The piles of clothes have been cleaned and put away, the kitchen is sparkling – untouched. I take a quick look in the mirror. I'm wearing my uniform of a black T-shirt and tired-looking jeans. The jumpsuit is slumped on the floor by the dining table where I left it, and I think momentarily about putting it on, before pushing the thought away.

I'm watching at the window when Detective Peters pulls up in his car. His hair has gone a little blonder in the April sunshine. He must be outside a lot, I think, exploring all parts of London, all manners of things. He must be used to odd people, concerned neighbours, people like me.

This time I'm ready at the door to greet him. His sleeves are rolled up to his elbows and he has removed his tie. He looks at me with an expression I find difficult to place. It's not pity, it's patience; he is here and he is trying to understand.

'Hi,' he says awkwardly. 'Everything okay?'

I nod. 'I just… I had a thought about Emily's parents.'

He holds up an arm and squints at me as the low evening sun blinds him.

'Sorry,' I say. 'Do you want to come in?'

He twists his head and looks down the street. 'We could go for a walk if you want?'

I like this time of the day, just as the sun catches the tips of the trees and the air starts to cool. It's the first warmth I've felt this spring and for a moment the detective and I stand staring at the low sun, squinting into its mellow heat.

'Yes, okay, let me just grab my keys.'

He nods.

I stuff my feet into my old trainers and grab my keys. I wince slightly as I pick them up; it's something I hadn't noticed in a while, but I notice it now. You colour-coordinated our keys, as I kept getting them jumbled up.

When we first moved in I laid all the keys out on the dining table and sat leaning over them smiling, exclaiming, 'They all look the same, they all look the bloody same.' How was I ever supposed to get it right? For the first few weeks I didn't and you'd hear the key scrambling around the lock and by the time I eventually worked it out, you'd be doubled over laughing. I'd try and mask a smile, but still laughing you retreated to the bathroom and came back with my nail varnish case.

'Come here then,' you said, taking both our keys.

I watched as you colour-coordinated each one. Orange is for the main door, green is for our front door, blue is for the back door and red is for the bike shed.

'This is very patronising,' I said smirking.

You frowned. 'I don't mean to be,' you said, holding up the keys in triumph. 'Our home,' you said, dangling them.

I grasp the keys in my hand. Memories bite like this occasionally and I know I should smile, laugh at them, but they are little pockets of time that we'll never have again and that's what makes them so painful, not just the moments when it was good, but the moments I can never change. They make me feel helpless.

'Hello?' Peters calls, gently pushing the main door open.

'Sorry,' I say, standing in my doorway. 'Just trying to find my keys.'

I follow him out into the hazy evening. An orange hue dusts the skyline as we walk towards the park, pale pink blossom lining the footpath.

'So, about Emily?' Peters prompts.

We reach the small strip of grass that joins two streets with slim gravelled pathways that weave between small stretches of shrubbery. We pause by a bench, but don't sit down. We both just look up at the pastel sky imbued with the late afternoon sun, as we're if searching for something.

'Are Emily's parents still in London?'

He frowns, turning to me. 'I don't think so, why?' He takes a step back. 'I don't have an update,' he says firmly.

'No, but—' I gaze back up at the sky, as the sun slowly starts to disappear behind the high-rise buildings in the distance.

'I know it's tough,' he says quietly. 'With everything that happened.'

I start to feel myself dampen with sweat, the backs of my hands prickle, the panic set in. I look at him. His face is twisted into an uncomfortable and awkward expression.

'What do you mean?' I turn my eyes away, not able to see his expression any longer.

'I know what happened to your husband. I'm really sorry.'

The last of the rays sink behind the buildings, the vivid colours lost in the grey evening, as a nearby streetlamp gently illuminates our bodies, casting slim shadows. I stare up at the sky. Billowing angry crowds circle overhead, and the gaps between the buildings are slanted like eyes, a menacing expression looking back.

'How do you know?' I say, my voice so small I barely hear myself.

'Inspector Freeman told me before we came back to ask you questions the second time. I'm so sorry. I saw that picture on the sofa and he remembered your name, your husband's name.'

'I have to go.'

'Please, Suzie, I didn't mean to upset you. I just wanted to say I understood.'

But I'm already walking away. I hear his footsteps behind me and I scream as loudly as I can, 'Don't follow me,' and they stop.

I wait until I'm at the end of my street and call my mum.

'Suzie, what's wrong?'

I cry at her until I reach my flat and stand at the front door, smacking it.

'Talk to me, honey,' she says softly.

I sit on the doorstep and let the overgrown grass tickle my ankles.

'Ben,' I say between waves of tears.

'Honey, I know,' she says, makes shhing noises, and I slowly begin to stop crying.

'Every time I think I'm ready, I feel something pull me back again. Mum, what if I can't move on?'

'Honey, maybe you shouldn't put this pressure on yourself. Maybe you're trying to move on from the wrong thing.'

'I don't understand,' I say, wiping my nose on my sleeve.

'You're blaming yourself for what happened.'

'What if there was more I could have done?'

'We've been over this. There isn't, you did everything you could to find him.'

'I don't know myself without him, Mum,' I say, rising from the step.

'You shouldn't be afraid to.'

I put my keys in the door and let the warmth encase me. I open the second door, wade into my flat and fall into the leather chair.

'I love you,' she says. 'Will you come home?'

I nod. 'I just have something to do first.'

'Do what?'

'Make things right,' I say.

'Please stop reliving what happened. Is that what this is about?'

'I can't... I'll never be able to forgive myself for what I said.'

'What you both said. It was a stupid fight; you were both so much more than that.'

'I hate that those were my last words to him.'

She doesn't reply.

'I'm going to sleep,' I say.

'Night, darling,' she says.

'Night, Mum. Love you.'

'You too.'

She puts down the phone and I hang up. I feel stupid for walking away from Detective Peters when he was just trying to be nice, to be there for someone he barely knows. I lean my head back onto the grooves on the leather chair where two dents used to sit. He's right, it is tough because of everything that happened. I lost you. I can't let Emily down too, I can't let me slamming the door on her be our last exchange. I open my laptop and start planning my route to visit Emily's parents, feeling like I have nothing to lose. Who are you, Emily?

# Chapter Nineteen

## Emily

'Who am I?' I tapped my pen against the notepad and ran my fingers across the dense ridges of the binder. Alice was lying on the bed humming gently, her own notepad pushed to one side and replaced by her phone. She looked up at me as I turned around, her wavy dirty-blonde hair stuck to one side of her face as she grinned.

'You know exactly who you are,' she said, scoffing. 'It's a stupid project.'

I swivelled back to face the desk and the empty notepad. Maybe Alice was right, it's stupid.

'Why don't we go to the pub?'

I didn't reply, because I didn't want to go to the pub. She sensed this, of course.

'Or we can stay here and not do this?'

'I like that plan better,' I admitted.

I closed the notepad and felt relieved. It was a project set by my creative writing tutor. I was supposed to write a piece that explores who I am, a way to 'bring me out of my shell' as she so kindly put it. She said my writing lacked emotion. A sense of self. Empathy for my characters. She wanted me to write about an experience that had made me me, as a kind of exercise for our poetry class.

'She's wrong, you know,' Alice said, 'You're an amazing writer. It's subjective, anyway.'

She jumped up from the bed and leant over me, her hair tickling my cheek as she swiped the laptop from her desk.

'Is she?'

'You know she is.'

I liked to write romance, but maybe it wasn't my genre, my place, maybe I lacked the experience. I loved watching romantic films late at night, even when I stayed on Alice's bedroom floor on a blow-up bed. She'd slowly doze next to me, insisting I didn't turn it off if it helped me sleep.

The way romantic comedies made me feel was something I could rarely emulate in real life, a euphoria that I struggled to capture. I desperately wanted to write romance and make someone else feel affected, to have that moment when it's nothing but two people's love for one another. My favourite was Strictly Ballroom, a 90s film about ballroom dancers. I loved watching the way the two main characters' body language changed throughout the film. How rigid they were at first and how they slowly intertwined, almost becoming one entity. I wrote a poem about love being like a dance, but my tutor said it lacked the raw emotion, the grit and passion you feel when you're dancing for love. It lacked love.

'What do you want to do?' I asked Alice.

She sat against the wall with the laptop perched on her knees. She looked up and flashed a wicked smile. If you won't go to the pub, then I will bring the pub to you. She raised her hand and brought a finger down to hit a key, the small speakers suddenly blaring The Smiths into her room. She pushed the laptop to one side and flew onto her stomach, stretching her arms to start grabbing for something underneath the bed.

'Aha,' she said, raising a bottle of spiced rum over her head.

'No,' I said, smiling, holding a finger up into the air.

She smirked. 'You always say that.' She tore off the bottle cap. 'Yet you always end up drinking it.'

She was right. We spent the rest of the evening curled up on her bed watching silly YouTube videos and listening to music. We got about a quarter of a bottle in when Alice grabbed her guitar nestled behind her pillow and started to strum along to the notes. She whispered the words quietly under her breath as she gazed out of the window. The giggling ceased, the noise softened and I just watched her play. Alice knows who she is, I thought, as her fingers stroked the strings methodically and her lips followed as if in a trance.

I looked back at the desk, at the closed notepad. It would be easy to write about Alice, someone who is a permanent fixture in my life, and I smiled at the thought of that.

We drank until we reached halfway down the bottle, then

hid it behind a pillow when Alice's mum peered around the door to say goodnight. Laughing when we asked ourselves why we were hiding alcohol at twenty-three like it was illegal.

Alice raised an eyebrow. 'Well, you know how disapproving my mum can be of my rock 'n' roll lifestyle.'

I laughed. 'It's all a façade.'

She smirked knowingly. Alice was an aspiring musician studying music at a college in Cambridge. I've known her since I was eleven, as we were both forced to mingle in the first year of high school and have been inseparable since. We've always been the opposite of each other: she's carefree, with a loud mouth, but also quietly vulnerable, with an innocent mischief. I've never seen her cry and she must have seen me cry a million times. I knew why were different, though. I don't remember the last time my mum peered around the bedroom door to say goodnight to me. I frown, looking over at the empty notepad. Who am I?

'What are you thinking?' Alice asked.

I forced a smile. 'That if I drink any more, you'll be clearing up my sick.'

'Beautiful. Well, let me get the blow-up bed out. I assume you're staying?'

I caught a look in her eye as she slid past me and opened the built-in wardrobe and pulled out the deflated bed. She knows I'm staying.

'You should keep more stuff here. My mum loves having you. She thinks you're a good influence on me. Little does she know.'

'A good influence?' I ask. 'I just drank half a bottle of rum.'

Alice laughed, but a seriousness creased the corners of her eyes and lines appeared on her forehead.

'I wish you didn't go back there.'

I know what she wanted to say, but she doesn't. Instead she unfurled the blow-up bed and gestured for me to move so she could lay it out.

'Go and brush your teeth. I can smell your rum breath from here.'

I wanted to reach forward and hug her, but she'd never been tactile, and I felt her tense as I stepped forward. Her quiet vulnerability.

When I came back from the bathroom Alice had set up the laptop next to my pillow. She'd even scrolled down to the romantic comedy section on Netflix. She was lying across the bed, propped up on her elbow.

'What are we watching tonight?' she asked.

I smiled, flicking off the light and stumbling towards the bed, my path illuminated by the glow from the laptop. I snuggled down into the bed Alice had set up for me, her comforting smell suffusing the pillow. I closed the laptop and we plunged into darkness.

'Oh,' said Alice's small voice.

'I'm tired,' I replied.

I was tired. Tired of living through those movies, those moments. I needed my own. Or else how could I ever know who I am?

## Chapter Twenty

As the train leaves London, I watch as the concrete skyline dwindles into fields and silently wish this was the journey to Hove. It takes over half an hour until London feels distant to me. The crowd on the train thins and I move to a window seat, watching flashes of green and crisp yellow dart past the window. I bring a hand to the glass and smile fondly, before an unease rests heavily in my stomach.

My mum called me on Sunday to check in, and when I didn't answer, she made Clara call me and then my dad. I told them all I was fine, not to worry, that I'd be home soon and this time, it was true.

The train pulls up at Audley End, and I clamber off with a few other people and walk through the barrier. I call a taxi and wait patiently for twenty minutes until it arrives to take me into Saffron Walden. We drive through narrow country lanes, skimming stretches of verdant fields and towering peat-brown trees. My heart soars a little. I ask to be dropped off further down the road so I don't pull up right outside the studio.

The roads are calm, with a few passing cars and a couple of joggers heading in the opposite direction. The air tastes different here; it's thin and clean as I take deep breaths towards the studio. Trees converge and arch over the pathway and I can hear the sound of birds singing in the dips of their branches. The walk is uphill and my thighs begin to throb as the road plateaus. I take a few moments to gain my breath and look up, seeing a neat white road sign, Church Street, and a small detached building, the art studio. I see the red painted sign hanging from the top window and a small ramp leading up to the front door. The brickwork has been painted cream and is flaking slightly on the edges. One side of the front of the building is glass and I can see into the small reception area, where a couple of paintings are propped up in the window.

Light cascades off the glass and dims the interior, but a figure appears and walks towards the front door, swinging it open. A bell chimes and I turn suddenly to see Emily's dad standing in the doorway, with one arm outstretched to hold open the door. He looks at me for a while, before pointing above my head.

I look up to see a small black camera poised just above the window.

'I thought I recognised you. Emily's neighbour, is that right?'

I nod.

'Well, come in,' he says, beckoning me towards the door.

I edge past him, taking in his smoky scent, and I'm greeted by the raw smell of acrylic drifting through the studio. He shuts the door and turns to me. He's wearing a red jumper this time, with a white shirt sticking out from underneath. He extends a hand.

'Sorry, I forgot your name.'

I shake his hand. 'Suzie.'

'Yes, Suzie.' He looks around. 'My wife's the painter. I work part-time now, so I help out around here.'

'It's lovely.'

He nods enthusiastically before his face droops. 'Is there news?'

'Oh no,' I reply quickly. 'No news, I just wanted to see if I could help.'

'Oh,' he says. 'Well, Christie's out the back painting, but I'm sure she'd be delighted you came. Do follow me.'

I follow him down several small wooden steps and a narrow corridor, which gives way to a large, light, open room, with high ceilings and paintings lining every wall.

'Darling, Emily's neighbour is here.'

Christie's face appears in the middle of the room, from behind a large wooden easel. Her tight blonde curls are pulled back from her face with a navy headscarf. She tips her head down and peers at me over the top of dark-rimmed glasses.

'Is everything okay?'

Emily's dad makes a calming motion with his hands. 'No news yet.'

Christie throws her paintbrush at the easel and pushes her chair back, raising a hand to pinch the space between her eyes.

'I don't know how much longer I can take this,' she says.

Stuart rushes to her side and places a hand gently on her shoulder. 'I know.'

Christie looks up at me, mascara smudging the corners of her eyes.

'I've been trying to distract myself, but nothing works.'

'I know,' he coos.

Christie composes herself and taps Stuart on the hand. He removes it and she smiles up at him. She stands and emerges from behind the easel, walks towards me and places her hands on her hips.

'Sorry, we've met before haven't we?'

'Yeah. I'm sorry if this is a little weird, me turning up like this.'

She looks serious now. 'You came from London?'

I nod. 'I just wanted to help any way I can. I didn't have your details.'

She looks me over, her mouth turning up at one

corner. 'What was your name again? Haven't you spoken to the police?'

'Suzie, I—' I bite my lip. 'I'm sorry if this was a bad idea. I just got to know Emily, well, kind of, I used to hear her above me.'

She looks surprised. 'You told us about her having a party,' she says, turning to Stuart. 'They never found those girls, you know.'

'I know,' I say.

'Well, how about we go back to the house, and you can tell us what you know. It would be nice to hear it first-hand, because if I'm honest with you, Suzie, the police have been shit.'

The word sounds unnatural coming from her, and I catch Stuart wince as she says it. She juts her chin out and turns to him.

'Let's go. Lock up,' she says to him vehemently. She grasps my shoulder and swivels me around to face the front of the studio.

'He'll meet us at the house,' she says, turning her head slightly.

We walk silently along the street and make a left at the corner. Christie is wrapped in her pale cream coat and she waves as several cars pass.

'It's a small town,' she says. 'We're up here on the left.'

I stand behind a large black metal gate and gaze up at their double-fronted brick house, surrounded by small green hedges. Christie dips into her bag for keys and stabs at a fob and the gates fold open for us. The driveway is lined with three cars – the Mercedes I've seen before, a yellow Mini and a sporty-looking Audi. Ivy crawls up the front of the house and each white-framed window hosts a nest of potted plants. There's something so theatrical about the house, like it's been painted this way. It's motionless; even the slight chill in the air seems to curve around us and the house remains untouched.

'It's beautiful,' I say.

'Thank you. It didn't look like this when we bought it,' she replies.

But I think that's untrue. The house is magnificent, the prettiest on the street, and Christie knows it. She looks at me.

'The yellow Mini is Emily's. She said she wouldn't need it in London.' She frowns, opening the door. 'Come in,' she demands.

I step through into the porch and she asks me to remove my shoes. I'm led through to a large hallway with cream carpets my feet sink into. The dark green wallpaper is covered in photographs, all in dusty pink and silver frames. There is an elegance about the place, a flair that only this house could pull off. I think about applying the same wallpaper to my flat and almost laugh. Pale pink chandeliers dangle from the ceiling and

I duck slightly as Christie leads me down the hallway and into the kitchen.

'Can I get you a drink?' she asks, pulling open a powder-blue cupboard to reveal a hidden fridge. 'Tea, coffee, orange juice?' She looks at me. 'Wine?'

I nod and smile.

'Please, sit down.'

I move through the kitchen, my feet cool on the terracotta tiles, and into the adjoining conservatory. I lower myself into a wicker chair covered in a light orange cushion. The garden is smaller than I imagined, but it's landscaped, with an imposing grey fountain covering most of the lawn. We have a large back garden in Hove, with overgrown grass, and when I was growing up my dad strung a homemade badminton net between the washing line and his shed. I smile at the memory.

'Lovely, isn't it, an antique,' Christie says, placing a small glass of crisp white wine in front of me. She clutches hers to her chest and sits opposite me, staring at the fountain.

'I've always liked sitting here watching it. We had it brought over from Italy. Have you ever been?'

I shake my head. 'No, I've always wanted to go though.'

'You should, it's lovely this time of year, just as it starts to heat up, and the water's just right.' She takes a sip of wine.

'Your home is lovely,' I say. 'I saw the pictures of Emily as a baby. She's an only child?'

Christie nods. 'Not planned,' she says bluntly. 'But loved all the same.' She looks at me sideways. 'Did she give you hell?'

I laugh awkwardly. 'Sometimes.'

'My daughter was like that – incredibly reckless with people. I know what she can be like.'

'You must be really worried. I'm sorry,' I say.

She nods. 'She kept to herself. I can't say we are a close family.' She crosses her slim legs and as the light hits her face revealing dense wrinkles through a layer of thick foundation. She looks older to me now, even smaller, and weathered. She drinks more wine and sinks lower into the chair. 'We sent her money for her birthday, became her guarantors so she could have that flat in London, but she wasn't grateful.'

'Do you think she ran away?'

Christie shrugs. 'It's not running away at twenty-three, is it? And she's left us to pick up the pieces. We'll have to pay rent on that flat she so desperately wanted.'

I follow her eyeline to the fountain.

'She hated it.'

'The fountain?'

She lets her head fall back onto the chair and stares at the ceiling.

'Being here.'

'Why?'

'I don't know. She hit that teenage-girl phase pretty hard, my art studio took off, the attention was no longer on her. She was a bitter person. Is that horrible? To think that your daughter is bitter?'

I consider this. 'I think if you love someone it's okay to see the bad in them, to want to help them.'

Christie smiles. 'Why are you here, Suzie?' she says, swallowing the last of her wine. She reaches forward and takes my glass with her to the kitchen. She fills both of them up, this time almost to the top.

'I just wanted to know if there was anything I could do. The officer said you'd be clearing out Emily's flat in London soon. Maybe I can help.'

'That's nice of you, but you didn't come all the way from London to say that.' She looks at me with piercing blue eyes.

I stare back at her, then to the fountain. 'I've been through something similar,' I say.

'Daughter?' she says, taken aback.

'Just… similar.'

'Say no more.' She smiles. 'I'm angry at her, you know, for doing this,' Christie continues. 'It's like her to run away when something fails, like her big move to London and glamorous new job, which,' she says, holding up a finger, 'I never approved of. But what she's done—' She looks away. 'You know why I was so upset the last time I saw you?'

I don't reply.

'Because of what she's putting me and Stuart through. If I'm honest with you I think she's done this out of spite.' She slumps further back into the chair. 'Of course I have to ring the police and I tell them, this is like her, but technically she's missing and this has been the longest she's been gone. I wish I could tell her she's too old to run away. It's so dramatic.'

'Why do you think she did?'

Christie eyes me. 'It's what Emily does when things don't work out her way – she runs.'

'That's sad.'

'No, you shouldn't feel sorry for her, nothing was ever her fault,' Christie says, taking a large mouthful of wine.

'What about if something happened to her?' I say quietly.

She looks at me.

'She's clever, my daughter,' she says, waving a finger. 'You'll only ever see what she wants you to see.'

I consider this. 'She had no friends in London?'

Christie shrugs. 'Not that I knew of, but as I said, when she moved to London we didn't have a lot of contact. That's why I'm thankful you alerted her landlord, and now the police are involved and she knows it's serious,' she says, threat tingeing her voice.

I nod. 'Where would she go? Hasn't she used any of her bank cards? Can't they trace that?'

Christie's eyes narrow as she faces me. A door slams

shut up the corridor and Christie's gaze rests on me for a moment before she turns to the kitchen as Stuart walks through.

'Not interrupting, am I?' he asks, placing his keys on the sideboard.

'No,' Christie says.

I place my wine on the table in front of me. 'I actually better be going,' I say, feeling the atmosphere change and Christie's mood shift. 'I'll leave my number with you, in case you need anything.'

'Thanks, darling,' Christie says, rising from her chair. 'For coming all this way.'

I shake my head. 'I just want to help. Would it be okay to use your bathroom whilst I'm here?'

'Yes, of course, up the hall, first door on the left as you come in,' she says, smiling.

I walk past Stuart, who glances away. I leave them in the kitchen, feeling the tension behind me and Christie's steady gaze as she watches me walk up the hallway. I pause outside the bathroom and rest my fingers on the handle, looking at the picture of Emily as a baby and then the other photographs that circle it. One of Stuart and Emily at the park with ice-creams, grinning at the camera. Another of Emily riding a horse, an outstretched hand stroking its mane.

I close the bathroom door behind me and lean onto the sink. The wine has reached my temples and pulses mercilessly as the warmth of the bathroom cocoons me. I suddenly feel very sick. I splash my face with cold water and let the cool droplets cascade down my clammy cheeks. I wash my hands and open the bathroom door and see Christie standing by the open front door. I've outstayed my welcome.

'We've got a lot to do today, but we'll make sure the police alert you to any changes,' she says directly.

I turn to say goodbye to Stuart, but I can't see him down the hallway. Christie smiles at me and stretches out a hand to gently rub my shoulder. 'Thanks so much for coming all this way, it's really appreciated.'

I step out into the sunny afternoon as the door closes firmly behind me. I make my way back down towards the main street to call a taxi and think I've never met a family like the Williamses, so much wealth circling them like piranhas. I've always thought that about money, that it's inevitable in some way that it will cause destruction. I think back to a very different conversation about money, an argument. The rotten taste of words I didn't mean resting on my tongue and the back of your head as you walked out of the flat. I wince at the memory, I can feel it itching my skin as the taxi pulls up outside the train station. Then the words are there like they've finally won.

'I'm doing this for us. This is the life we want.'

'If this is the life you want, then I want no part of it.'

The sound of a door slamming and the instant regret.

# Chapter Twenty-One

## Emily

A lice asked me to meet her at a pub right by her college. I couldn't wait for a long, cold beer and a greasy burger to see off a tiring day at University. I still couldn't get my creative writing piece right. Self-expression, my tutor had said this afternoon to try and unburden me from the obvious despair I was feeling. I fussed with the conversation I'd had, playing it over in my head on the walk to meet Alice, the habitual feeling of doubt creeping into the backs of my eyes.

I was also becoming painfully aware that I'd have to go home at some point as well. I'd been staying at Alice's for over a week and the pile of dirty clothes at the foot of my makeshift blow-up bed had been slowly rising. Alice had offered me clothes; she told me to pick up some knickers today and borrow her T-shirts. I'd eventually given in to her thrusting a knitted jumper at me this morning as we stepped outside to a light chill in the air, too cold for April, I'd thought. I'd accepted reluctantly and she helped me pull the jumper over my head, giggly as we both knew it was too big for me. But all of Alice's clothes were designed that way, big baggy black jeans that swamped her slight frame and chunky jumpers to match. As I marched across the park, almost at the pub, the jumper rode up slightly to the tip of my nose, masking my lips. I inhaled and pulled the jumper closer, the familiarity and comfort drowning my thoughts for a moment.

As I reached the pub, I was welcomed by the rich smell of beer-infused wood and oily batter. A plate of onion rings wafted past my nose as I crammed past a group of students huddled by the bar. A waiter headed towards me and I stepped to the side, accidently treading on one of the students' feet. A guy turned around, an apologetic hand already raised in the air, his other hand clutching a dark bottle of beer.

'Sorry,' he said, hesitating before turning back to his group.

I waited for a second before scanning the room for Alice. I spotted her sitting in the corner, perched on a stool at a two-seater table. She was looking my way, but her eyes weren't focused on me; they were glaring at something to my right, behind me. I turned around and saw that the guy I'd bumped into was looking over his shoulder at me, his lips sealed around the bottle of beer that he clumsily pulled away when he caught my gaze. Liquid spilled from his parted lips and flecks hit the top of his polo shirt, leaving dark patches. He looked away embarrassed as his friends poked his chest, teasing him. Alice was laughing now, her slim fingers cupping her cheeks.

I made my way towards her and had barely sat down when she leant over and grasped my wrist.

'What are you doing walking away? That guy is adorable.'

I dragged the stool from the wall to sit opposite her, facing away from the bar to avoid making eye contact with him anymore.

'I ordered already, a double cheese for you and a pitcher of beer with two shots of tequila.' She winked. 'The usual.'

'Lovely.'

'Maybe you could ask that guy if he wants to join us?'

I shook my head. 'Unless you fancy one of his friends?'

She cocked her head to the side and pursed her lips, before flicking her eyes back to me, a smirk drawn across her features.

'A bit young. They must be in their first year.'

She looked bored suddenly, tilting her head back the way she did when her mind became preoccupied. Something was gnawing at her; she sucked her cheeks in and blew out loudly, smiling as the waiter plonked down the pitcher of beer and the shots.

'Everything okay?' I asked.

She ran her finger around the rim of the shot glass and looked up at me very seriously. Her thin, dark eyebrows sat in deep creases as she slammed the glass on the table and threw her head back for the shot.

'Oh, don't wait for me then.'

I swallowed the tequila and set the glass down gently.

She laughed. 'I don't know how you don't wince. Such a cool cat, aren't you?'

I interlaced my fingers as Alice poured out two pints of beer and pushed a glass towards me.

'A lovely burn, as you describe it,' I said.

'Speaking of a lovely bum,' she said.

I raised my eyebrows. 'I said burn.'

Alice's eyes darted behind me and she suppressed a laugh.

'Hi.'

I turned around to see the guy standing there, his polo shirt now dry and beer-free.

'I'm Zak.'

I didn't reply. Alice frowned, thrusting out a hand. 'I'm Alice and this is Emily.'

'Hey,' I whispered.

'Sorry,' he said. 'For knocking into you. I could buy you a drink, if you want?'

'Oh, you're a confident one,' Alice said, that look of danger in her eye. She was enjoying this, and it just made me shrink further into her baggy jumper. I felt the subtle rub of her boot against my thigh under the table and it made me sit up in surprise. I looked at her. Her twisted grin, her dark green cat eyes.

'I'd like that,' I blurted.

Alice clasped her hands together. 'Give us your number, Zak, we'll be in touch,' she said, taking a sip of beer. I sighed *inwardly, pulled my phone out of my pocket and handed it to him. He keyed in his number and handed it back.*

*'It was nice to meet you, Emily,' he said, smiling slightly, his cheeks flushing as he ran a hand over his closely shaven head. He was handsome in a clean-cut way. I could see he was smart and clean, with dazzling blue eyes and a dark hairline. I smiled, flattered, and he grinned, revealing straight white teeth.*

*As he walked away, Alice muttered, 'Probably from Cambridge.'*

*'Should I have asked?' I said.*

*She shook her head, taking a long glug of beer. 'I guess you'll find out on your date.' She wiggled her eyebrows.*

*'We'll see,' I said.*

*'Ever since I've known you, Em, you've never been interested in putting yourself out there. Your creative writing tutor wouldn't be happy, would they?'*

*'Not you as well.'*

*'Seriously, Em, you love, well, love. Yet you don't want to put yourself out there. How can you write about romance if you don't experience it?'*

*I looked at her then, thinking how innocuous the comment was, but just how clumsy and ill-conceived she could be in a naïve and unapologetic way. I saw all the mischief and sincerity all at once, how much she cared for me and wanted me to be happy. But there was something etched in the undertones of what she thought was her being helpful. She was concerned.*

'I'll text him,' I said.

She nodded triumphantly.

I pulled the jumper around me, feeling the tickle of loose threads, and took a deep breath. I couldn't help but think she was wrong.

## Chapter Twenty-Two

When I arrive home, I see Detective Peters parked in a car outside my flat. The rush of guilt floods my body. Does he know where I've been? And then something worse, a danger in seeing Emily's parents, going to her work, being involved in her disappearance when I've been told to leave it alone.

He gets out of the car, but his expression is relaxed. He doesn't look angry, he looks sad.

'Please let me explain,' he says, digging his hands into his jeans pockets as I approach him.

I stand next to him for a moment, the exhaustion of the day dripping from swollen bags under my eyes. I don't know what to say to him. He chose not to tell Inspector Freeman that he saw me in South London, and I owe him for that, and more. I went to Emily's work, I went to see her parents. I've wronged him too. I think about him reading through the details of your incident and wince, rattling around for the keys in the bottom of my bag. Detective Peters smiles weakly and turns to leave.

'Detective,' I call.

He turns to me.

'Do you want to come in?'

He nods and follows me up the path into the flat.

I open the door and let him in first. He waits patiently for me to pour a glass of water and finish it in the kitchen. The wine has left my mouth dry and swollen.

'I always thought London water tastes really shit,' I say.

I turn to face him and he is wearing a sad smile as he stands in the middle of my lounge.

'Do you want a glass?'

'No, it's okay. I agree, it does taste like shit.' He pauses. 'I'm so sorry for how it came out. I never intentionally went looking for the information, I swear.'

I nod for him to continue.

'I did tell Inspector Freeman that I found that wedding photograph of you and then he remembered the name. Ben Arlington.'

I wince as he says it.

'He looked it up on the system and showed me, and it felt wrong at the time, like an invasion of your privacy. I'm just really sorry, but I didn't want to lie to you, I didn't want to pretend like I didn't know.'

I smack my lips together and grit my teeth and will myself not to cry.

'He went missing,' I say.

He nods. He looks younger in jeans and a white shirt, maybe late thirties. He must be new to this kind of position, working his way up through the ranks from patrolling the streets to finding missing people. It can't be easy dealing with that every day, dealing with people like me.

'It happened two years ago. It was three days before they found him.' I start to cry. 'He was coming home after a night out with his friends, it was dark along the canal and he tripped and fell.'

He knows all of this, but I need to say it now, maybe not for him but for me.

'He hit his head and fell into the canal. His body was found under a riverboat.' I let the tears trail down my face as I lean onto the kitchen sideboard. 'You know what I don't understand, all these fucking people in London and no one saw or heard anything, it's like London was the one that took him from me.'

We don't speak for a while, until he lowers himself slowly onto the sofa and I sit opposite him in the leather chair.

'I don't want you to think that what happened explains me.' I look at him, but he is already facing me. 'I have enough people in my life who do that,' I say, wiping my nose on my sleeve.

'Why stay here,' he asks, 'if you feel that way about London?'

I look around at the flat and glance towards the closed bedroom door. 'This is our home,' I reply.

He nods slowly. 'I'm sorry.'

'I wish people would stop saying that too.'

I think about telling him what I said to you before you left that night, but I swallow the words. You always told me to put a positive spin on things, to see the world in a way where it wasn't against me. Since you left me, I've found it even harder to do so, and whenever I think about that night, different scenarios play out in my head.

You'd been out drinking with work friends, we'd had an argument that morning and in my head our argument had left you feeling destructive. You'd gone out and had shots of rum and told your friends that it was over between us. You'd taken the quick route home, along the canal at 2am, but it was dark and poorly lit, the flats lining the canal asleep.

But then, I know you. And I'd heard your friends tell me over and over again. You loved me, it was never over between us, it was a fight, and it was a mistake.

'I lost someone too,' he says suddenly and I see how he recognises my kind of pain now. I want to ask him who, but he shakes his head slightly.

'You've obviously got a lot to deal with and I think with Emily going missing, it's resurfacing, what happened. Is that fair, for me to say that?'

'I hated how I left things with Ben,' I say quietly. 'I hated my last words to him.' I look up at the officer. Does he think I'm a terrible person for that? He smiles sympathetically.

'At first, maybe, I didn't want the last thing I said to her to be about that stupid council letter, I didn't want it to happen all over again, but…' I swat at my face, but the tears won't stop. 'Now it's like I'm the only person that really cares about her, like something bad has happened and no one's doing anything.'

'We are,' he says. 'I'm sorry that you think that.'

He looks away. 'I better go,' he says, rising from the sofa. 'I hope you feel better, and again, I'm really sorry about what happened.'

I follow him out and place a palm up to the door as he closes it and then let it glide away. This time when I turn back to the flat I see it in a new way, the way you would have wanted me to.

## Chapter Twenty-Three

### Emily

I didn't text the guy from the bar – well, not at first. Weeks passed, my creative writing project looming nearer, with my tutor insisting we all read our work aloud to the class. She was all about building confidence, how could she not realise how much she was breaking it down? I had to return home eventually as well, a place that completely uninspired me.

When I pushed the door open, I couldn't help but think how much it looked like a show home. It's what my mum wanted you to see when you walked through the door, smiling photographs of an adoring family, posed and contrived. I stared at the picture of my parents and me in the garden in front of the Italian fountain my mum had had shipped over. She always thought I didn't like the fountain; she said I didn't understand art. It's not true, I just didn't like that picture.

'Is that you, Emily?' my mum called from the kitchen.

I followed the parade of photographs down the hallway into the kitchen and saw my mum sitting in her usual spot in the conservatory, a glass of white wine nestled on the table next to her and a book in hand.

'Where have you been?'

'Alice's.'

'You could have called.'

I didn't reply.

'It's been awfully quiet here. Your father is on a business trip.' Her voice was laced with cynicism and I saw her wash the bitterness down with a large mouthful of wine.

'It's just easier to stay at Alice's for uni.'

'How is school?'

'Fine.'

She twisted her body to face me. 'Is that all you can say? Fine?' She turned away. 'Come and sit with me.'

I dropped my backpack on the floor and sat down opposite my mum in the other wicker chair. I could see she'd already been drinking quite heavily; her eyes looked sleepy and her cheeks were flushed.

'Tell me.'

'I have a project on at the moment, it's taking up a lot of my time.'

'That's exciting,' she said flatly. 'What's it about?'

'Me, I guess.'

She raised an eyebrow, pushing back her soft locks from her shoulders. She was interested now.

'What about you?'

I fidgeted awkwardly. 'A self-expression piece.'

'Well,' she said, splaying a hand to her chest. 'I am an artist, so I know all about self-expression. Maybe I could help you.'

I smiled feebly at her. 'I'm trying to write romance.'

She didn't look surprised. 'You always have your nose buried in those Austen books, don't you? Or those tacky romcoms you watch. They hardly qualify as romance.' She looked at me solemnly. 'Love is a lot more complicated and a lot more painful than that.'

I looked out of the window at the fountain, how out of place it looked.

'Do you have a boyfriend, Emily?'

The question took me by surprise. I shook my head.

'Have you ever been in love?'

She said it like I was a stranger to her. I didn't answer the question, but she continued anyway.

'Then you can't understand it, and shouldn't write about it, that's my advice.' She waved her hand in the air and emptied the remains of the glass into her mouth. She stood up and paused for a moment before walking away, leaving me sitting there staring out at the garden.

I grasped my phone and hovered over Alice's name in my contacts; I just wanted to hear her voice. I wanted her to tell me to come over and pull up the plans for our London apartment and tell me we would get out of here soon. Instead, I scrolled all the way down to Zak, and typed out a message.

*Hey, we met the other week, sorry it's taken so long to message, how about that drink?'*

*I pressed* send, *but felt nothing. Love is painful, love is complicated.*

## Chapter Twenty-Four

'Suzie, you need to get up now,' Ben says, nudging my side. I flip my head lazily to the side and see his concerned brown eyes gazing down at me.

'Now,' he repeats, smiling.

I throw the covers back and let the icy December morning pinch at my joints.

'It's fucking freezing,' I say.

'Come on, you'll be late,' he says, throwing his green T-shirt onto the floor.

'I can't be bothered with work today.'

'What's wrong?' he says, sitting down on the edge of the bed.

'I don't know, I guess I'm just restless, that's all, not enjoying my job at the moment.'

'It pays well.'

I shrug. 'I don't care about that.'

'If you don't like working there, then resign. We'd be all right for a bit until you found something else.'

'I'm not sure it's the job.'

'What about looking at something to do with food? You are an amazing cook. You could be the next Nigella.'

'You dream too big,' I say with a smile.

'What's wrong with that?'

I stop smiling. 'I just don't think it's the job that's the problem.'

'I can't have this conversation again,' he says, rising from the edge of the bed.

'I'm not asking you to.'

'We're in London because we both wanted to be here.'

I look at him. His cheeks are puffed out, the way they get when he's angry but trying to suppress it.

'What about if we both wanted to leave?'

'I don't want to leave. Do you?'

But I can't say it. Instead I clamber out of bed and grab a towel from the radiator.

'Do you need the bathroom? I'm going to shower.'

He follows me, pulling on dark jeans and stumbling with them halfway up his legs into the hallway.

'Do you want to leave?' he repeats.

I turn to him and see the person I love most in the world, and I can't hurt him, even if it means hurting myself.

'I just don't want this to be about money.'

He raises his voice now. 'We're here for us, our future,

of course it's to do with money. Everything is to do with money.'

I shake my head. 'No, not everyone makes decisions for money.'

'I wish you would stop comparing yourself to other people. It's what we want.'

I know internally it isn't what I want. I shut the bathroom door and turn on the shower, letting the argument simmer on the other side. I hope he'll be gone by the time I get out, so I don't have to look at him, so I don't have to hurt him.

Ben knocks on the door and gently pushes it open. His brown eyes have a defeated look and he leans forward to hug me. He pulls me in and strokes my hair gently, and kisses my forehead. The steam from the shower rests on us and I throw my arms up to hug him back. I can hear the shuffling of the upstairs neighbour in the bathroom above us and the rush-hour traffic roar past the lounge window.

'This isn't what I want,' I say quietly.

He stiffens and pulls away, grasping my arms.

'I just want to go home.'

'This is our home,' he says.

'I don't want our home to be here anymore then. It's London… I can't take it, the people, the crowds, the commute, the air, it's everything. I don't know why you're always so against going back home.'

'It's not that I'm against it, but if we'd stayed in Hove, I wouldn't have had the opportunities I've had here.'

'We wouldn't have the money, is what you really mean.'

'I'm doing this for us. This is the life we want.'

'If this is the life you want, then I want no part of it.'

He pulls away and stares at me, open-mouthed. I go to speak, but I can't take it back, because the longing to leave London, to go home and live the life I want, is too overwhelming. It wins.

Ben shakes his head and walks into the hallway. I follow him, but I can't speak. He picks up his backpack and slips his keys off the small coffee table. He doesn't turn to look at me before he closes the door firmly behind him.

## Chapter Twenty-Five

### Emily

I didn't tell Alice about the date with Zak. I knew she'd fuss over me and that I'd feel my phone buzzing in my jacket pocket the whole time, even if I put it on silent. I'd know she would be trying to contact me – wouldn't she? I left my phone on loud when I pushed through the door to the wine bar Zak suggested meeting at – just in case.

I saw him sitting in the corner, a bottle already on the table, a small lit candle flickering against the glass and emanating a raspberry glow. I didn't like that. I walked over to the table and saw his eyes travel down my body and up again to meet my gaze. He rose quickly and leant forward to kiss my cheek, delicately placing a hand on the small of my back. The formality of it made me feel uncomfortable.

He pushed a glass brimming with red wine towards me clumsily and presumptuously.

'I ordered my favourite, I hope you don't mind.'

I took a small sip and winced slightly, the tannins scratching the back of my tongue, its acidity nothing I cared for. Alice always poked fun at my love of wine. I smiled. She'd say that I dressed wine up in a pretentious way to make it acceptable to get pissed. Sophisticated drunk, she'd call it. She was always happier necking bourbon straight from the bottle.

'It's nice.'

'It's a cool spot, quiet. Sometimes I study here,' he said, taking a sip.

I stroked the stem with my fingers, but didn't want to take another sip. Alice bought me a Malbec for my twentieth birthday. She'd gone – in her words – 'to the fancy part of town where all the poshos shop'. I loved it – she'd written down all the flavours I'd mentioned on a scrap of paper and produced it for the owner. I laughed suddenly, imagining her shoving this small, blotchy bit of paper at the owner – probably covered in doodles – her loquacious manner coming across as completely incoherent.

'What's funny?' he asked.

I noticed myself then and felt embarrassed. 'I was just remembering something funny someone said to me about wine.'

'Oh, please share.'

I smiled, sitting up straight. 'They said wine was an adult fruit shoot.' I took a sip then.

He smiled. 'A bit of a silly thing to say.'

I screwed up my face, but he wasn't looking.

'What are you studying?' I asked.

'Geography. I know,' he said, holding up his hands. 'What am I going to do with that degree?'

I smiled. 'I know what you mean. I'm studying creative writing.'

'You said in your texts, that's very cool – we're studying the Mickey Mouse subjects, eh?' He raised his glass. 'At least we're having fun.'

I didn't raise my glass. He didn't seem to care. He took another sip anyway, smacking his lips as he did. I could see the lines on his forehead deepen, the red wine sticking to the rim of his lips, and every time he spoke, a pearly red sheen coated his teeth. This was not his first glass. I realised the bottle was nearly empty. Was he nervous? I felt apologetic, I wanted to say sorry, that he didn't need to be nervous. Instead I said, 'What's your favourite film?'

He looked offended suddenly, a slight eye roll. Was I not being interesting enough?

'Looper.'

I shrugged, leaning forward. 'What's that?'

He looked engaged, twisting his body back to face me. 'It's a sci-fi, where people called Loopers are paid to terminate people sent from the future.'

'I don't really watch sci-fi.'

'It's a tame sci-fi, futuristic, but don't worry, there aren't aliens or spaceships or anything, but Bruce Willis comes back *from the future to exterminate someone called the Rainmaker, but his present self – Joseph Gordon-Levitt – is waiting for him.'*

*'Who's the Rainmaker?'*

*He smiled. 'You should watch it.'*

*I nodded. 'I will. I mean, I used to watch* Star Wars *with my dad, but I never liked it, and my mum said films are for people who have nothing better to do.'*

*He glanced away awkwardly.*

*'She doesn't mean it, she's just—' I don't finish, because I don't know the answer.*

*'What's your favourite film?'*

*'Strictly Ballroom,' I say, holding the wine to my lips.*

*'Dancing?'*

*I nodded. 'It's a romance about two people—'*

*He grabbed the bottle and didn't offer me any, instead filling his own glass up, emptying the remains. I felt myself sink into the chair. I didn't want to be there, I wanted to be in Alice's bedroom. I wanted to see her face when she propped herself up and said, 'What are we watching tonight?'*

*I waited until he'd finished his glass of wine, before standing up and swinging my jacket around my shoulders.*

*'So, do you want to come back to my place?' he slurred.*

*I stared at him. I wanted to cry. I shook my head, biting my lip as I collected my stuff. He stumbled back slightly, his eyes glazed over, as he blew into his top lip.*

*'I have to go,' I said.*

He didn't reply, just furled his lips and widened his eyes expectantly.

'Looper,' I said dumbly as I started to leave. 'Thank you for the wine.'

I went home that night. To a silent house void of lights, of life – to a thousand messages from Alice on my phone about where I was and what I was doing. I traipsed up the stairs and shut my bedroom door, pulling the blanket over my head, and booted up my laptop. I put Looper on. I watched until the tears finally came, and I pulled a bottle of red wine from underneath my bed – another bottle of the Malbec Alice had got me. My favourite wine.

I cried harder than I'd ever cried. It was a love story. Something I could never understand.

## Chapter Twenty-Six

Do you remember how we met? We'd been together for so long the story became a well-choreographed dance when people would ask. You loved to tell it. We were so young, weren't we? How much we changed as we grew up, but still those same twenty-year-olds, still us.

I remember striding over to you first. I'd had a couple of glasses of wine and I felt confident. It was your boyish looks that attracted me, the smile you flashed me as I stood with my friends on the other side of the sticky club in Brighton. 'I'm going over,' I remember saying to my friends. I didn't know what it would turn into, I didn't know a drunken night when I invited you back to my hotel room would lead to this.

You tell the story better, of course. It's more romantic

191

when you say it; you always describe it as a wonderful whirlwind. I guess our whole relationship was. When you asked me to marry you on the beach, we'd only been together for a year but I knew that you were the one I wanted to spend the rest of my life with. It sounds so cheesy when I say it but you made it sound just right. What I'd do for a moment like that again, for a moment of such intimacy with you.

I love that you are romantic and spontaneous and all the things I'm not. I love that you can be serious and funny in one breath. I was so envious of your ability to show your emotions, so easily and with no embarrassment. Whenever we fought, whenever I was sad, or happy, you beat me to solving it each time, knowing the perfect thing to say. You never gave me room. You never gave me room to feel as much as you did.

I resent you for that. I don't want to, but I do. Now you're gone and it's like I'm unable to process my thoughts anymore, because you did that for me. You solved all the problems, but you couldn't solve that one, could you? Me, silently loathing London, letting it fester, and you watching me take it. Why did you not say anything sooner? Why did you not make one of your big cheesy moves? Why did you not listen?

I'm sorry, I don't mean to blame you, but now I have all this time to think, desperately trying to let my thoughts form and take shape. You'd be disappointed in me now.

I remember the first meal I made you was homemade arancini. You'd come to meet my parents for the first time and I cooked for everyone. I expected that first meal with my family to be awkward, for my dad to say something silly or Clara to recount her most embarrassing story of me – and they did, but I didn't care. I just saw the way you looked at me across the table, accepting every part of me. I laugh again, as I remember you patting your belly, saying you couldn't bear another bite. Then me laying a raspberry trifle in the middle of the table and you quoting something from Monty Python, a wafer-thin mint, and my dad laughing and me not understanding until years later when you made me watch all the sketches.

We were so different and I think that's why we worked, but you were too ambitious sometimes, ahead of me before I could catch up.

I pick up my jacket and wander out onto the streets. This time I imagine you're next to me as I take each step, heading towards the shops. I'm going to cook tonight, arancini and raspberry trifle. Your favourite. I'm going to sit at our small dining table and have a meal. I can't give up on something I love, not again.

After dinner I walk to the bedroom door and push it slightly open. Preserved, just the way it was the day you left. Your green T-shirt sits on the floor next to your side of the bed. Your bedside cabinet is ajar and socks tumble out. Your *Avengers* figurine and personalised coaster with a picture of us from our wedding sit next to your side of the bed.

Our bed is unmade, with navy and cream sheets dispersed across it. Your proud collection of vinyls fans the wall, alongside a small framed picture of us on the beach. On my side of the bed is a small white box, and inside are my wedding and engagement rings. I feel along my empty finger. It felt so light when I took them off, but I couldn't stand the questions – the weight of explaining my loss so much heavier than the rings ever felt.

When your parents had arrived to help sort through your things, I had a panic attack at the thought of anyone entering the bedroom. I lashed out and screamed, begging them to take it all, everything else of yours but that. The bedroom is a picture frozen in time. I step inside and the stale scent of dust flies into the air. I sob quietly and whisper into the stillness of the room.

'I stayed for you, Ben, I would have always stayed for you.'

I bend down and pick up the green T-shirt and hold it in between my fingers.

'But now I have to go.'

---

The next day I call my boss. She picks up after the third ring and I sense the disappointment in her voice.

'Hey, Suzie, everything okay?'

'I'm not calling in sick again,' I say.

'Are you coming in for our meeting?'

'I don't think we need to have it.'

'I think we should,' she says bluntly.

'It's been a difficult few years.'

'You know I've given you time, Suzie.'

'I know you have, and I'm really thankful for that, but I haven't given myself time, and I don't think being in London is the right thing for me now. I want to hand in my resignation.'

She is quiet at the other end. I can hear the soft office chatter in the background and then it grows quieter as she walks away to somewhere private.

'I understand, Suzie. You can take your resignation notice as leave for the full month,' she says quietly.

'Thank you.'

'I hope you feel better, Suzie. I think you're doing the right thing.'

'I hope I am too.'

I hang up the phone and relief floods my body. I let

out a gentle cry. I pick up my phone again to call Clara. I look around the flat. I'll need her help.

I hear traffic sifting in the background when she picks up. 'Hey, I'm just on my way to pick up the kids from school.'

'I handed in my notice at work,' I say.

She's silent. In the background I can hear only the sound of the indicator and the gentle hum of the car's engine. 'Is that good?' she says finally.

'I'm coming home.'

'Really?' she says sceptically.

'Really. I'm going to let out the flat until I can sell it. I'm going to chat to Mike, who lets the flat upstairs, to get some advice.'

'Zee,' she whispers, her voice strained. 'I'll come and help you?'

'Can you come next weekend?'

'Of course. I'll bring Ian and his van and ask if Mum and Dad can look after the kids until we get back.'

'Thank you.'

'What's brought this on, anyway?'

'He'd want me to be happy,' I say. 'He always wanted me to be happy.'

'I'm proud of you. I have to go, but I'll call you later, okay?'

'Okay,' I say, hanging up.

I look around the flat and see all the memories I've had here. When you cooked us dinner for the first time and the smoke alarm went off. When I came home and flowers sat on the kitchen table with a note saying 'Just because', and the nights spent drinking whisky and watching films, coiled around each other. I do what you always told me to do: I see the positive. I see the moments when I laughed and sang and danced and was incredibly stupid with you. I see all the beautiful mistakes we made and times when we were more important than anything and anyone.

I go to the kitchen, pull out bin liners, shake one open. I bend down and pick up old junk mail and the empty bottle of whisky, and stuff them into the open sack. I empty a plastic container in the bedroom full of shoes I don't wear anymore and start to fill it with all the memories of our first home.

I pull loose the old cream throw from a stack of books and they topple over onto the floor. Sighing, I bend down to shuffle them into the box and see Emily's name scrawled across a thin white envelope. I lean back onto my heels and reach forward to pick it up. Shit.

I think about putting it back on the table in the communal hallway. I'm about to open the door, but pause. It's something Emily's mum said. It was her birthday, and she wasn't grateful for the money we sent her. I look down at the card and take it to the kitchen counter. I stare at it, pacing back and forth, deliberating my next move.

I can't open it, that's illegal. I can't return it, it was

supposed to have been sent weeks ago. I should have given it to the police when they first came round. How did I forget? How stupid.

*That family*. I grab a knife from the kitchen drawer and slowly slick it in between the fold, pressing against the envelope, hearing the satisfying sound of the adhesive prying free.

I release the card and open it carefully. Placed in the middle is a cheque for one thousand pounds. I see the same handwriting scrawled across the top, saying 'Emily Williams'. I push the cheque to one side and read the message.

*To our darling daughter Emily,*

*Let the past be the past and focus on your future. You never have to do this alone, we love you. Happy Birthday.*

*Love, Mum and Dad*

I place the cheque back in the card and close it gently. I slip it back into the envelope and use a Prittstick to seal it back shut.

I grab my phone and think about calling Detective Peters. I have to tell him. I have to give it back. It might help – it might not. Shit. I decide to text him.

*Need to speak to you, can you call me.*

I press *send* and regret it. He doesn't know any of what I've been doing. Maybe I should just leave it outside and carry on with sorting out my flat.

My phone rings. It's him.

'Hi,' I answer.

'Suzie, is everything okay?'

I stare down at the envelope.

'I found some of Emily's mail wedged in between mine. It might be important.'

'Oh.'

'Do you want me to leave it on the table in the hallway? I don't know if you'll need it for your investigation.'

'Yes, please. I'll come and collect it.'

'I'm really sorry, I feel stupid.'

'It's okay, at least you found it and told me.'

I nod. 'Okay, well, I'll leave it outside, and again, sorry.'

I hang up the phone and take the envelope and place it on the table in the hallway in front of the main front door. I look down at Emily's red wellies, with dried mud flaking around the soles. I feel the urge to clean them, to make them look nice for her when she arrives home, but I turn away.

I close my door and continue to sort through the flat. I make a separate box for your things. I find the lost wedding picture of us and smile. I hug it to me, before wrapping a tea towel around it and placing it in the box.

I hear a rap at the front door and look around the curtain, seeing Detective Peters standing outside. I press the buzzer, but I don't open my door. I stand next to it, listening to the heavy tread of his work shoes and the shuffling of letters on the table.

I can hear him breathing, steady outside my door; he's facing this way. I try to ease away, but I want him to know I'm in here. I want him to knock. I deliberately push the coffee table so it scratches along the floor and turn to face the door expectantly.

I try in that moment to understand what I want him to say. The first person I've told about you, whether I was pushed into it or not. It led me to this moment and I can't ignore that. I feel grateful.

Before I know it, I'm leaning forward and yanking the door open quickly before he can leave. He is standing outside with a hand poised to knock.

'I didn't want to disturb you,' he says quickly.

I gaze up at him, his large frame shadowing my doorway, his blue eyes bright, his unassuming look back. He lost someone too and he recognises my pain, but now I'm looking at him, it feels like more than that. He seems hesitant and careful around me, like he's trying not to blur the line between his job and concern.

'I just wanted to see how you were feeling.'

'I'm okay. I'm just packing.'

'Oh, are you going away?'

'Moving away, actually.'

I look down at the letter in his hands, the happy birthday card from Emily's parents. Guilt brims to the surface.

'I haven't been completely honest with you.'

He frowns. 'About what?'

'Emily.'

He takes a step back and follows my gaze to the envelope.

'What about her?'

'I just felt like there wasn't enough getting done.'

He shifts to one side. 'So you didn't think we were doing our job properly?'

I go to speak, but can't.

'What's happened, Suzie?'

'It just made some old emotions resurface, from when Ben went missing.'

'This is different, Suzie, she's done this before.' I shake my head. 'I'm really sorry about what happened to Ben, but it's not the same thing.'

'No,' I say desperately, 'because I did everything to find him, so did his friends, so did his family. I trawled the streets for three days and three nights. I followed his route home, I knocked on every door, I did everything. No one is doing anything for Emily. Her parents have just accepted that she's run away, like that's even what's happened here. You know what her mum said when I went to see her? That her daughter is bitter. No one is looking for Emily.'

He is silent. He purses his lips and says, 'When did you go to see Emily's mum?'

I flick my head towards him. 'Last week. It was stupid.'

'Why did you do that, Suzie?' he says calmly.

I look at him squarely. 'I think her parents know something.'

'Jesus,' he says, waving the envelope. 'Did you open this?'

I bite my bottom lip, pressing hard until I can taste blood.

'I can't help you anymore, Suzie. I mean, what can I do, what can I do?'

'I know it was stupid, but—'

'You're accusing me of not doing my job properly,' he says.

'That's not what this is.'

He holds the envelope between us in both hands.

'We're not actively investigating this anymore, Suzie.'

'I don't understand.'

'Her parents say she's done this before and we can't find any evidence to say otherwise. I'm sorry if that's not what you want to hear, but you need to let this go now.' He looks down at the letter. 'Emily's parents will be collecting her things next week. I suggest you make yourself scarce.' He turns to leave.

'All I did was offer to help them, that's all I did.'

'How can you even think they know something?'

I think back to the receptionist at PBL Associates, her wrathful stare as I opened the bathroom stall, her vicious words. *That family.*

'Why run?' I say quietly.

He studies me, then turns silently and leaves.

## Chapter Twenty-Seven

### Emily

I sent Alice a message the next day saying I was just busy working on my writing project for Monday morning. She messaged back saying,

*Gotcha, give 'em hell.*

I spent the weekend in my room, staring out of the big bay window onto the quiet street, with my notepad nestled on my knees.

On Monday morning I wandered downstairs and saw my mum sipping coffee at the kitchen counter. She gave me a meek smile.

'Your dad is still away.'

She didn't ask how I was, she just said exactly what was on

*her mind, what was always on her mind. This is how it was with us. There had been other things since my first memory of my parents. My mum violently slapping my dad as he staggered through the door, liquid dripping from the corners of his mouth and the smell of him so unnatural.*

*I don't think I was better off when it was just Mum. She'd have all this pent-up rage and she'd redirect it at me. Silently hating me, whether it was forgetting to pick me up from school or saying things across the table at dinner time. You're the only reason I'm here. It wasn't comforting, the words were resentful, and I never knew what her goal was.*

*One night, when my dad had been gone for over a week, I found her crying in front of the TV. She was clinging to a glass of red wine, streaks of deep red staining her mouth like fangs. Mascara trailed down her face. She turned to me slowly, as I placed a hand on her knee. I wanted to tell her we were better off without him, I wanted to say that I loved her and it would be okay. She leant forward, her hand cupping my cheek and I let myself cry with her, gently, into the palm of her hand. Then a flicker of recognition and the hand clamped down on my cheek, pinching me. I don't remember it hurting, I just remember letting her, if that's what she needed.*

*Six months ago, my dad had been gone for three days and now I'm older the routine has become so normal. Mum and I adapted as I grew up and instead of remarks across the dinner table or filthy looks as I walked through the door, she ignored me completely. I floated through our large house like a ghost, trying to find a purpose, to prove to her that I was nothing like* my dad and that we could be in this together. I'd ask how she was, but blue glassy eyes washed over me like she'd forgotten something, then trail away, like she suddenly remembered.

Sometimes, when things were really bad between my parents, I'd stay with Alice's family for weeks. Her mum would make a massive fuss over me when I arrived, embracing me in a big hug and demanding that the table be set for one more person. Dinner time was chaotic, an eruption of noise as we all took our seats. Alice's two younger brothers squealing over a toy, Alice's dad's low belly laugh as her mum placed piles of food – too much food – in the middle of the table. Alice grinning at me across it all, our friendship unwavering.

Alice's mum asked me once if I wanted to call my mum and tell her where I was, but I shook my head. She never asked any more questions after that. I think maybe she called my mum herself and, whatever was said between them, she understood that my house wasn't like theirs. My parents didn't check up on me, they didn't care, and whenever I arrived home my mum would say the same thing: 'I thought you'd run away.' She always sounded so disappointed that I'd come back.

'I'm going into the studio soon, you should pop in.'

'I have uni today.'

'Oh, yes, how is your project going?'

I gripped the notepad in my hand. 'Fine.'

She pursed her lips and moved one of her locks behind her shoulders, the way she always did when she was preparing to say something she knew I wasn't going to like.

Instead, she said, 'He should be back soon.'

*I was her sounding board. Wherever my dad was, a business trip or elsewhere, he was just teetering on the edge of being away for too long. A couple of days, sometimes a week, but I hadn't seen him for nearly a week and a half now and I could see my mum thinking the same thing.*

*She gnawed at her thumbnail and swivelled the chair to face away from me. I wanted to hug her in that moment, but she swung back around, and I saw that determination in her face. She compartmentalised the thought, tucked it away in a drawer and closed it firmly, her eyes boring into me.*

*'Are you going to show me?'*

*'Show you what?*

*She held out a manicured finger and pointed to the notepad clutched by my side.*

*I didn't know what to say.*

*'Whatever,' she said, flying out of the chair. 'Have it your own way. I'm going to get dressed, I have a busy day.'*

*She left me standing in the kitchen, the words caught in my throat.*

---

When I arrived at uni, my friend Elisa was leaning against the wall in our usual pre-uni meeting spot. She grinned when she saw me, waiving the usual greeting with, 'How much are you dreading this?'

I nodded grimly.

'I don't understand why she's so keen for us to read this out.'

She peered down at me, her tall frame nudging me slightly.

'Did you get it finished?'

'Yes, just.'

She sighed. 'Same. I'm pretty sure it's awful, though.'

'I'm sure it's not.'

We walked into the classroom and sat in our usual seats around the large round table that took up most of the room. Our tutor was already there, her head bowed, reading as she waited for everyone to find a place.

She clasped her hands then, coming to life as if someone had wound up a battery on a mechanical doll. She grinned.

'Who's first?'

We went around the table until it reached Elisa and she stood, confidently grasping a notepad and pushing her glasses up her nose. I couldn't hear her. I looked down at my own notepad and felt sweat prick the backs of my hands and heat travel across my chest into the crook of my collarbone.

I didn't realise that Elisa had finished and sat down. I didn't hear the rest of the class give feedback and discuss Elisa's poem. I just heard our tutor cough loudly and through the drones of static, I knew it was my turn.

Suddenly the room was silent. I cleared my throat and bent my neck, grasping the notepad in both hands. I said the words, but I can't be sure if I said anything at all.

The words came alive on the page. I traced my finger over

them, realising how harshly I'd dug into each letter, pushing the pen into the page and leaving jagged marks that I could only just make out. My lips were moving but it was like someone had stuck a syringe into my jaw; it ached to talk, and my tongue was starting to swell. The words became blurry but I didn't stop.

It was only when I felt Elisa's gentle touch on my elbow, and then a soft push, a whispered 'Let's step out,' that I came to. I looked around at the bewildered faces and up at Elisa's concerned expression. I saw my hands shaking and tears smothering the page, smearing the words.

'Let's go,' she said again.

I swiped at my stuff and clumsily rushed out of the classroom with it clutched to my chest. I heard Elisa calling after me, but I kept going until I was outside and I could finally breathe.

## Chapter Twenty-Eight

When Emily's parents arrive the following week in their Mercedes, I immediately jump up from my place by the window and rush to the front door to greet them.

My flat is mostly packed away now, and Clara has confirmed that she and Ian will arrive with his van next week to help with my things. I've arranged for an estate agent to value the property and plan to let it out until it sells.

I haven't spoken to Detective Peters since he left last week. I think about texting him, but can't seem to find the right words. I know he's right, I didn't think the police were doing enough. I can't blame him for being angry at that. Even now, as I stand in my doorway waiting for Emily's parents to come through into the hallway, I still don't think they're doing enough.

Emily's father opens the door, waving an umbrella back into the folds of rain. He closes the door and turns, jumping slightly when he sees me.

'Suzie,' he says, but something catches his eye. He looks down at Emily's red wellies sprawled across the hallway floor and then back at me with a false smile.

'Christie isn't coming today, she's not feeling very well.'

'Oh, do you need any help?'

He shakes his head. 'That'll be okay.'

He eases past me and starts to climb the stairs.

'What if she comes back?' I say.

He pauses. 'We can't continue to pay rent for her, that's not acceptable,' he says, before continuing up the stairs.

For the rest of the day I listen to him shuffle around Emily's flat. I can hear objects spill across the floor and the flattening of boxes and bottles clinking together. He makes several trips outside, carrying black bin liners that I see him squash into the large black bins in front of the house.

I follow him from room to room, hearing drawers slide open and wheels churn across the floorboards. In the bedroom, I stand gazing up at the ceiling, listening to cupboards slam shut and boxes scrape along the floor, until there is silence. I hear the floor give way slightly to the gentle creak of Emily's bed and then I stand for minutes hearing absolutely nothing.

Then, soft sobs flutter through the hollow ceiling and into my bedroom. I stand motionless, listening to Emily's father cry in his daughter's bedroom. The bedsprings screech and Stuart's footsteps are heavier now. I trail after them into the bathroom, where his cries echo. The toilet-roll holder spins, and then there's the sharp sound of a nose blowing. Stuart says something, but his voice is muffled and I can't make out the words. He cries harder now and speaks through each exhalation, forcing the words out like vomit.

'I'm sorry,' he cries, 'I'm so sorry.'

---

She immediately answers, on the first ring.

'What's up?'

'Emily's dad picked up all of her stuff yesterday and it just doesn't feel right. Her parents, the police, they all think she's run away but I just can't let it go. Something's happened to her, I know it has.'

'Zee, you've got to let it go. You're coming home at the weekend, and you've got to concentrate on you. If her family and the police aren't concerned, then you shouldn't be either.'

'I just don't understand. Why would the family call off the search? If Abigail went missing, even if you thought she'd run away, wouldn't you still do anything you could to find her?'

I can hear Clara sighing down the phone.

'Yes, you know I would. Be careful, Zee. The police have already told you to keep out of it so don't do anything stupid.' She sighs again. 'I mean it, you need to be careful.'

'I will be.'

'I'm going to come and get you this weekend.'

'I know.'

'So just hold off doing anything stupid until I get there.'

'I'll try,' I say.

'And for what it's worth,' she says, 'Emily is lucky to have a neighbour like you.'

I smile before hanging up. I did everything to find you. I remember that morning so vividly as my hand reached over to your side of the bed and felt across the cold sheets, but after that it was a blur of phone calls, everyone's voice so calm at first and then panic rising as the day went on.

I shake the thought loose and start to pack more things away, bunching up two bin liners into my arms and shifting them into the communal hallway. I bend down and start shovelling piles of junk mail from old upstairs tenants, estate agents' pamphlets and takeaway menus into the bin liners. There's a slim folded note wedged in the letterbox and I pull it free, expecting to see an advertisement for movers or a cleaning service. Instead I unfold it to see the words:

*I'm watching you, bitch*

I freeze. The scrawled handwriting looks rushed and angry as the words bounce around the page. It wasn't here before – I would have noticed, wouldn't I? I stare down at it, before stepping quietly to the front door and releasing the peephole to stare out onto the street. No one is there; the space between the front door and the street is completely empty. Is someone hiding around the corner under the low arched brickwork? I hold my breath. Was this note meant for me, or Emily? I scrunch it up in my hand and desperately want to throw it away, but I retreat back to my flat and smooth it out on the kitchen table. 'I'm watching you, bitch,' I read again. Who's watching me? I think about all the things I've done in the last week: Emily's parents, going to her work. I look at the ceiling, all the things I've heard. I'm involved, aren't I? I'm a part of it. I trace the dense scratches and chilling words burning into the paper. I think for a moment I recognise something in the handwriting, but I can't make it stick. Someone's watching me, because I know something.

## Chapter Twenty-Nine

### Emily

That night I was upstairs in my bedroom, a place that never felt like mine. I never slept much. The silence pierced the evenings and left me feeling restless and uneasy, broken only by the noise of my dad stumbling to the spare room when he got home in the early morning. I was sitting in my window, perched on a padded chest. I looked out at the still evening, so unbearably quiet.

A streetlight flickered restlessly, and when a car pulled up underneath it, it illuminated Alice's powder-blue Fiat 500. I was confused at first. Had she sensed that I needed her? I felt fortunate in that moment. Some clarity washed over me, and I saw a future surrounded by good friends, my soulmate – a place far away from here. Alice and me in our London apartment with a small balcony, 'So I can play my guitar on it *like in a film,' she'd say, pushing her hands together and clapping, long blonde hair caught between her fingers. We'd go on Street View and move through the congested streets teeming with people and the hubbub of the city. I could imagine the raucous chants and drum and bass music vibrating from a nearby bar. I longed to climb onto a sticky bar stool and wrap my fingers around a martini stem, dressed in a silky black dress. Like something out of Sex in the City, we'd giggle.*

*I pulled on my jogging bottoms and Alice's baggy jumper. It was a sticky, humid night; the last rays from the burgeoning May sun had disappeared and the whole house felt close and suffocating. I always left my curtains open – I welcomed any outdoor sensation, any small light, any noise.*

*I carefully made my way downstairs. I didn't want my mum to think my dad had arrived home and commence the ritual of cries, my dad falling into objects, at least one broken ornament or picture. I couldn't hear my mum tonight; the house sat in silence, but there was something inevitable about it.*

*I trod along the gravel driveway, pebbles crunching underneath my feet, and looked back at the house, but only the dim light from my lamp projected back. I held up a hand and waved as I approached the car. The windows were blacked out, but I could see a shadow moving inside.*

*'Alice,' I called.*

*The shadow froze and the car tipped slightly, as if crushed under a weight. I walked around to the passenger side and yanked on the door. At first, I couldn't process what I saw as I* stood in the middle of the quiet street, the handle still gripped in my hand. Alice's head slotted into a bent neck, her hair coiled around their shoulders. I glanced down and saw a hand working up the top of her thigh, fingertips brushing her knickers. Had they not seen me? Then Alice's face appeared, distorted in the glow from the streetlamp. Her eyes were half-closed, her lips smudged pink, and then realisation dawned on her and she pushed the person back, pulling on the hem of her skirt.

The man just slid his hand higher before Alice could react. Her eyes were wide with alarm, but drooping slightly as if she was drunk. The man twisted towards me and I saw grey stubble stream from the tips of dark, neatly cut hair. My dad looked up at me, his grey eyes piercing, affronted, annoyed at the disturbance. He looked right at me but I don't think he really saw me.

'Emily,' he slurred.

I looked back at Alice, searching her face for an explanation. Had my dad forced himself on her? Had she found him wandering the streets after being kicked out of the local pub and brought him back on the way to see me?

'Alice?'

But she didn't say anything, just released my dad from her fingertips and turned her attention back to the wheel. She started the car and I almost thought she'd drive off with my dad's hand still fighting its way around her thigh, the car door open and me standing there.

'What's going on?'

My dad leaned forward and took my hand, pushing me back as he staggered out of the car. He swiped the door behind him, and Alice immediately drove off into the night.

'Let's go inside,' he said, pulling on my wrist.

I obediently wandered after him as the grip tightened and the pain reverberated up my arm. We didn't stop until we were inside and the darkness of the house encased us. My dad shut the door firmly and grabbed me by both shoulders. I thought he was going to explain himself, or apologise, but he didn't, he just breathed musky breath laced with wine into my face, his glistening eyes the only light in the darkness of our hallway.

'Don't tell your mum,' he said slowly.

'Don't tell me what?' my mum said from the shadow of the staircase.

She bent to switch on the light, her body wrapped in a pale pink dressing gown, her blonde locks falling effortlessly next to her face, her skin, paler than usual, glimmering in the artificial light.

In that moment, I felt trapped, like a broken dial on an old clock, stuck on the same second, unable to move time. I saw the defeat in my mum's face, what she would lose if she ever left my dad. I saw Alice's battered expression, the way she almost didn't consider me until she realised she had to. I saw my dad, his hand sliding up my friend's thigh. My future in London, our small apartment with hanging plants lining every wall. I wanted to swat at it, scrub it clean and start all over again, make it all disappear into inky blotches and forget it all.

'Emily?' my mum asked. 'What's going on?'

'I don't know,' I said, pulling away from my dad's grip. I trailed past my mum on the stairs, leaving them suspended in the silence of that hot May night. I couldn't think in the heat. My eyes felt heavy and when I closed them I just saw Alice.

It wasn't until the day after when the rain came and cleared the humidity from the thick, cloying air. Not until I came downstairs and saw my parents sitting at the kitchen table, my mum still wrapped in her dressing gown, her locks messy, my dad resting a hand on her knee, sitting so close to her. They both clutched coffee, my mum taking silent sips as my dad frowned at her.

I hovered by the door, listening in on the low conversation, my mum nodding every so often.

'It's over,' my dad said. 'I don't want to lose our daughter over this. Things have always been different between us since we had Emily. We need to get us back again. Don't you agree?'

My mum tilted her head. 'You need to make this up to her,' she said slowly. 'I can't believe you've done this to us, to Emily.'

'Her friend came on to me. I promise you, there was nothing in it from my side.'

I cleared my throat, knocking on the kitchen door awkwardly. My mum didn't turn to me, but my dad got up immediately, striding over to me.

'I owe you an explanation. What you saw'—he ushered me into the kitchen and over to the dining table—'it's not what you think. Your friend, she's not a good person. She came on to me and I told her to stop. She became obsessed with me.' He threw his arms up into the air. 'She didn't want to hear no, and I'm just so sorry for what you saw.'

He continued, 'But we were thinking, it might be nice for you to get away for a bit? We could pay for you to go to London?'

I stared up at my dad, a hopeful grin plastered on his face.

'If that will help,' I said dumbly.

My dad's grin widened like a Cheshire cat's and he pulled me into him, squeezing me tightly into the collar of his shirt. I smelt Alice's perfume and like the dial I was stuck again, frozen in time.

## Chapter Thirty

One of Ben's old friends used to work in finance in the city. He used to describe the job as 'hardcore', not because of the hours but because of the after-work socials that inevitably followed. The boozy client lunches and dinners and the pace of the industry. It was part of the job, he'd say, a requirement that came with the territory of working in finance.

Emily knew people at work, and they knew her too. On Friday night I slip on my best skinny jeans and a white blouse that skims my hips. I lather my face in make-up and paint my lips red. I strap on my tall, slim leather boots and stand in front of the mirror, taking in the sight of myself. I've filled out in the last few weeks, my skin has more colour and my lips are full.

I nod to myself, you can do this. The note is lying

folded on my desk. I think about telling the police, but it will have to wait. I won't be made to feel afraid.

If you were here, you would ask me why I'm doing this. What would I say to you? That I'm doing this for you? Because that's not strictly true. I'm also doing this for myself.

The heels slow me down on the way to PBL Associates, but it gives me time to think and plan. I need to find the receptionist and ask her what she meant and what she knows about Emily's family.

I find a spot opposite the offices, where I'm concealed from the lobby. I prop myself against the brick wall and watch the exit. After half an hour, I see Brittany with a group of women, but the receptionist isn't with them. Brittany laughs and strides slightly ahead of the group, wearing slim black stilettos and a knee-length blue dress. She grins playfully and waves her hand for them to follow.

I push myself off the wall and follow them, remaining concealed in the dense Friday crowd. Brittany pulls away and stops in front of a lively bar, where people have spilled out into the summer evening clutching colourful cocktails and bottles of beer. They are penned in behind a neat white fence and I struggle to squeeze past, staring up at the light grey sign that says 'The Fence Bar'.

I lose them in the crowd as I slink into the cramped space full of suits and tailored dresses. I manoeuvre to the bar and wedge myself in between a group of squealing women clutching small purses and throwing their heads back to the low beat of the music. The bar is dimly lit, with thin strips of white light lining the walls. I crane my neck to try and spot Brittany, but I'm pushed back by two men either side of me vying for the bartender's attention.

I feel a touch on my hand and flick my head towards the bar.

'What can I get you?' the bartender shouts and I see the men eye me bitterly.

'House white, please.'

He nods and walks off.

'It's on me,' a man's low voice says into my ear. I stiffen as I recognise the smell, so close it pervades my nostrils and I almost choke.

I turn to face him and see Emily's old boss, Darren. I move back into the crowd to let him through. He turns and hands me my wine, clutching his pint of beer, the metallic scent saturating the space between us. He takes a long swig.

'Are you here with work?'

I shake my head. 'Just some friends.' I gulp. 'Thanks for the wine.'

'Do you want to join us?' I'm so close to him, I can smell sweat from a hot day spent in his slim-fitting suit.

'I better get back to them,' I say, contorting away into the crowd.

'Brittany spotted you,' he says, raising a hand over

my shoulder. I gaze up to see Brittany with her lips upon a tall glass. She takes a sip and angles her eyes towards me.

'No news on Emily,' he states.

I shake my head.

'I'd love to meet your friends,' he says. He walks around to face me, blocking Brittany from view. 'Where are they?'

I'm silent as I stare up at him.

'You know,' he says, 'Emily doesn't have a sister.'

My eyes widen and my throat thickens. I go to sip my wine, but someone behind nudges into me and it spills down my white blouse. Darren steps closer, until I can feel the warmth of his stale breath.

'So I wonder what the police would think about that.'

'She has friends though,' I reply.

He considers this, before leaning closer. 'Is that what you are? A friend?'

I say nothing.

'If I see you around here or near my employees again, I will call the police,' he says, his smile dipping into a frown. 'Do you understand?'

I nod.

I gasp as I pile out of the bar and into the busy street. A cyclist rings his bell and I fall to the side out of his way. A group of men with ties slung around their necks heads towards me and complain as I don't move for them. I run my hands through my hair and chew on my bottom lip as I rush in the direction of the tube station.

Something tugs at the back of my jacket, but I ignore it and press on until I hear a voice.

'Wait, please wait.'

I turn around and see the receptionist standing in front of me.

I cling to my jacket and shake my head. 'What are you doing?'

'I have to get back, before they see I'm gone. I could lose my job,' she says. Her black hair is gelled back, clinging to her scalp, and her green eyes are frantic.

'What did you mean by "that family"?' I say, stepping closer.

She eyes me. 'She wouldn't let me speak to the police.'

'Who wouldn't?'

'Brittany,' she says.

'I don't understand.'

'You're her neighbour, aren't you? Her eyes slanted in sympathy. 'I heard them say that's who you are.'

I nod. 'Do her family know something?'

'I don't know, but she didn't trust them.'

'Why?' I press her.

She looks down at her feet. 'Her dad did something. He was involved with one of Emily's friends, and she left home when she found out.'

I glare back at her. 'Are you the only person she told about this?'

She shrugs. 'Maybe, I don't know. She told me on her birthday. She was really upset.'

'Why were you told not to talk to the police?'

She shakes her head, looking confused, as if she might cry. 'I was just told not to say anything about that night.' She glances behind again. 'I have to go back, before they notice I'm gone.'

'Wait,' I say, 'does Casse-Croûte mean anything to you?'

Her eyes widen. She turns to leave, but pauses, then nods slowly. 'I've seen it on company receipts, why?'

'You go there with work?'

She shakes her head. 'No, client receipts.' Her forehead wrinkles. 'For when clients come into the city for pitches, they dine there and stay at a hotel down the road. Why?' she urges again.

'What hotel?'

'It's not far from here, The Royal Oak,' she says.

'Who gives you these receipts?'

She looks up at me, her face red and flustered, alarm convulsing her features.

'I have to go,' she says, turning away. 'Please, don't follow me. I don't want to get into trouble.' But her eyes give her away. She doesn't want to put herself in danger.

## Chapter Thirty-One

### Emily

The months after I found my dad with Alice in her car were the hottest summer I could remember. I spent a lot of time in my room, spread across the floor in front of my wide-open windows. Clouds stretched across the sky and the sun sparkled between dashings of large trees that lined our street. A pain in my chest.

I was thinking about my future. I could still go to London anyway, without Alice. I could start fresh. Somewhere away from here. I decided not to attend my graduation. I didn't want to risk seeing Alice, or even to know that she was there in the crowd, her eyes on me.

My mum spent the summer sending me applications for jobs in London and my dad was persistent about helping me with flat searching. Not the two-bed place like Alice and I had planned, just a single room for me. He sent me potential places daily and my mum began filling out some of the applications. They were in this together now. They were ready to be rid of me for good. That had been the plan anyway, hadn't it? To move to London.

I ignored the applications my mum sent; they were irrelevant and I realised how little she knew me and how desperate she was for me to leave. Instead I found some graduate positions in sales to apply for, something that paid well but didn't need relevant experience or qualifications. I'd write on the side, I promised myself. I still had that dream. They offered to fund renting a place for me, which I tried to decline, but they insisted on being my guarantors. My dad had been around more, coming home straight from work, bringing my mum treats like flowers and expensive bottles of wine. They started drinking them together now though, my mum perched at the breakfast bar as my dad cooked dinner.

I finally heard from Alice, a short message.

I know you'll never forgive me, but please know how sorry I am.

It made me feel sick. How little I could know her. How wrong I've been. I think about her smiling at me, her cheeks bunched by two hands cupping either side. Her low belly laugh and slight smile. My chest implodes every time I think about her.

Not just her. The dynamic at play, and all facets of my dad

rotating and revealing themselves. The pathetic drunk, the rich sleazebag, the loving and devoted husband – the caring dad. I could barely look at him, at either of them. I moved silently around the house, avoiding them as much as I could. I didn't know who to be angrier at, my dad for taking Alice away from me, for not thinking about me once, or my mum for accepting every time he messed up. I settled on being angriest at myself, for not shouting and screaming at them. For just silently tiptoeing around their feelings, like I was in the wrong.

They seemed elated at the news that I'd be moving to London. My dad offered to help me with applications for the positions I found, but I thanked him and said no. I came downstairs one day to a brand-new yellow Mini sitting on the driveway, my dad dangling the keys above the entrance of the door, like I would run underneath and reach up and grab them, us both bundling in the car and driving off for ice-cream. I took the keys begrudgingly but let them grow dust on the side table – I didn't drive it once. He asked me why and I would just look at him, until he walked away.

I had my mind made up that it would be simple and easy to cut them out, leave them and never have a reason to reach out again. I'd given them too many lifelines, a piece of me always hoping my mum would see sense and leave.

It would have been so easy after it happened, her ghost-like figure standing on the staircase that night. She just needed to knock on my door and tell me, 'We're leaving,' and I would have packed my stuff and followed her. But I overheard her on the phone one day, whispering quietly on the edge of her bed when she thought no one else could hear: 'I'd lose the art studio,' and that was it. Her creation. Not me, but what she considered her real calling in life, not being a mother, being an artist.

It seemed incredibly futile needing something like that more than people. I never understood it – maybe I should have tried. I never liked my mum's paintings, slops of colour spread across canvases, mostly deep reds and snakes of blue, like dismembered body parts intertwined with deep purple veins. I felt queasy whenever I saw one of her pieces.

I found a graduate scheme at a firm called PBL Associates. They invited me in for an interview the following week. When I got the train, I felt the thrill of speeding towards London, as if all the rotten parts of me were dropping away under the sheer force of it. There was a new kind of sensation pinching at my insides, all the possibilities of the friends I'd make, the people I'd meet. Of exploring the city together.

I paired the job interview with flat hunting. Alice and I always spoke about living centrally, just north of the river, by a canal. I stepped off the tube at Angel in Islington, the autumn leaves chasing each other between the flurries of pedalling feet racing in every direction. The smell of peppered, salty meat and ripe flowers and sweet lager flew through the air. I wanted to consume everything, every stand spilling with antiques down Camden Passage, every oversized pastry tipping from wooden boards, every smoky hit of coffee. The noise almost blew me backwards, the roar of traffic, the crowds, the bells, the buzzes, the chimes, the clinking and clacking of glasses and shoes. I loved it. Everything was perfect.

I disappeared into the noise and came out a few streets away from the station. My parents said that central London would be too busy, but I didn't want peace, I wanted life, constantly. I wanted noise, constantly. At home it was always so quiet. So still. So nothing. I longed to look out my window and watch London's movement, in every sense. All the rawness of it felt palpable as I lunged further to the house viewing.

The flat sat on a corner of a long road running parallel to the high street. The lettings agent said the landlord would show me around himself, but they would deal with the paperwork. From the outside the flat didn't look like much. I waited outside, staring up at the window, curtains drawn. I thought about ringing the bell until footsteps stopped behind me.

'Emily?'

I turned to see a man, short, with a closely shaven head and deep lines across his forehead. He held out a hand. 'Mike,' he said.

'Emily,' I replied, taking his hand.

He dived into his jeans pocket, rummaging for keys, and grinned at me awkwardly.

'I know I've got them,' he said. 'Ah.' He produced the keys and we walked up the overgrown pathway.

He lowered his voice. 'Sorry it's a bit messy, this is the downstairs lady's garden, but she's not very good at keeping it cut back.'

'Oh, that's fine,' I said. 'Is it just her downstairs?'

'Yeah, her husband passed away a couple of years back.'

'Oh, how sad.'

Mike nodded, holding the door back for me.

'This is the communal hallway, so you're welcome to keep bits and pieces here. My other tenants have. You know, a bike if you have one, that sort of thing.'

He trailed upstairs. 'There are only two flats in the building, so you won't get much noise. These old buildings are pretty solid.'

'I don't mind the noise,' I said quietly.

'Where did you say you were moving from?'

'I didn't. I'm not far from Cambridge, moving here for work.'

'Right.'

Mike opened the front door to Flat 2, and led me in. The lounge was bigger than it looked from the outside: it stretched across into a narrow kitchen, where a small dining table was propped up against the wall.

'I'm getting some new furniture put in,' Mike said, pulling open the curtains.

A film of dust rose into the air, and the sunlight trickled through onto the floor. I followed Mike through to the bedroom, a small room with a king-size bed, and poked my head into the bathroom, noticing the grime lining the bath.

I don't know what I should be looking for, the questions I should be asking. So I just asked myself. Could this be your new home Emily? Could you be happy here? I walked over to the lounge window and cast my eyes over the street dappled with people, some huddled under umbrellas as the sky loosed specks of rain. A steady flow of traffic hummed into the flat, and a group of schoolchildren sang impatiently as they traipsed after their parents. It didn't have a balcony like Alice and I had imagined, but it won't have her either. I could be inspired here, write the stories I always wanted to write. I could put a desk close to the window so I could look out at the city. I'd slowly forget what happened and write happy, beautiful stories, ones that made people smile – stories with a happy ending.

'I'll take it,' I said, turning to Mike.

He looked at me curiously, and I had a different thought. Am I acceptable? Does he want me as a tenant? I suddenly felt very silly waiting for him to respond.

He did finally. 'Okay, well, if you put an offer in with the lettings agency, they can explain the fees and documents I'll need.'

'Great, thank you.'

I felt elated, giddy, drunk on the noise that perforated me as I wandered away. I took one last look at my new flat before I rounded the corner. This is it. I'm home

## Chapter Thirty-Two

W hen I return home, I stand in the shower and let the water wash away the make-up casing my face. I put on my warm jogging bottoms and familiar cosy fleece socks, closing the curtains to the unbridled Friday night noise.

Emily didn't trust her parents. She left home when she found out one of her friends was involved with her dad. Poor Emily. I think about her dad, Stuart. Something had felt off about him, hadn't it? So why the money from her parents on her birthday? Why the change of heart?

I know I should call Detective Peters or Inspector Freeman, tell them about the note and that it all feels connected to her family in some strange way. She was distant from them, her parents cut her off, but there'd been something in the receptionist's tone. It was more than that, like it wasn't just Emily's family anymore, it was someone else too.

I sink further into the chair. Why would Emily hide the bits of paper under the tile? Was she afraid as well? I punch The Royal Oak Hotel into maps to see where it is. So close to her work. I think about the receptionist's wild eyes. It was on client receipts along with the restaurant – is that coincidence or something more? None of it makes sense and I have to find out why. I bring up LinkedIn and go to Emily's profile. I hold my phone up to the screen and take a picture of the small framed photo of her, and hold it up to my face. I slide the laptop off my thighs and put it on the floor.

Grabbing my jacket and slipping on my shoes, I call a taxi and give them the address of The Royal Oak Hotel and Spa. This is my second journey to Bermondsey tonight, but I feel so close now. It's been weeks, not days like before when you left me, but I know Emily needs me.

I think about the receptionist's face when she told me about Emily's dad. How Emily must have felt when she found out, like she couldn't trust anybody. She was cast out, not because of her behaviour but because she threatened her parents' life and they made a decision about what was more important and it wasn't Emily. The birthday money feels like a payout: 'let's forget the past – here's some money'. They were scared that she was going to tell someone. I struggle to fit the pieces together.

Do they know where she is and have they paid for her to go away and keep quiet? Or was it worse than that? Had Emily refused? How does it connect to the restaurant and the pieces of paper she hid or the note that was stuffed through my letterbox? *I'm watching you, bitch.*

The taxi skims across Tower Bridge and I disappear in and out of the blue arches that line the way. The traffic is thicker tonight, full of black cabs and Toyotas carrying drunk passengers and meaty midnight snacks. I smile, remembering the big slices of pizza you and I would carry home after a night out drinking. We'd stay up in the lounge drinking pints of water and talking about our day, oil from the pizza dripping down our faces as we grinned at each other. The memory fades as the taxi slows to a halt outside the hotel. I pay the driver, thank him and slip out onto the busy street. I stare up at the luminous sign plastered across the front: The Royal Oak Hotel and Spa. A group of women in short dresses and high heels staggers past me, giggling into the night. The rest of the street is dark apart from this one building. The lobby is full of curved navy seats and plush silky pink cushions. I can smell chlorine from a swimming pool and the sweet floral scent of spa products. I hesitate, feeling stupid, as I watch a man sharply dressed in a grey suit and a woman in a flowing maroon dress holding hands ahead of me at the reception. The woman slips off her black stilettos and holds them playfully in one hand, taking the man's hand with the other. He looks down at her and I turn to walk away.

'Hello, can I help?'

I look back and the couple are walking towards the lifts. He bends down to kiss her. The man behind the reception is looking at me expectantly. He looks impatient, his mouth set in a straight line as if I'm wasting his time.

'Can I help?' he repeats.

'No,' I say.

He frowns. 'Are you waiting for someone?' he says, gesturing towards the sofas.

I shake my head, turning fully towards him. 'No,' I repeat.

'Are you a hotel or spa guest?'

I approach the desk and lean awkwardly, intertwining my fingers.

'Neither, I just needed to ask something.'

The man looks confused; his eyes glaze over me and his eyebrows narrow. I pull out my phone and bring up the picture of Emily from her LinkedIn photo.

'Have you seen this woman at all?' I say, holding up the phone to meet his eyes. He keeps them on me for a few seconds before looking down at the picture.

He cocks his head to the side and I see a flicker of recognition.

'Are you his wife?' he asks suddenly.

I frown, looking at the photograph. 'Whose wife?'

He looks down at his lap and stands up, leaning towards me.

'Look, I don't want to get involved in other people's affairs.'

I shake my head. 'I'm looking for her.'

He squints at me. 'I don't know her.'

'But you know the man she was with?'

'Like I said, I don't want to get involved.'

I clench my jaw and hold the phone towards him. 'You are involved,' I hiss.

'I will call security,' he says, raising his eyebrows.

'Fine,' I say, my voice rising. 'Call security, and then you can explain to them why you won't tell me about this girl.' I pause. 'This missing girl.'

He flicks his head towards me. 'Missing?'

I nod fiercely.

'This is serious.' He looks me up and down again. 'You're not police?' he asks, knowing the answer.

I shake my head. 'I just know her.'

'I'm so sorry,' he says. 'Maybe I should speak to the police?' He pauses. 'Has it been reported?'

I withdraw the phone. 'Yes.'

'Are you her friend?'

I don't respond.

'Who was she with?' I say.

He looks at me, sympathy now dancing across his features.

'If she's missing, I think I need to speak to the police.'

I stare back at him, and he looks away, a sadness in his eyes.

'I understand,' I say quietly. 'I'll call them.'

He hesitates, 'Maybe this should wait till tomorrow. I'm the night manager here, but the general manager will be back tomorrow.'

'I don't think this can wait,' I say impatiently.

He nods slowly.

I glance at the time on my phone, before calling Detective Peters. What must he think at eleven o'clock on a Friday night? Maybe I should call Inspector Freeman and tell him instead, but he'll have more questions than I can answer right now.

'Suzie?' he says. He sounds tired, a slight croak in his voice.

'I know it's late.'

'Is everything okay?' he asks.

'Not really. I'm at The Royal Oak Hotel and Spa in Bermondsey.' I hear the release of springs and a cover being thrown back. 'I'm sorry to wake you.'

'Are you in trouble?'

'No, but Emily was here,' I say.

He is silent.

'I know you've closed the case, but this feels important.'

He sighs. 'What do you mean, she was there? Did you see her?'

I shake my head. 'No, the night manager did. She was with a man.'

'I'm on my way,' he says. 'I'll be forty minutes.'

I hang up the phone and wave it in front of the night manager.

'The police are on their way, about forty minutes,' I say.

He nods, glancing away. 'If you want to sit down, I can bring you some tea or coffee?'

'Tea would be nice, thank you.'

I turn towards the curved sofas in the lobby and flop onto one of them. I can feel the night manager looking at me from over the reception desk.

He disappears into a back room and emerges with a cup of tea. Sauntering over, he places it in front of me. I smile gratefully and he retreats behind the reception desk. A man in a robe walks through the spa doors, rubbing his damp hair with a towel. He looks at me distastefully and the night manager notices, glancing at me, embarrassment spreading across his face.

'Good evening, sir,' he says quietly, but the man is already halfway into a lift and disappears into the night.

I let my mind rest on the receptionist, her face when I asked her about the restaurant. A client receipt? An affair? It made sense, a purchase you wanted to keep off your phone records, a way for it not to be traced. It has to be someone she works with.

The hotel doors slide open and Detective Peters walks into the lobby. He's dressed in dark jeans and a creased checked green top. He has his phone in his hands, like he's just been on a call, and his light hair is flopped unevenly to the side. He has dark circles masking his grey eyes and uneven stubble circles his downturned lips.

I hold my arm in the air, feeling self-aware and unnatural. He catches my eye and grimaces as he approaches me. I rise from my seat and see the night manager get up from his place behind the reception desk and come over.

'Officer?' he says, before I can speak.

Detective Peters turns to face him and holds out a hand. 'Detective Sergeant Noah Peters,' he says, as the night manager extends his arm and fidgets nervously and Detective Peters reaches into his pocket to produce identification that the man studies carefully.

'This is just unusual,' he says carefully.

Detective Peters nods. 'Would you mind me having a moment alone with the woman that called this in and I'll be right with you.'

'Of course,' the night manager says, adding, 'Tea, coffee?'

'A coffee,' Peters replies, exhaustedly, 'black, no sugar, thank you.'

He gestures to the sofa and I lower myself back down. He doesn't meet my gaze, instead walks around to one of the wing-backed grey suede chairs, swivels it towards me and sits down. He rubs his thumbs awkwardly over his eyes and loosens his jaw.

'Suzie,' he says, looking up to face me.

'I can explain,' I say, reaching forward. He tips back into the seat and his eyes flicker away.

'Why am I here?' he says slowly.

'I know, I've done some things I shouldn't have...' I pause. 'But I was right not to trust her parents. Emily knew something about them, about her dad.'

He squints. 'Knew what?'

'Emily's dad, he was involved with one of her friends. That's why she left home.'

He shakes his head, and breathes out a heavy sigh.

'That's why she came to London.'

'How do you know this?' he says bluntly.

'I... her friend told me.'

'I thought she didn't have any friends?'

'She did, at work.'

He nods in frustration. 'Of course, and you'd know that how?' he demands.

'I'm sorry,' I say, 'but you closed the case and I couldn't let it go.' I think about the note. Should I tell him?

Detective Peters's eyes widen and he goes to speak, but shakes his head. 'I'm going to call Inspector Freeman,' he says, reaching for his phone. 'You'll have to explain this all to him.'

I nod. The night manager walks over with a small cup

of coffee propped on top of a saucer. 'Do you want this here?'

'Do you have somewhere more private we can talk? I'm going to call my colleague and then I'll need to ask you a few questions.'

The night manager hesitates and then nods. 'We can talk in the back office. I'll ask someone to cover the reception.'

'Thank you, and please could you phone a taxi for Mrs Arlington?' Detective Peters says, turning away from me. He starts to walk away. 'I'll ask Inspector Freeman to contact you, seeing as you're involved in the case now.'

'I'm sorry,' I call. He pauses. 'I'm leaving tomorrow,' I say quietly. 'I'm going back to Hove.'

'I wouldn't,' he says, without looking at me, and then I feel the full weight of what I've uncovered and I sense he does too.

## Chapter Thirty-Three

### Emily

I was offered a graduate position at PBL Associates the next week. They asked if I could start full time at the end of the month. I was thrilled, but I felt a pang of disappointment that I couldn't call Alice and share my excitement with her. I had to move forward. I didn't reply to her message and I desperately tried to remember every interaction she'd had with my dad when she'd visited the house or picked me up, or when I'd tell her fragments of his actions. I don't know when it began, how far back their relationship went, how they met or if there was anything charged between them when they passed each other in the hallway at our house. I remember her sunken features in the bar by her work a month ago. Something was on her mind, wasn't it?

I tried to remember if she'd ever mentioned him, but she

must have been careful not to. I rarely had her over to the house, so the opportunities to meet him, speak to him, must have been so minimal. Maybe all it took was a look. I pushed the thought away. My parents hadn't spoken to me about Alice. I almost asked my mum about it on one occasion, because I wanted to know how she was feeling, but she was so buried in her art, so consumed with my dad's presence around the house, that it was like the limit of what he'd done had been a blessing. My parents needed something from each other that no one else could give them. A unit, fuelled by greed and wealth. My dad started cutting back on hours at his company and putting the time into my mum's art studio, saying he wanted to focus on her. They grew, mutated, until by the time it was ready for me to move out at the end of summer, they had become the parents I wanted – but it was too late.

The day I left, I didn't take much. Only one suitcase and a backpack. I wasn't really one for sentimental items, maybe because I didn't have any. Alice's jumper sat scrunched up on the floor at the bottom of my bed and I blinked back the tears, thinking of her smell, and then, worse, her smell on my dad. When I looked around my room for the last time, it felt like shedding old skin.

I only took what I really needed. The rest I'd buy in London, in the bustling Saturday morning markets and vintage shops tucked away down forgotten streets. I was excited to touch every part of London, to absorb all these new memories and to create a sanctuary to call my own.

When I arrived at the flat, Mike was waiting to greet me

and hand over the keys. He was already inside the flat as I made my way up the narrow staircase. The door was wide open and he was sitting on the sofa. He patted it as I walked in.

'This is new. The old sofa was falling apart a bit.'

The flat still looked sparse, but I wanted that, I wanted to fill it with all the treasures I'd pick up along the way. I stared at the space beneath the large bay windows where I planned to put a desk. I'd fill this place with beautiful stories I'd write.

'That's okay, I'm planning on getting some bits and pieces.'

Mike nodded. 'Of course. Well, if you have any problems then you've got my number.'

He dropped the keys into my hand and paused in front of me, as if waiting for a reply.

'Thank you,' I fumbled.

'Do you need any help with your things?'

I shook my head. 'No, I've travelled light.'

'Ah, well, I'll leave you to get settled in.' He smiled and closed the door behind him.

A week later I started working at PBL Associates, I set my alarm extra early, so I could make myself look perfect, in a grey pencil dress and my smartest black blazer. When I arrived at the office, I was greeted in reception by a woman called Brittany. She was beautiful, with wavy blonde hair and full red lips. I felt intimidated as she stood watching me as I had my picture taken for my work pass.

She whisked me off upstairs and introduced me to the rest of the team.

'I think Darren was away when you had your interview.

He's the department head. He's in a meeting at the moment, but should be out soon.'

I was shown to my desk at the end of the aisle. The row was mostly empty, but the team was growing, they'd said in the interview. I was one of many new additions.

I was keen to get stuck in, learn the ropes. I spent the morning setting up my computer, with IT coming over to sort out various emails and logins. I'd get a plant for my desk, I thought, and maybe my own mug and coaster. I smiled.

The receptionist, whose name I learnt was Anna, showed me around the kitchen and stood with me whilst I made a cup of tea. I found it easy to talk to her; she was nothing like Alice. She liked the same films as me, she wore her emotions on her sleeve, and her eyes hid nothing.

When I carried my tea back to my desk, I saw a man exiting one of the meeting rooms. He was broad, with greying stubble neatly blanketing his face. His eyes scanned the room and settled on Brittany. He strode over to her, a firm smile plastered upon his face. Brittany rose from her desk. I guessed she was his PA, but I wasn't sure. He said something to her and she nodded, flicking her head towards me and smiling with round blushing cheeks. The man followed her eyes and rested his gaze on me. I stood and made my way clumsily down the row filled with twirling office chairs.

'Darren, head of sales,' he said, extending a hand.

'Emily,' I said, shaking it.

He couldn't be more than forty, with a boyish smile that

revealed deep dimples on both cheeks. He was the most handsome man I'd ever seen.

'Are you getting settled in?'

'Yes, thank you.'

'Good, well, it would be great to catch up properly as I didn't get to meet you at the interview stage. My office is through there.' He pointed to a small glass-walled room next to the meeting room. 'If you want to pop in after lunch.'

'Of course,' I said.

He smiled again, before turning his attention to Brittany. As I waded back to my desk, I felt my legs shaking and a small tingle in the bottom of my stomach. I was excited about my meeting after lunch, excited to find out more about Darren.

As the weeks progressed at work, I had regular one-to-ones with Darren, mainly to talk about how I was enjoying the job, any KPIs I wanted to focus on, and if I saw myself staying at the company. When I entered his office for the first time, I saw a framed photo of a woman with short, dark hair holding a baby. My heart sank.

'Your baby is beautiful,' I said. 'A girl?'

He nodded, smiling at the picture. From then on I just enjoyed his company. I laughed at the things he said, because they were funny. I always attended the meetings, because he asked me to. He was my boss and it had to stay that way, but I struggled to suppress my attraction to him and the tightening in the bottom of my stomach whenever I saw him.

As Christmas approached, the office started to get more social, with boozy lunches and Friday drinks after work. I revelled in it, cramming into a sticky pub and making friends. The carpet thick with the stench of beer, every seat taken, the music thrumming along to our laughter. I started to become close to Anna. She was my age, and we'd do rounds at the pub, both awkwardly slotting into the older crowd. Brittany always led the after-work march to The Fence Bar. She'd say 'pencils down' at 5pm and everyone would simultaneously jump up from their seats.

Darren never came for drinks. He had a baby, a wife to go home to. So much better than my dad, I thought.

When the Christmas drinks rolled around, we all got dressed up in the toilets. It was how I always imagined having a tight-knit group of friends would be. Compliments strung through the air, glittery eyeshadow smudging the mirrors, the clinking of smuggled-in gin as our heels smacked against the bathroom tiles.

The venue was one of the breweries that the company had rented out in the Bermondsey archways. It was beautiful. Fairy lights laced the walls, tinsel streamed from the ceilings and Christmas music chanted from the speakers clinging above the bar.

I left Anna dancing in the corner to squeeze past to the bar. The Christmas party was full of so many names and faces I couldn't place, but I didn't care. I loved the noise, the chaos.

'What're you drinking?' a familiar voice said.

Darren was standing next to me, draining the last of a pint of beer.

'Oh, you came out?'

'Well, I'm not going to miss the annual Christmas party. What would that do for staff morale?'

I nodded. 'Christmas miracles do happen,' I said, adding, 'a brandy and lemonade, please.'

He looked at me quizzically. 'I wouldn't have guessed that.'

He ordered us the drinks and we stood awkwardly in silence.

'Thanks,' I mumbled. 'I'm going to find Anna.'

I found Anna with a hand on her hip watching me as I emerged from the crowd clutching my brandy and lemonade.

'You were talking to Darren,' she stated.

I nodded. 'Yeah, he never comes out, does he.'

'Well, now he and his wife have split up, I'm sure he'll be out a lot more.'

Anna turned away like the comment didn't mean anything and continued to gently sway to the music. I couldn't help but look back towards the bar, to catch Darren's eyes resting on mine.

---

It felt like everything was finally slotting into place, like I'd just been trying to make the wrong piece fit for so long, but now, here in London, in my new life – it was effortless. I adjusted to a new routine of lazy work lunches and cocktails in the pub after work. Time spent with new friends. Soon Alice and my parents became like a grey cloud I had struggled to see through. I'd spent a long time trying to make sense of what happened, but now, as I settled into a new normal, it was special – I just had to be patient.

In the weeks after the Christmas party, I noticed Darren finding more ways to speak to me, whether he conveniently made coffee at the same time as I did or would find a way to sit next to me in the pub.

As we grew closer, I opened up to him more and he told me about his marriage breaking apart – how hard he'd tried to keep on track, but his wife just wasn't his soulmate. He looked defeated as he said it and I wanted to share a part of myself with him. One night, after too many cocktails, I told him about my family, about Alice. He listened intently, nodding rhythmically as I relayed everything. He smiled afterwards, but not in a crude way – it was as if he understood. He didn't judge or offer advice, he simply replied, 'Sounds like they messed up on the chance of something wonderful.

I cocked my head. 'What's that?'

He blushed. It was adorable. 'You,' he said quietly.

After that there was no denying my attraction to Darren and the way he made me feel, treating me like no person ever has. He got to know me, but really know me – not just my favourite flowers or film, but who I am. I started to discover myself through him and one night as I arrived home at my flat and turned up the music, I started dancing, flicking through playlists and singing loudly as I made dinner, imagining a future of us dancing together in a place of our own.

I thought of Alice in that moment, how I'd always imagined it would be us dancing together. Her soft blonde hair trailing down my arm as it rested on my shoulder. I pushed the thought away. Alice never let me be honest with myself. I stopped dancing, realising it was the first time I was being honest with myself, like I could finally breathe, and it was all thanks to Darren. He didn't tell me what was good for me, he didn't make me feel like I was always one step behind, he didn't accuse me of not understanding love. In fact, he made me feel like I understood it better than anyone. He told me, 'Heartbreak is the purest form of love.'

Darren and I started meeting at a hotel near work. He wanted to keep it private, our secret, and I understood that. I didn't want people at work to start talking and thinking I was getting any favouritism because of our relationship.

He had the most romantic way of letting me know when to meet him. On the week we'd meet, he would write the day and time on a pink Post-it note and stick it to my coffee cup. It was always at our favourite French restaurant. He knew how much I loved the place, somewhere I could people-watch and be consumed by the noise of the city. Somewhere where we blended into the endearing chaos of Bermondsey High Street. I always loved to come in in the morning and see it there, knowing we would be alone soon, just the two of us. The notes meant so much to me that I started to keep them, tucked away in my jewellery box – our secret.

By March, I decided I was ready to let people at work know about me and Darren, so we didn't have to sneak around anymore – we could hold hands down the High Street and he could join us for drinks on Friday night, and people would say *how wonderful we were together. I longed for it so badly, and I wanted it to be special, so I waited until the Post-it note came. He was working late, and wanted to meet at the hotel instead. As I entered the hotel, I smiled at the same desk clerk I saw every time Darren and I checked in. He gave me a key to the same room, and this time I decorated it with rose petals and scented candles. I put on a new piece of Victoria's Secret lingerie I'd received from him as a present.*

*When he arrived, he was grinning and it felt so perfect. I flew into his arms and he encased me, pulling me in tighter.*

*'I want to tell you something,' I said.*

*'Oh, yes,' he said, reaching down to kiss my neck.*

*'I love you,' I said passionately into the air, and he didn't stop, he kissed me harder.*

*'I want to be with you,' I breathed. 'I want to tell everyone.'*

*He stopped and lowered me to the floor, my arms still folded around his neck.*

*'Emily, we spoke about this.'*

*'But I'm ready, aren't you ready?'*

*He pulled my arms away and walked over to the bed. He sank onto the edge, not noticing the swarm of petals that fell into the dip he made.*

*'Emily.'*

*'What?' I said, standing in front of him.*

*He wouldn't look up. He pinched his temples and then stood suddenly.*

*'Maybe this was a bad idea. I've had a long day.'*

*'Don't be like that, please. It was just an idea.'*

'I'm getting back with my wife, so we can be a family, with our baby girl.' He faced me then. 'You're not going to stop a family being together, are you?'

What was the answer to that? Of course I wouldn't be that person and he knew that. He knew I would never come between him and his family. He knew, from the moment I set eyes on that picture, the way my feelings changed towards him, the shift in my emotions.

'Do you love me?'

'Emily, you know I do, but this is my family.'

Am I as bad as Alice? Or the other countless women that my dad would stay out with all night? Am I a lie? No, I'm not any of those things, because I'll let him go. I stepped nearer to him.

'Leave,' I said. Before it's too late, before your family shut you out and your daughter learns what you are, leave.

'I love you,' he said. And I felt stupid, standing in a room of candles, in lacy underwear, surrounded by masses of crumpled roses. He took one last look at me before he turned and walked out the door.

## Chapter Thirty-Four

I waited up most the night to hear from Detective Peters or Inspector Freeman, but no one showed up at my door or rang my phone. Now, I stare out of the window as specks of cloudy rain obscure the low, fragmented sky. Slices of sunlight brim over the currents of sombre clouds and I feel trapped. Since I made the decision to go home, it feels like anything will keep me from it.

I pull the curtains closed and take in the flat. I'm sitting amid piles of stacked boxes and large black bin bags. Your box is separate, full of things I wouldn't let your parents take, that I wouldn't let anyone touch. Resting on top is your *Avengers* mug and a stack of vinyls I peeled carefully from the wall and bubblewrapped three times. This doesn't mean I've put you away.

I've never been religious, you know that, but it feels good to have faith in something right now. I've always spoken to you, ever since you left me. I asked you to come home when we couldn't find you for three days. I asked you to not be dead when they told me they'd found your body and for the last two years I've waited for you.

'I've got myself into a mess, haven't I?' I say, knowing you'd be proud.

Stubborn, that's how you described me, but with a smile across your face when you said it. I never told you how proud I was of you, but I tell you now.

I sit down in the leather chair. Our place. I smile. We'd always opt to squeeze into the chair instead of sprawl across the sofa, that's how we liked it.

My doorbell buzzes and I jump up, expecting the police at the front door, but instead, when I peer through the curtains, I see Clara. She's already looking at me, her hand held up in a half wave. I smile back, so grateful that she's here.

I open the door and she flies into me. Her taller figure wraps around me and she pulls me in. Her long strawberry-blonde hair tickles my face and I take in the scent of her, the same sweet smell I've missed so much.

'Come in,' I say, taking her hand and leading her into the flat. She gazes around, a sadness etched across her sharp features.

'You said you had to speak to the police?'

I nod. 'You did tell me not to get involved.'

'Since when do you ever listen to me?' she says smiling. 'Is it serious?'

'I haven't heard anything yet.'

She walks slowly around the flat, before dropping onto the sofa. She looks up towards the ceiling.

'Poor girl,' she says. 'I hope she is okay.' She lowers her head to meet my gaze. 'Are you okay?'

I nod. 'I think so.'

'I didn't tell Mum,' she says. 'Didn't want her to worry.'

'I can't leave yet.'

'I know you can't, but I'll be here,' she says, leaning forward and pulling my hand into hers. 'No more doing this alone, okay?'

I smile. 'What did you tell Mum?'

'That we were going to have some girl time in London before Ian came up to help with your things.'

'Do you think she bought it?' I say.

She raises an eyebrow, something I've always been jealous of. 'Not even a little bit. You just need to be honest with the police.'

'I will be.' I hesitate. 'I just don't want Detective Peters to get in trouble.'

'I think it's really cool what you've done,' she says suddenly.

I screw up my face and Clara leans towards me.

'Really,' she continues. 'What that girl's been through, and God forbid anything has happened to her, you didn't give up. I'm proud of you,' she says.

'You shouldn't be,' I reply.

'About Ben—' I go to interrupt but she holds up a hand stopping me. 'You've beaten yourself up about this for too long now.' She presses a hand on her chest, shaking her head. 'It was constant, you asking yourself the same questions over and over again.' She doesn't need to say them, I know what they are.

When you went missing I always thought there was more I could have done. I could have reached out to your friends when I didn't hear from you that night. I could have walked towards the pub I knew you'd be at when you didn't come home, traced your steps and found you before it was too late.

Clara interrupts my thoughts. 'You know there was nothing anyone could have done.' She struggles to say the next part. 'He died instantly, and all these "what if"s are only damaging. You need to heal,' she says, bending forward and squeezing my hand.

She hauls herself up and disappears into the bathroom. I see her pause by the bedroom door and her face turn slightly. She looks back at me and smiles before disappearing into the bathroom.

'Shall we get some food?' she calls from behind the closed door.

'Yeah, let's do that.'

Clara and I decide to order in Chinese and we open a bottle of red wine she brought with her; she never did like my taste. She sips it delicately as we discuss the future. What I'll do when I get back to Hove, whether I'm looking forward to living with Mum and Dad again, what I'll do for a job.

The tension slides away with Clara here and I can't think why I didn't give in sooner to her company. She focuses on what's to come, saying that she'd love me to spend more time with my niece and nephew. She starts tidying away some of my stacks of books into boxes and I gaze at all the faded covers from afternoons spent reading in the sun, and thick coffee marks from lazy Sunday afternoons when you'd rest a mug on top of them. She smiles at me as I watch her, seeing how painful it is for me. She furrows her brow as she picks up a folded note from the dining table and flicks it open. Her face falls in shock.

'What is this?' she says, thrusting the note towards me.

I shake my head. 'I don't know.'

'Answer me,' she says firmly. 'What is this?'

'It came through the door,' I say quietly.

'Have you told the police?' she demands.

I shake my head again. She lowers herself into the chair. 'What does this mean? What have you been

263

doing?' She marches towards the window and pulls the curtains closed.

'You need to tell the police about this. It's fucked up,' she says.

'Please just drop it.'

'Why haven't you told the police?' Clara yells, waving the note.

'Because I'm scared,' I cry, sinking into the sofa and burying my face in my hands. Clara joins me, resting a hand on my shoulder.

The buzzer rings for the Chinese and I edge off the sofa, grabbing my purse from the coffee table. I pull open the main door and my face sinks as Darren turns slowly to face me. He frowns at me, his usually groomed face streaked with stray hairs and his hair flat against his forehead. He's wearing the suit I saw him in yesterday, but his navy tie has been loosened from around the collar and his dark grey blazer is slung over his shoulder.

'Suzie,' he says, as if he couldn't remember what to say. It rolls off his tongue and he recoils as he says it.

'What are you doing here?' I ask quietly, closing the door slightly.

He looms forward, slipping a smart black shoe into the space between the door and the jamb.

'I'm here to see you,' he says. This time his tone contains menace and I flinch. 'Can I come in?'

'My sister is here,' I say dumbly. But he is already

forcing the door inwards and moving into the small corridor.

'That's okay,' he says. I close the main door and turn to see him waiting by my front door, gazing up the stairway towards Emily's flat. He turns to me expectantly and points inside my flat. 'This way,' he says.

I follow him as he wanders in. He is already smiling at Clara, who looks confused. She flicks her head towards me and her faint smile slips as she sees me glare at her in horror.

'I'm Darren,' he says, holding out a hand to Clara.

Clara takes it, but doesn't introduce herself. She goes to speak, but I shake my head slightly and she retreats.

'Okay,' Darren says. He lowers himself into the leather chair and my lungs push against my ribcage as I dart forward.

'Not there,' I say quietly, but he doesn't move.

'I think we need to have a chat, don't you?'

'This isn't a good time,' Clara says cautiously.

Darren leans forward and pinches the space between his eyes, before glaring back at her.

'I think it's an excellent time,' he says spitefully.

He turns to me. 'Sit down, Suzie.'

'Who are you?' Clara says more forcefully.

He lifts his hands in the air and slaps his thighs.

'Your sister can tell you,' he says, leaning towards me.

I walk forward to stand next to Clara and take her

hand, lowering us down into the sofa. I stay silent, gripping Clara's hand.

He points towards Clara. 'Is this another one of Emily's sisters?'

I shake my head slowly.

'No, because she didn't have any sisters, which makes me wonder why her nosy neighbour was prying into her business, because,' he says, 'you two weren't very close were you?' He looks at me, his dark eyes piercing and full of rage. 'In fact,' he continues, 'you hated living downstairs to Emily. You'd complain about her, wouldn't you.'

'I didn't hate—'

He interrupts me. 'I was there that night when you came up and told her to turn off the music,' he says. 'Seems like you didn't stop there, did you? Ratting her out to the council.'

I can't breathe. I squeeze Clara's hand tighter, but she stares forward, horrified, so I place an arm around her shoulders and she swivels to me.

'It was just an affair. She was in love with me, infatuated by me.' He stops. 'She was a really stupid girl.'

'Thanks to you the police came round, and now the police – and my wife – know every sordid little detail.' He shakes his head and bites his nail, gazing blankly into the distance, as if lost in thought.

'You've ruined my life,' he says finally, pointing at

me. 'I'm married... happily,' he says, convincingly. 'Emily was just fun, until it wasn't fun anymore.' He looks at me trying to find some understanding.

I nod, and clear my throat. 'Then where is she?'

He shrugs. 'It's none of my fucking business.' He rises from the chair, pausing in front of me, casting a shadow across the sofa. 'Emily is a vicious little bitch.' He bends down slightly until I can smell the remains of booze on his breath. 'No one cares where she is, except her lonely, pathetic neighbour.' He straightens his back, opens the door and pauses for a moment before slamming it shut.

Clara lets out a small, painful breath. She turns to me with wide eyes.

'I'm sorry,' I say, and she squeezes my hand tighter.

'How does he know you, Suzie?' she says quietly.

I don't reply.

'Why does he think you're Emily's sister?' She leans in closer. 'What have you been doing?'

'The police, they weren't doing anything. They'd stopped looking for her.'

'Oh, Suzie,' she sighs. 'Did he send that note?'

'I don't know.'

She falls backwards into the sofa and cups her head in her palms. The front buzzer rings and I go to collect the takeaway. I feel my phone buzzing in my pocket as I hand the money over, and, holding the bag in one hand, I dig my hand into my hoodie pocket and see a number I don't recognise.

'Hello,' I answer.

'Suzie, it's Detective Inspector James Freeman.'

'Hi,' I breathe, entering my flat and placing the Chinese on the kitchen counter.

'We'll be needing to speak with you regarding the development in the case. Are you around tomorrow?'

I stare at Clara across the room, who is fidgeting with her long hair whilst chewing the corner of her mouth.

'Yes,' I mumble.

'Can we stop by?'

'Yes.'

'Midday okay?'

'My sister's here.'

'That's not a problem.'

'Okay, it's just—' I look at Clara's delicate features, her thin face and bright blue eyes. 'Darren turned up.'

Inspector Freeman is silent. I can hear a siren in the background and a nearby chime of laughter. A door shuts, muffling it.

'When?' he asks.

'He just left.'

'What did he say?'

'Just that he doesn't know where she is. Is he a suspect?' I ask.

'I can't talk about that,' he says sternly.

'I understand,' I say. Clara is staring at me intently across the room, her eyes searching mine for answers as she listens to my conversation.

'Did he threaten you?'

'He's upset. He blames me.'

'We'll come by tomorrow.'

'With Detective Peters?'

Inspector Freeman exhales awkwardly. 'As you know, myself and Detective Peters stopped investigating Emily's disappearance but,' he pauses, 'as new information has come to light, we are looking into other possibilities.'

'That she didn't run away?'

'Just other possibilities. I must go, but if Darren contacts you or turns up at your residence, please contact me urgently.'

'There's something else,' I say. 'I received a note through the main letter box, an angry note.'

'What did it say?'

'"I'm watching you,"' I wince, adding, '"bitch."'

'When did this happen?'

'I found it a couple of days ago. I'm sorry I didn't say anything.'

He sighs. 'I'm sorry this has happened. We'll have to investigate this. It's a serious offence.'

'I think it's related to Emily.'

'We'll collect it tomorrow, please don't touch it anymore.'

'Okay. I'm sorry I didn't say anything sooner.'

'If you get any problems, be sure to call me.'

'Okay, thanks,' I say, hanging up.

Clara walks into the kitchen and starts unloading the bag of Chinese food. She takes a long sip of wine and wipes her lips with the back of her hand.

'We need to get you out of here,' she says quietly. 'If you're not in trouble, then I don't see why we can't leave after you've spoken to them tomorrow. I can call Ian and ask him to come.'

I nod slowly.

Clara discards the empty pots and picks up the two plates. She hands one over to me and slumps down next to me.

I lean forward, dump the plate onto the coffee table and bend down towards the floor, letting my head hang between my knees. Clara's hand gently strokes the top of my back as I sob quietly into the floorboards and let a steady stream of tears fall into the splinters by my feet.

'I don't want to put you in danger.'

She makes shhing noises and lets her fingers splay across my shoulder blades. Leaning forward, she bends down to join me.

'We'll be fine.'

'He must hate me.'

'Who?'

'Detective Peters.'

Our heads dangle next to each other, our blonde hair smothering our faces.

'I'm sure he doesn't hate you,' she says, dropping an arm and brushing my face with the back of her hand.

'That's the same hand you used to wipe the wine from your mouth,' I say.

'Yummy,' she says, smiling.

'I'm sorry about Darren, that must have been scary.' I straighten up and Clara does too. She put a hand on my knee and smiles evenly at me.

'We need to leave,' she says.

I shake my head. 'I can't believe he doesn't know where she is. Maybe her parents are right, maybe she did just run away.'

Clara nods. 'Try not to think about it. I know that's difficult.'

I puff my lips out and nod.

'Detective Peters doesn't hate you,' she says again, seeing how much it means to me.

'He looked so angry the last time I saw him, he just put me in a taxi home.'

'He had a job to do,' she says.

We eat our Chinese in silence. I run my fork through the strands of noodles and move slimy orange sauce to the side of the plate. I think about Emily, the times she sat upstairs eating Chinese alone. Was she lonely? I think about her now, where she could be, and I want to stretch my fingers up to the ceiling and tell her to come down, to join us. We'd drink wine together and it would be a different conversation to other ones we had. We'd shrug it off and laugh, our glasses clinking together. It would be a different kind of noise.

'I'm sorry,' I say out loud.

Clara puts down her half-empty plate and pulls me in, letting her hair fall into my pile of egg fried rice and sweet and sour sauce. She sighs heavily into my ear.

'It'll all be over tomorrow,' she says encouragingly. I glance up at the window, at the heavy traffic and shadowed figures moving between streetlights just visible behind the curtains. No it won't, I think.

## Chapter Thirty-Five

### Emily

The following week at work, I struggled to focus and Brittany noticed. She stalked over to my desk and bent down slowly next to me, how teachers used to when they wanted to single you out.

'Is everything okay, lovely? You don't seem quite yourself.'

I turned to her, the frustration suffocating me.

Darren's office door swung open and I immediately swivelled my head. He strode out, a grin from ear to ear as he shook the hand of another man in a navy suit. He didn't seem to notice me, he didn't seem to care. He went about his day, avoiding my gaze in meetings, skimming past me in the kitchen. I felt so desperately sad.

'He's married,' Brittany said, surprising me.

She looked at me in a different way, sympathy etched across

*her round features, but there was an edge, a sharpness in the corner of her eyes, and I felt like there was more to say, but she just continued to look at me until we felt someone standing next to us.*

'Lunch?' Anna asked.

*I nodded. Brittany smiled and got up from her squat on the ground.* 'Maybe some drinks on Friday will cheer you up.'

'Do you need cheering up?' Anna asked. 'Why?'

'No reason,' *I said, eyeing Brittany.* 'Just work stuff, a lot on, need to blow off some steam.'

'Oh,' *Anna said, clasping her hands together.* 'Well, it's your birthday coming up, we could do something nice for it?'

'That sounds like a great idea,' *Brittany chimed in.*

*I smiled, thankful for the distraction.*

'Yeah, you guys could come over if you want, Saturday?'

'Perfect,' *Anna said.*

'I just need to speak to Brittany a moment. Can I meet you in the kitchen?'

*Anna nodded.* 'Yeah, okay,' *she said, smiling at Brittany before walking away.*

*Brittany stooped over me expectantly.*

'Please don't tell anyone.'

'Who would I tell?' *she said, puckering her lips. She swatted her hand in the air.* 'Don't think you're the first heart he's broken,' *she said, seriousness plucking her strained voice.*

*I felt sick, and stupid. I looked back towards his office, but the door was firmly closed.*

I don't know why, but I convinced myself as I walked home that evening through the electrified London streets that Brittany had only said those things to be spiteful. I couldn't believe that Darren had been with other people in the office. He wouldn't do that. It's almost like Brittany was alluding to herself, but I chose to push it away. The thought of Darren and her together made me feel queasy.

When I got home, I started cooking dinner, turning the music up loud, starting to cheer up slightly as I poured myself a large rosé and began pulling leftover ingredients out of the fridge. I poured a tin of tomato sauce and basil into a saucepan. A cacophony of noise wrapped itself around me as steam floated up from the pan and masked my face. My phone chanted above the noise and I picked it up reluctantly. I saw Darren's number flash across the screen and I felt extremely hopeful.

'Hello.'

'Emily.'

'Why are you calling?'

'I needed to hear your voice.'

I laughed.

'And I needed to hear your laugh.'

I laughed again, but tinged with sadness. 'It's so difficult seeing you at work. All I wanted was to know you still cared.'

'I care, Emily. Can I come round?'

I stared around the flat. He'd never been here before, but I couldn't refuse him. I needed him.

'Yes,' I said, before hanging up. I jumped in the shower and prepared myself. I wanted him to tell me he loves me, I wanted him to say he couldn't make it work with his wife, that he couldn't lie to us both and he was picking me.

I discarded dinner, instead pulling on my tight jeans and a velvet cami top. Looking myself up and down in the mirror, I applied a coating of lipgloss and pushed my dirty clothes under the bed out of the way. I waited patiently for him to arrive, swapping my rosé for a glass of red wine – more sophisticated. I was nervous about him seeing my flat, letting him into this small part of what's mine.

When he arrived, I wanted to throw myself at him, but he was reserved. He barely looked around my flat, he just stared straight at me. His tie was loose around his throat and his jacket was slung over his shoulder.

'Did you work late?'

He nodded, falling into the middle of my sofa.

I turned the music up and joined him, handing him a glass of wine.

'Why are you here?'

He turned to me. He took a long, deliberate swallow of wine and pulled me in, kissing me with sweet, wet lips. I kissed him back, harder, and let his hands travel across my back and pull at the waist of my jeans.

There was a knock at the door, but Darren didn't stop. Another knock.

'Who's that?'

'I don't know, shall I answer it?'

*Another hard thud at the door. Darren leant back, frustrated.*

*I walked to the door and opened it slowly.*

*'It's my neighbour,' I said, to stop Darren joining me.*

*I'd seen her before through the lounge window, returning from the shops or putting her rubbish out. I'd never passed her in the hallway, but I knew it was her. I was surprised, seeing her up close for the first time. I'd thought she would be older, having lost a husband. Mike didn't tell me what happened to him, but whenever I caught her features when she was walking towards the house from down the street, she looked so sad. Her honey-blonde hair circled her face. Sleepy blue eyes glistened in the faint glow of the landing light. Her lips trembled.*

*'It's your music.'*

*She shifted uncomfortably and I wanted to tell her I'm sorry, but it was the way she looked at me. She's small and fragile and I realised in that moment I felt incredibly guilty. It's the way my mum would look when she thought I wasn't looking, so broken. There was an intensity in her stare and I wanted to shut the door on it. It made me feel rotten, selfish. It brought me back to a reality where I couldn't be with Darren. That I'd become all the things I'd set out not to be.*

*'I'll turn it down,' I said, closing the door on her.*

*When I turned back to Darren, all I wanted was to feel him, even if it was just for one last time.*

*'Turn the music off. Let's go to the bedroom,' I said.*

*A smile slipped across his lips and he switched the speaker off. He took my hand and led me to the bedroom, shutting the* door behind him. Now his touch felt wrong on my skin, stinging me as he pulled me in. I placed a hand on his chest and buried my head in his neck. He tried to move my neck to kiss me, but I pulled away.

'Everything okay?' he asked.

'Yes.' But it's not.

We lay tangled in the bed sheets and I fought for the words to ask him.

'Be with me,' I said suddenly.

'I can't,' he said.

'But I can't do this to your family.'

He took my hand and kissed the palm. 'You know how I feel about you, but I can't do that to my family either.'

'Then this really has to be over.'

He ran a hand up my thigh and I stared down at it, remembering my dad's hand making its way up Alice's thigh. I yanked myself away.

'No.' I rolled across the bed and stood up.

Darren wasn't listening, he just stared at my naked body. I scrambled for the bed sheets and pulled them over me.

'This isn't right,' I said fiercely.

'Why are you trying to make me choose?'

'You cheated,' I said, tears spilling down my cheeks. 'And I'm just as bad.'

I wanted him to leave. I wanted to scream at him to get out of my life. I shook my head, swallowing all the urges. I needed him.

'I need you,' I said and it sounded so desperate and lost.

'I love you.'

'You need to tell your wife about me. You can't have both, or...' I let the words trail off. Or what? What would I do? Would I tell his wife? I don't know anymore. Would my mum have wanted to know? Is Darren's wife anything like her? Is she playing happy families too?

'Or what?'

'You can't have both.'

There was a change in his eyes. He rubbed his stubble, climbed out of bed and started getting dressed. I didn't want him to leave. I cried harder.

'Don't,' I said.

'I told you,' he said curtly, 'I love my family and I won't break them.'

'But you already have,' I said. 'Don't leave.'

He pulled on his jeans and draped his shirt across his shoulders. 'Bye, Emily,' he said, a finality about it. He walked past me and I clawed at him desperately. I wrapped my arms around his waist and he stopped. 'Let go, Emily,' he said. Instructions: do it.

'No,' I cried. 'I'll tell her,' I said, 'your wife. I kept those notes you left me at work.' But I didn't mean it, I know I didn't.

'Where are they?'

I loosened my grip and he turned in my arms. I'd say anything for him to stay. He looked down at me, his eyes searching mine. Does he see it? All my misery, my self-loathing, my insecurities laid out for him to shatter? Instead he *bent down and kissed me, but I didn't want him to, I wanted him to speak. I wanted him to tell me he'll do it – that he's mine. I shrug.*

*'I have to go. Get rid of those notes, for me, please.'*

*I let my arms drop to my sides. He left silently, and I didn't move, I just stood in the darkness of my empty bedroom, the silence piercing me. I am so alone.*

---

Darren wasn't in work the whole of the next week. I wanted to ask Brittany if he was coming in, but she knew about us and I didn't want her to tell anyone else in the office. I tried to act as casually as I could, keeping my head down, keeping busy.

I tried to call Darren the next day – I just wanted to explain myself – but he didn't pick up. I left a voicemail, my anger sizzling and fighting my desperation to want him to call me back. He sent a short text telling me to stop and I felt like my heart would explode. I started to cry, silently at first and then louder. I stalked to the bedroom and pulled out the notes he'd written me and left on my desk, notes that I'd so lovingly stored in my jewellery box, when really it was because he didn't want to be caught texting me, I knew that. I was about to rip them up, but I couldn't bear to part with them. Instead, I went to the bathroom and pried open the loose tile next to the bath and stuck them behind it and forced it back into place. Maybe it was just in case he ever came back. I wouldn't *actually use them, would I? It felt so final, so childish – so necessary.*

*I turned up the music louder, opened a bottle of wine from the fridge and took long, deliberate gulps until my legs felt like they'd give way. Then there was a loud, sharp thud underneath my feet. I thought I'd imagined it as I stared down at the floor, my eyes slightly bleary from the wine. Then it was louder. I looked over at my speaker – is it the music? I went to stomp my foot back on the floor, but something struck so hard that I could feel the vibrations in my feet. Was that a broom? I swatted at my phone to turn down the music and press off the TV. I tried to listen for the sound again, but I didn't hear anything.*

*I stomped down the stairs and stood outside the downstairs flat holding a bunched fist up to the door. Then I withdrew it. Should I be doing this? It's my flat, my home, I reasoned. I knocked loudly and after a couple of seconds my downstairs neighbour appeared meekly around a sliver of her doorway. She gripped the door in both hands, her knuckles turning white from the pressure.*

*'Was that a broom?'*

*She looked me up and down, considering me as she opened the door a little wider.*

*'Yes, I—' she said, and stopped.*

*'This is my home,' I said before she could finish. I couldn't believe her, how selfish she was being. 'This is my home,' I repeated.*

*'This is also mine,' she said.*

'I am not making too much noise,' I said, thinking about the size of my speaker. 'My speaker is tiny, tiny.'

'I don't think it matters about the size of the speaker,' she said.

I craned my neck, trying to see in her flat, but she pushed the door defensively. Why would she live in a ground-floor flat if she doesn't want noise? I think about her complaining the other day. Does she just enjoy it? I looked at her. Or is she just bored?

'You shouldn't live in a flat if you don't like noise.'

She didn't reply and I felt rotten as soon as the words left my mouth. She cowered slightly, looking defeated, and I wanted to cry and say I'm sorry. She lost her husband. How could I even begin to understand that pain?

'I'll try and keep it down,' I said, before turning and walking away. I'm sorry, I thought, I'll be better.

---

On Friday, I'd promised I'd go for drinks, but all I wanted to do was go home and curl up in front of the sofa with a glass of wine. I usually went out for drinks on Fridays, and I didn't want anyone noticing that I wasn't there, that something was up.

After work, Brittany was the first up. Turning to the rest of the department and winking, she said, 'Boss isn't in today, so we could leave a bit earlier.' She smiled at me. 'Coming, Emily?'

I nodded. I didn't have any choice. I dragged behind the parade of work people following Brittany to The Fence. We slotted into our regular table at the front, always reserved for us on Fridays. Anna waded through the crowd towards me and clung to me. 'What're you drinking? I'll buy the first round.'

'Wine,' I said bitterly, secretly wanting something stronger. I was about to suggest doing a shot when Brittany interrupted.

'Are we all set for your birthday night out tomorrow?'

I nodded. 'Yeah, I don't want to be out too late tonight.'

'Is it just me and Anna?'

'I just want to keep it small. I'm not really into celebrating my birthday.'

Brittany pushed back her thick blonde hair and tilted her head. 'It will be a good distraction,' she said accusingly.

I nodded.

Anna returned with our glasses of wine and I swallowed mine quickly, before she was even halfway through hers. I leaned over to her and asked if she wanted to do a shot, but her forehead creased and she smiled. 'No, I don't want to be hungover for your birthday tomorrow.'

I shrugged and headed for the bar. I felt reckless, the surge of alcohol burning the back of my throat and loosening my legs.

'A shot of tequila,' I demanded.

'Just the one?' the bartender asked, trying to look over my shoulder.

'Make it two,' said a familiar voice next to me. For a moment I thought it was Darren, but when I turned I saw Mike, my landlord, standing there.

'What's the occasion?' he asked.

I shake my head. 'I don't know if there is one,' I replied.

'Even better.'

'Do you work near here?' I asked.

He dived into his jeans and produced his wallet, but I shook my head. 'No, it's okay,' I said.

'It's fine,' he said, producing a twenty and throwing it onto the bar. 'I've been over this way for a meeting.'

We each picked up a shot and raised it to each other. I swallowed mine quickly, wincing as the liquid burned my throat. I relished the numbness that followed, my head loosened and my shoulders sunk.

'Do you want to put your business card in?' said the bartender, holding up a large goldfish bowl. 'You can win a bottle of champagne tonight.'

I shook my head.

Mike grinned, producing a business card from his pocket. 'Not interested?' he asked me, releasing his card into the bowl.

'I've got to get up early.'

'Oh.'

'It's my birthday tomorrow.'

Mike's grin widened. 'Well, that is cause for celebration. I hope I win the champagne then.'

'Well, I better be going, thanks for the drink.'

'Have a nice birthday,' Mike said.

I felt him watching me as I broke through the crowd. Brittany grabbed my hand as I was nearing the door.

'Are you leaving?' she said, surprised.

'I just want to get back, but I'll see you guys tomorrow, right?'

'Looking forward to it,' she said, squeezing my hand.

I pushed through the heaving crowd to the doors and out onto the damp street. The air felt thick and the mugginess stuck to my skin as I made my way towards Bermondsey tube station.

## Chapter Thirty-Six

L ast night, for the first time since you left, I slept in our bed. Clara curled up next to me, filling your empty space so I wouldn't have to face it. The weight of the mattress felt uneven, sagging under my weight instead of your own. A spring I never noticed dug into the bottom of my back and the sheet kept peeling away from the bottom corner and wrapping itself around my leg. Things I never noticed when you were here.

I lie awake for most of the night, the last night in our flat. Do you remember the first? We gathered on the lounge floor surrounded by pizza and cheap red wine. The memories that once stung now thaw me a little, like a small fire, and I relish the heat of them.

I don't want you to think that these memories aren't painful, but the pain has adjusted itself; it's shifted into another emotion, one where I smile instead of cry. I remember people saying it's something I would never get over, like that was a condolence, a comforting notion I could sit at home alone with, night after night. I know what they mean now. I won't ever get over it, but I'll live with it and I'll remember you and smile. I'll talk about you to friends and family. I'll remember from when I first met you in a bar at twenty years old up until the moment you walked out of the door.

I'm looking at the door now, knowing you won't come back. Clara places a hand on my shoulder. She's wearing a dressing gown and pink fluffy socks. She flashes a sleepy smile at me and then looks towards the door too. She pats me gently on the shoulder and shuffles towards the kitchen.

'Ian will be here at three,' she says, flicking the kettle on.

'If you want to get out of the flat while the police are here, it's fine,' I say.

'I'd rather not,' she says, eyeing me.

We spend the rest of the morning shifting the remaining boxes into the lounge and piling cutlery and plates into empty spaces inside boxes. We work silently and methodically, both of us checking the time every now and then, until the buzzer echoes in the cavernous flat.

Clara is already looking out of the window. She nods slowly to confirm that the police have arrived and I smooth down my hair and lick my lips before buzzing them in.

I open the door and Inspector Freeman is filling the hallway. I tip my head to look towards the front door, but I don't see Detective Peters.

'Hi, come in,' I say, forcing a smile across my face.

'DS Peters couldn't make it today,' Freeman says quietly. He walks through the door and looks surprised to see Clara.

'Hi there, you must be Suzie's sister,' he says, extending an arm towards her. 'Detective Inspector Freeman.'

Clara smiles awkwardly and shakes his hand, then quickly lets her arm fall back to her side.

'I'm sorry about what happened last night with Darren. We have spoken to him and he has been given a warning.'

'He should be arrested,' Clara says, 'for scaring us like that.'

Inspector Freeman smiles sympathetically. 'It's not as easy as that, I'm afraid.'

Clara ignores him. 'Is Suzie in trouble?'

Inspector Freeman moves forward and looks around the flat at the piles of boxes and bags. 'I just need to ask some questions.'

'That's not what I asked,' Clara insists, taking a step towards the inspector.

He shakes his head.

Clara's head shoots towards me.

'I'm here to find out what you know, Suzie,' he says, turning to face me, 'and how you know it.'

'And the note?' Clara asks, pointing to the folded piece of paper on the small dining table.

'That as well. I'll need to take it with me.'

'Could it have been Darren?' Clara asks.

Inspector Freeman forces a smile. 'We don't want to speculate,' he says, producing a slim plastic bag. He unfolds the note and his eyes widen. 'Handwritten,' he states.

I nod, looking at the words with him.

'Do you recognise the handwriting at all?' he asks.

I shake my head slowly. I thought I had, but there's so much anger in the words that the writing is distorted and disguised.

Inspector Freeman places the note in the bag, seals it and carefully slips it into his jacket pocket. I shuffle awkwardly, before sitting down in the chair and gesturing to a spot on the sofa for him. Clara sucks in her cheeks and looks down at her phone.

'We're leaving at three,' she says firmly.

Inspector Freeman smiles. 'That's fine. I'm sure we'll be finished by then.'

'I'm going in the bedroom, if you need me, Suzie,' she says. Her eyes widen as she looks at me and she gently nods towards me, looking for some understanding. I nod back.

'Okay,' she says defiantly, before leaving me and the inspector alone in the lounge.

Inspector Freeman turns to me. His smile fades and I can see the tiredness he is wearing in thin lines creeping down his jaw, undulating his unshaven cheeks.

'I wanted to ask you about Friday night, and how you knew to ask the hotel about Emily,' he says.

I clench my jaw and stare up at him. 'I visited Emily's workplace,' I say quietly.

He doesn't look surprised. 'How many times?'

'Once. Well, twice,' I correct myself. 'The first time I went to her office, I told them I was Emily's sister and the second, on Friday night, I followed a group of them to a bar.'

'Which bar?'

My face tightens. 'The one near her office, in Bermondsey, I think it's called The Fence Bar.'

'You followed them?'

I nod.

'Why?'

'The first time I went to the office, the receptionist there, well, she approached me in the toilet,. She was friends with Emily.'

'What did she say?'

'That I wasn't Emily's sister. She was angry.'

'Did she say anything else?'

'She said'—I swallow hard, but my throat is dry and I

choke on the next words—'she asked how I could be a part of that family.'

Inspector Freeman writes that down, then looks back up at me, his eyes narrowed accusingly.

'What did you do with that information?'

'I thought her family...' I look up at him. 'I don't know what I thought.'

'What did you do with that information?' he repeats.

'I went to visit them,' I say.

His eyes widen. 'Right, what did you hope to find out from this visit?'

'I was just worried about Emily.'

Detective Peters slumps back into the sofa. 'Why were you worried about Emily?'

I look up at him. 'Because she's missing. And because no one is doing anything about it. No one knows where she is.'

He nods slowly. 'I'm sorry,' he says, but I can tell he doesn't mean it.

'She didn't have anyone, her family didn't seem to care, and they said she didn't have friends in London. Well, she did, and they lied.'

Inspector Freeman presses his thumbs over his eyelids and takes a deep breath. 'What did you discuss with Emily's parents when you visited them?'

I think back to the conversation, the sting of wine as it flooded my body, Christie's sharp look as she said, 'My daughter was like that, incredibly reckless with people. I know what she can be like.'

'I offered my help,' I reply.

'Okay, so you went all the way to their home to offer your help?'

I shake my head.

'Well, then, why did you go?'

'I thought…' I look outside as the clouds disperse and the fierce midday sun blisters the window and sunlight cascades onto the low brick wall, casting a shadow over the overgrown garden. 'I thought they were involved,' I say quietly.

Inspector Freeman pauses. 'Why did you go to Emily's offices the first time?'

I freeze, thinking about pulling apart the damp pieces of paper attached to the tile in Emily's bathroom. The look in Detective Peters's eyes when he said he knew about you. Inspector Freeman knows, too. I bite my lip hard and flick my eyes towards the closed bedroom door.

'I remembered something.'

'Remembered what?'

'A conversation between the girls that were round Emily's flat. They were talking about work.'

Inspector Freeman nods. 'Why didn't you tell either me or Detective Peters when you remembered this?'

'Because those girls lied to you. They told you they weren't there that night.'

Inspector Freeman frowns before stabbing at his

notepad. 'That was information you shouldn't have withheld.'

'She was scared,' I say. 'The receptionist.'

Inspector Freeman looks up at me, his eyes bloodshot and sunken. 'How did you know about the hotel, Suzie?'

I stand up.

'She hasn't done anything wrong.' The bedroom door swings open and Clara storms across the hallway towards us. 'I asked you if my sister had done anything wrong,' she says, pushing herself into the space between me and the inspector.

'Did you see what was on those pieces of paper?' Inspector Freeman raises his voice over Clara and steps to the side.

'Yes,' I shoot back.

The flat is quiet apart from the sound of traffic outside and the low buzz of next door's television.

'I'm sorry.'

'Suzie just wanted to help,' Clara pleads. 'The police stopped investigating Emily's disappearance and all Suzie wanted to do was find her.'

Inspector Freeman rises from the sofa and edges past Clara to the front door, opening it slowly.

'We're leaving London,' Clara says adamantly.

The inspector nods slowly, his head bowed in disappointment. 'Thank you for your help. If you get any more trouble from Darren, let me know,' he says quietly.

'I am sorry,' I call after him, but he closes the door firmly behind him.

'You haven't done anything wrong,' she says, turning to me. She blows her hair off her face, anger pulsing across her features. 'They're the ones that haven't done enough.'

She embraces me, her long hair tickling my nose, and I fold into her neck, breathing in her sweet, comforting smell. She holds me tighter.

'Maybe they're just mad you're a better detective than them.' She leans back, a half-smile on her lips. 'We should get a move on,' she says.

An hour later the buzzer thrums into the flat and Clara jumps up. 'That'll be Ian.' She stops halfway through packing the toaster, pats my shoulder gently and walks over to the intercom, calling, 'It's open.' Ian lumbers through the hall, his large frame filling the doorway.

'Hey,' he says to me with a charming grin.

I smile at him as he hugs my sister. 'Any chance of a cuppa?' he asks.

'Nope, the kettle's packed. We'll pop out soon, but I want to make a start first on packing up all of this,' Clara says gesturing to the flat.

We start to pack the van, a box at a time, leaving the bulky furniture until last, taking pictures to try and resell them later online, everything apart from the leather chair.

Ian and Clara walk down to the local café to grab us sausage sandwiches and hot drinks for lunch.

I hear Clara and Ian talking in the hallway and the main door close as they arrive back. The familiar sound of bags rubbing against my wall. I reach back a hand and place it on the wall, letting the noise vibrate my fingers. They bustle through the flat door, sweat lining Ian's receding hairline, a firm smile plastered across my sister's face.

'It's really hot out there,' she exclaims.

'And there's no air-con in the van,' Ian adds.

I go to the window and watch as light cascades in between the elongated concrete buildings, a slim shadow cast over my home. Not my home anymore. Another memory, of seeing this place on the outside for the first time, standing in the street and bathing in the possibility of it all. The gentle nudge of a passing stranger and hearing pulsing music from the block of flats opposite. Ben's reassuring gaze as I fix on him: it will all be okay. I run my fingers down the window and become aware of the silence in the flat. I feel a hand on my shoulder, and turn to see Clara looking sympathetic.

'Let's have some lunch, yeah, and then we'll pack up the remaining bits,' she coaxes, almost before I can change my mind.

We spend the rest of the afternoon silently packing up the remainder of the flat. The emptier it grows, the more does my longing to stay. I catch Clara's eyes as we clear the last of the bags from the bedroom and I twist my body to avoid her. Standing in the doorway, I stare at the empty bed, the spot where you used to lie. I reach forward to pull the door closed, hesitating as the last slice of our bedroom disappears.

'Suzie,' Clara calls from the lounge.

'Coming,' I call back.

I walk into the lounge and see my door wide open and Detective Peters standing there, wearing a creased light blue shirt and dark grey trousers.

'What are you doing here?' I ask, eyeing Clara.

'Emily,' he says bluntly.

'What's going on?' Ian says, appearing in the hallway.

Detective Peters steps back to let him through and follows him into the lounge. He looks around at the boxes and back to me.

'Inspector Freeman told me about the note. I just wanted to see if you were okay.'

'And Emily?' I ask.

He looks up at me. 'We've reopened the case.'

'So what now?' I ask.

'Well, we need to speak to Emily's parents again.'

'And that slimy shit that came around here last night, what about him?' Clara demands.

Noah's eyes flicker to Clara. 'We'll be bringing him in again.'

Clara looks at me and then back to Detective Peters. 'Ian, could you help me with some boxes in the bathroom,' she says, taking Ian's hand and leading him away.

'No, it's okay, Detective Peters was just leaving,' I say, holding up a hand. 'We've got to get going,' I say to him.

He nods emphatically and turns to leave, resting his eyes on mine for a second more.

'Thank you for your time today and for all your help on the investigation,' he says, before smiling at Clara and Ian and turning away. We stand in the lounge waiting for the click of the front door. I hear the gentle tread of the detective's footsteps down the path and feel Clara's steady gaze waiting for me to react.

'So that's the officer you've mentioned,' she says finally.

I nod.

'Not what I expected.'

'What did you expect?'

She shrugs. 'Not a blond,' she says.

'Funny business about that girl,' Ian interrupts.

'You did good, Suzie,' Clara says, reaching out a hand to grab mine. 'Maybe they'll find her now.'

'I hope so,' I say quietly.

'I still think that snake that visited here has something to do with it. He'll be in so much shit anyway, for lying to the police.'

'I would have beaten the shit out of him,' Ian says.

'I know you would,' says Clara, smiling at me, rolling her eyes.

'Right, this is the last of the boxes,' he says. 'Is there anything else you want to put in the van before we set off?'

I turn round in a circle, taking in the bare bones of the place I've called home for the last five years.

'I don't think so,' I say.

'Do you want us to give you a moment?' Clara asks.

I shake my head. 'I've had a lot of moments.' I smile.

Clara rests her head on my shoulder and loops her arm through mine. 'I'm so proud of you, Zee.'

I nod slowly, and bite my lips hard to stop the tears. Clara holds on tighter and I smile up at her.

'Let's go home,' I say. She smiles back.

## Chapter Thirty-Seven

### Emily

I wanted an early night to clear my head and freshen up for tomorrow. *It will be good*, I repeated, *something to take my mind off Darren.* When I got in, my head slightly foggy from the tequila, I stripped off my work clothes and pulled on loose shorts and a baggy jumper, and scraped my hair back into a tight bun. I looked around the flat. *I'll get up early and tidy it, a proper spring clean.* I made myself a cup of green tea and snuggled into bed, pulling the duvet high over my chest and placing my laptop on the bedside table.

I woke to the sound of buzzing and opened my eyes to an episode of How I Met Your Mother still playing on the laptop. *It couldn't be late*, I thought as I checked my phone for the time. *Not even midnight.* The buzzer drummed through the flat and for a moment I wasn't sure if it was mine or for the woman downstairs.

I swung out of bed, feeling the cold on my bare legs as I made my way towards the intercom. It buzzed again, definitely mine. 'Hello,' I answered, still disoriented from being woken up.

'It's Darren.'

I froze, my stomach tightening, my mouth dry and fuzzy. 'What—' I paused. 'What do you want?'

'I just wanted to see you,' he slurred slightly.

'I'll come down.'

I didn't attempt to smooth out my hair or wash my face, although my eyes felt sticky from sleep and there was saliva around the corners of my mouth. I felt angry, and I realised how forcefully I was treading down the stairs. I swung the door open and saw him huddled under the low brick porch, rubbing his hands together. He smiled at me, revealing his dimples, and pushed into the small hallway, closing the door behind him. He went to embrace me but I took a step back.

'You can't keep doing this.'

He looked confused, like he'd misunderstood what I'd said.

'You have to make up your mind.'

He didn't respond, just looked at me sheepishly, his eyes drooping from the alcohol. He sighed, the stench of beer pervading the hallway.

'Leave,' I said quietly.

He shook his head.

'Make up your mind then,' I said, this time a little louder.

He twisted away from me. He was really drunk, but he looked wounded and in pain. But I was in pain too and this was my new life, my silver lining after years of misplacing my trust. I couldn't let him take that from me. I felt so angry and betrayed and sick of not confronting it. I stared at him.

'Make up your mind,' I shouted at him.

I thought he might, in that moment, as he stepped back and looked up at me like I was the only person in the world. He reached out a limp hand and dared me to take it, but then he averted his gaze and made a deep noise in the back of his throat. Then he turned, opened the door and closed it firmly behind him.

I stood for a moment, trying to listen to his footsteps. Silently begging for him to turn back and fight for me. I thought I could hear his breathing on the other side of the door, but it was just the wind. I turned to go back upstairs and saw the light on in the downstairs flat. I wondered if she'd heard me and what she must think. I had an urge to knock and apologise if I woke her, but instead I turned away and trailed back upstairs.

---

The next day I got up early and started cleaning the flat. I hadn't heard from Darren, but I kept my phone on loud and with me as I moved around the flat tidying away clothes and cleaning the kitchen surfaces. I headed to the shops in the afternoon to pick up wine and snacks for later. I couldn't face a night out, so I loaded my shopping basket with enough wine and food for a good night in. When I got back from the shops, there was a bottle of champagne sitting in the hallway, with a card propped next to it. I turned it over and read,

Happy Birthday, Mike.

I cringed, remembering seeing him the night before, us necking a shot together.

I hadn't had a proper girls' night since that night in the pub with Alice. She'd messaged me this morning, for the first time in a while. It said,

Happy birthday, I hope you have a lovely day.

It seemed so generic, but I know Alice, the number of times she would have written it and deleted it and rewritten it. I missed knowing her, the familiarity of what she would say, what she would do. But maybe I didn't know her at all.

When the girls arrived, they brought large carrier bags overflowing with wine. Brittany had a whole suitcase of clothes, because she couldn't decide what to wear tonight. They immediately cracked open a bottle of the sparkling rosé I had bought and started dancing around my flat with large glasses of the sweet, fizzy wine. I got lost for a while in the noise of it. The joy of strutting out into the lounge in different dresses. The way they pored over my shoes, matching them to outfits. The feeling of Brittany's fingers coiling through my hair as she curled it with her tongs. The music was loud and I swayed gently to it as they paraded around me, singing 'Happy Birthday' and presenting me with a small chocolate cake, a single candle poking out.

We left the flat at gone 11, Brittany insisting we go to a club. We decided to head into Shoreditch, to a small corner bar with a rooftop terrace. The bar had a queue, but Brittany breezed to the front and spoke briefly to the bouncer, pointing at me as she did. I smiled awkwardly, but we were led straight in and to a small booth with a piece of velvet rope sectioning us off from the rest of the room. I imagined Alice cupping my hand in hers in that moment, pulling me in the other direction and rolling her eyes, saying, 'VIP is for dull people, and you, Emily, are not dull.'

'VIP baby,' Anna yelled.

'Did you guys do this?' I asked.

'Of course we did,' Brittany shouted. 'Only the very best.'

My head was pulsing from the bottles of wine we'd already consumed, but I felt alive, my legs longing to dance. I started chanting along to the music and Brittany joined in.

'I'm going to get shots,' Anna yelled above us.

We didn't respond, we just sang louder and she rolled her eyes, smiling.

Brittany tapped me on my knee and beckoned me to lean in. Her green eyes looked iridescent in the strobe lighting. She opened them wide and puffed her cheeks.

'I know what happened with you and Darren,' she said.

I nodded casually, the thought of him I'd suppressed

*bubbling to the surface.*

*'He told me,' she said.*

*I frown. 'Told you what?'*

*'About you two, about you asking him to leave his family. We're close, me and him.'*

*My cheeks felt hot.*

*'That you'd tell his wife. That you kept those notes of his.' Her eyes pierced mine. She shook her head. 'I've been there,' she said, leaning back and closing her eyes. She tipped her head back and forth to the music.*

*I stumbled to my feet and thrashed at the velvet rope.*

*'Where are you going?' she shouted after me, but I ignored her, pushing my way through the crowd to the bathroom. I locked myself in a stall and took deep breaths. Rifling through my bag for my phone, I called Darren. It was stupid, but the buzz from the wine propelled me forward.*

*'Emily?' he said.*

*'You told her.'*

*'Where are you?'*

*'You told Brittany,' I repeated. 'You two are close, right,' I said angrily.*

*'Emily, I can't talk to you right now.'*

*'You will talk to me,' I demanded, 'or I will tell your wife. I'll tell her fucking everything, how you fucked me and you fucked Brittany and I don't know how many other people you fucked. I have those notes, remember.'*

*The line went dead and I started to cry as I realised he had hung up on me. There was a small knock on the toilet cubicle. I* pulled open the door reluctantly and Anna was staring back at me.

'What's going on, Em?' she said.

I cried harder. She eased me back and joined me in the toilet, shutting the door behind her.

'What's happened?'

'Everything, it's all so fucked up,' I blubbered.

She placed a hand on my shoulder and gazed up at me.

'Tell me what's happened.'

I told her about my parents who'd spent half my life ignoring me, and how they tried to pay me off so they could keep their lifestyle, so my mum didn't have to be a mum and could carry on being a painter. I told her about my dad and my friend, but I didn't talk about Alice. I thought about the words but as I was about to say them the familiar pain in my chest rose and I choked. When I thought about Darren, even telling Anna about him, it wasn't the same pain, and I fell into Anna's arms and she held me in her small frame. Love is painful.

---

Once Anna had managed to coax me out of the toilets, she herded me back to the booth, where Brittany was waiting with a bottle of champagne.

I spent the rest of the night quietly drinking, until I didn't remember much of what happened. We woke the next day in my bed, all of us still wearing the clothes from the night before. Brittany and Anna left early. Anna gave me a small squeeze *before she left and I had a flashback to the toilet and what I had told her.*

*When Monday rolled around, I still hadn't recovered from my hangover and I was thirty minutes late for work. My tongue was dry and heavy, no matter how much water I consumed, and my body ached from the alcohol and dancing.*

*I saw Anna first. She nodded, smiling as I walked in, as if to say, 'Yeah, me too.' I hurried to my desk and saw Brittany coming out of Darren's office. I shielded my gaze and began setting up my computer. Brittany walked down the aisle towards me. She looked perfect, not a sign that the weekend had been a heavy one.*

*'Darren wants to see you,' she said robotically, before racing back down the aisle and towards the kitchen.*

*I got up from my desk, and walked towards Darren's office, remembering everything I had said to him on Saturday night. I stood in the doorway clenching my teeth.*

*'I'm sorry,' I said, when he looked up.*

*'Emily,' he said in a businesslike way. 'Please sit down.'*

*I took the seat opposite his desk and started to bite my lip.*

*'I wanted to call you in here, as it's come to my attention that you've been late over six times this month.'*

*I looked at him, my mouth open. I shook my head. 'I don't think so.'*

*'I've also noticed mistakes in the reports you've been turning in, even when asked to correct them.' He doesn't look at me. His eyes remained fixed on his screen as he scrolled down as if reading off a list.*

'I'm sorry if that's happened,' I said.

'Look, Emily, as you know, you have a six-month probation and in that time you have targets to meet and it's a chance for us to decide whether we're a good fit.'

'I don't understand,' I said.

He leant back in his chair and met my eyes. 'I don't think this is working out,' he said directly.

I didn't know what to say to him. I stared back, trying to make sense of it.

'Everyone else here has to complete the same KPIs in a six-month period, but we have seen no improvement from you and we can't let the standards of this department slip. I'm sorry, Emily, but we will not be continuing your contract of employment here.'

I stared at him, trying to find some understanding in his eyes, but he just averted his gaze and looked back at his screen.

'Sorry, Emily,' he said diplomatically.

'Is this about us?' I said.

He lowered his gaze. 'Thank you, Emily. Best of luck in your future career. We would be happy to provide a reference if needed.'

I stood up and opened the door. 'I wouldn't have said anything,' I said, looking back at him, but he didn't reply. I closed the door and walked back towards my desk, feeling eyes on me. I collected my things from my desk and walked through reception. Anna wasn't there, but I saw Brittany emerge from the kitchen carrying two mugs. She stood in the hallway staring at me, waiting for me to leave.

## Chapter Thirty-Eight

The sun feels stronger now. It's 3pm and I watch as Ian ties down the last of my boxes in the back of the van. He smiles at me reassuringly and I nod, before twisting my body away. It's difficult to look at our life like that, packed up in the back of a van. The last time I saw our things packed away, we were unloading from a van rental in London. We had a conveyor belt system, you passing stuff down to me, me handing them over to Clara. You and Ian sliding our leather chair off the back and watching it just squeeze through the narrow frame of the front door. It had been hot that day too, five years ago, when we moved from our rented flat up the road and saved enough for a small ground-floor flat. Putting down roots, that's what you'd said. Now I'm digging them up, I'm branching out, away.

Guilt congeals in my throat, pressing at the back of

my chest and threatening tears behind my eyes. I blink quickly and slide my sunglasses down from the top of my head. I watch the steady stream of traffic, people moving in and out of the off-licence and parents trailing back from the school run, children in tow. The heat feels like an extra chore, another obstacle for Londoners to battle against. Am I a Londoner? Has someone silently watched me, my face agitated as I move to the next destination? A to B to C. Now I'm leaving and the thick air and sun penetrating the windless road have me trapped.

'Are you ready?' Clara calls, swinging open the van's passenger door.

I nod, pulling my gaze away from the busy street.

'A lot of good memories,' Clara says, sensing my mood.

And all those memories swim to the top of my mind, giving way to a painful knot of confusion. I've longed for this moment for so long, I fantasised about it for years before you left me, but now it's here I can't bring myself to leave.

'I would have stayed for him,' I say to Clara, tears escaping down my cheeks.

'You did stay for him,' she says, rubbing my shoulder.

I nod. 'Let's go.'

We climb into the van and Ian asks, one last time, if we're all ready to go, and I see Clara shoot him a look. He starts the van and we set off down the road and as I glance in the rear-view mirror I can't help but feel I'm leaving you behind.

———

'Which road is it again?' Clara asks, stabbing at the sat-nav.

'I gave you the postcode,' I reply.

'Yes,' she says shortly. 'But I need the number and name of the street.'

'I'll recognise it. It's the road after the Chinese takeaway place, the one in yellow.' I look up. 'That one,' I say, pointing.

'Very useful directions,' she says sarcastically and leans back.

We pull around the corner, into Mike's street. I need to get the spare key that I'd given him four years ago in case of emergencies. There had been a leak in the flat upstairs and when we returned from a two-week holiday, our entire bathroom had been drenched in water, and the smell was something that took nearly three months to get rid of. Apparently the student upstairs had panicked over being charged and decided to wedge a towel into the rusted rip in the toilet pipe. That was the first time I complained about the neighbour upstairs, and Mike had accepted the key begrudgingly, a responsibility he didn't like. 'Don't become a bloody landlord then,' I'd said on the bus ride home to you. I flinch at the memory.

'Just pull up here, I won't be long.'

'Will I get charged?' Ian asks.

'Probably,' I say, closing the passenger door behind me. I can hear Clara through the door whining about the price of parking and saying she'll go find out.

I pass a couple of slim terraced houses, black-railed balconies protruding from the first floor of each. The road is well maintained and the vehicles lining the preened verges are either work vans or pricey cars. The street is cramped, too many cars compressed into the narrow spaces. Half these people won't need a car in London, they'll just like having it. The thought niggles at me as I squeeze past a hedge and up Mike's tiled terracotta pathway.

I glance down the street and see Clara backing Ian into a spot, her hands thrust against her hips and neck sticking out like a crane. I smile as her voice carries down the road. 'A little further,' she says. Knocking on the door, I realise I forgot to let Mike know I was stopping by. I wait patiently outside and lean forward to try and see down the hallway, but it's masked by frosted glass. I see a flash of colour and step back as Mike walks into view. He swings the door open and frowns at me.

'Suzie.'

'Hi, sorry about this, I completely forgot to call you.'

'Everything okay?'

'Yeah, I just came to get my key.'

'Oh,' he says, looking surprised. 'I forgot today is the day.'

I nod. 'Big changes.'

'You never liked London,' he states.

'Was I that transparent?'

He laughs. 'Let me get that key for you. Do you want to come in?'

'No, it's okay, I've got to get off.'

Mike smiles. 'Be right back.' He walks off down the hallway and disappears to the left. I lean in and take in the size of Mike's place. I peer through a door that's slightly ajar and see a large cream sofa and a TV mounted onto the wall. I hear the jangle of keys and step back, and my foot catches on something. Mike rounds the corner and looks down at my feet, where a promotional leaflet has stuck to my shoe.

'Want me to get that?' he asks, smiling.

I fumble awkwardly, leaning against the door frame, pry the pamphlet free and clutch it in my hand.

'Sorry,' I say, looking down, not knowing where to put it. 'I was being nosy,' I say coyly.

His eyes flicker down to my hand and back up. 'I'll take that,' he says, his smile broadening.

'Oh, okay, sorry,' I say. Stretching out my arm, I look down at the paper and catch the grey logo blazoned across the top, and below it 'Mike Tellar. The Fence Bar'.

Mike snatches the leaflet from my hand and screws it tightly into his fist. He bends down to the floor, collects the rest of the post and straightens up. 'The amount of junk,' he says.

'I didn't know you'd been there?'

He looks at me evenly and back down at the scrunched-up leaflet in his hand. 'Yeah, for a couple of networking events,' he says, shrugging.

I nod. 'Emily used to work near there.'

'Did she?' Mike asks. 'Anyway, I think your key is in the office upstairs. I thought it was in the kitchen, but I must keep it with my tenancy documents. Are you okay to wait?'

I nod.

'Could you close the door? I've got the air-con on in the lounge, so I'm trying to keep the hot air out,' he says, turning back down the hallway.

'Sorry, yeah,' I say, closing the door behind me.

'Have you heard anything more about Emily?' he calls, as he ascends the stairs.

'No,' I reply.

'I thought you'd helped out a lot in the investigation?' he says, his voice fading.

'Not really, I just did what I could.'

Mike's hallway is bare; there aren't any pictures on the walls or photographs of family members or friends. I think about Emily's parents' house, all the pictures of her crammed on the wall by the door, how false it is that they present themselves that way to visitors, that they care about their daughter. Mike has placed the leaflet on a small radiator cover with other post piled alongside it. The Fence Bar – what a small place London can seem sometimes. I see a lined notepad with various names and numbers scrawled across it. I lean in closer and see a message:

*Drop chairs off at new flat*

A reminder. I frown. There's something familiar about it.

I can hear Mike moving about above me, the sound of drawers being pulled open and closed, the heavy tread across the landing, and then he appears at the top of the stairs triumphantly holding a bunch of keys in one hand.

'Got it,' he says, as he follows my gaze to the note and frowns. There's something deliberate about the look, and although Mike has the air-con on, the hallway feels stifling and I want to leave, quickly.

I smile gratefully. Mike walks slowly down the stairs, dropping each foot deliberately, making the floorboards creak uncomfortably underneath him.

'I better be going,' I say, staring up at him.

'Of course,' he says, fumbling with the keys. 'I'm just trying to remember which one's yours.'

I glance at the notepad again, the scribble of handwriting, the way the letters dart into each other. It's rushed, but it's not that, is it? I look up at Mike. *I'm watching you, bitch.* Anger, that's what I saw in his look, an irritation I'd never seen before. He had only ever been patient with me, the widow who calls him and complains about his tenants. He was always softly spoken and gentle. He asked how I was and handled me carefully, never quite asking directly about you, but insinuating. I can't imagine him saying those words, but what do I really know about him?

He stops in front of me, and I see the flash of colour, the nail vanish you painted on each key. I go to speak, but Mike interrupts.

'I had a call earlier, from Inspector Freeman. He said there's been a development in Emily's disappearance.' His eyes grow wider as he pulls aside each key, freeing one from the chain. 'He said you'd given them some new information and they needed access to the flat again.'

He stops just in front of me until I can feel his breath on my face, dense with stale red wine and cigarettes. He doesn't feel short anymore, like he did when I saw him in the hallway hidden behind the police, his face so close to mine. He reaches a hand up and grazes days-old stubble with his fingertips. The noise makes my ears itch and I edge back. The same noise I'd heard on the phone when I imagined Mike walking back from the pub after an afternoon of drinking beer and watching football. I don't know him and I'm suddenly very aware that the door is firmly closed, and that the house is sticky from the high afternoon sun.

'I think they're looking into a man she was involved with,' I say, meeting his gaze.

Mike's lips unfurl revealing stained red teeth. 'And how did they find out about him?' he whispers.

'I don't know,' I stutter, stretching a hand back slowly to grab the door handle.

'Because you're nosy,' he snarls, holding up the key in front of my face. I pinch the key with my free hand and slowly turn to face the door. Mike's body heat radiates against me as I feel him press closer. The words sound jarring coming from him and I flinch, but I can't react.

'Thanks for the key,' I mumble, stuffing it into my jeans pocket and tugging at the door handle.

There's a sharp pain in the back of my head that spreads to my temples. My legs collapse underneath me and my right knee smashes onto the bare stone tiles. I go to scream, but Mike's warm hand is already coiled around my mouth, gripping me tightly.

I thrash with both arms, but the pain in my head tremors through my senses and I instinctively reach back to stop it. Mike's other hand is gripped firmly around my pony tail and the harder I try to pull free, the worse the pain gets, as Mike pulls harder.

'You're a nosy bitch,' he spits, 'a fucking nosy bitch.'

It's the way he says it, *bitch*, angry like the note he slipped through the door. I desperately try to make sense of why. Then I think of Emily and my body goes limp.

Mike's sweaty hand slips from my mouth and I'm

about to scream, but I feel a sharp blow on my right cheek and heat vines across my face. My eyes water with pain as I swallow large mouthfuls of air. Through blurred vision I see something come towards me and then there's only darkness.

## Chapter Thirty-Nine

### Emily

I didn't know what to do. I'd spent the last few days curled up on the sofa nursing cups of cold tea. I felt my exciting new life, my escape, my plan B, all disintegrate into nothing. I'd been naïve, foolish. Maybe the woman in the flat downstairs is right, I thought, as I stared at the letter from the council lying on the floor. Maybe I am selfish. I'd been quiet in the week, but not for her, for me. Because noise suddenly felt like a frivolous excursion from reality and if I spoke, what would I say?

Anna called me. She asked me what happened at work and I told her I had to leave London, a family emergency. I was embarrassed, and now I'm ashamed.

I looked around the flat. It was a mess, not like me at all. There were pizza boxes strewn across the kitchen floor, and bins overflowing with empty wine bottles and scraps of food. The desk I bought and placed lovingly by the window for writing remained untouched. I hadn't written anything since I started living in London, no beautiful stories. I wallowed in it, I thought, traipsing to the bedroom, but all I wanted to do was wallow a little longer. Then pick myself up, dust myself off, find a new job, and make a new plan. I slumped onto the bed and let the heat from the duvet absorb me as my head sunk deeper into my pillow.

I thought about Alice. I started to address the pain I felt in my chest whenever she popped into my head, which happened more frequently when I was alone in the flat. Other times it was when I saw something that reminded me of her, or sometimes I could hear her voice reacting to something I saw, as if she was standing beside me. What would she say about this?

'You've got yourself into a right state, haven't you, Em?'

I nodded.

I silently hoped Darren would call me and say he'd made a huge mistake. I longed for him to turn up at my front door and say he'd left his family for me. But was that really what I wanted? I thought about Darren's little baby, its soft gurgles when she sees her dad appear at the bedroom door. The loving kiss he gives her mother's forehead as he leans over them both – protecting them. Who protected me?

I wanted to show my parents I could be something, I could be successful and happy without their guilt money – without them.

*When I peeled myself from the bed sheets the next morning, I walked into my lounge and didn't recognise it as a sanctuary anymore. The sofa where he sat and sipped my wine and felt me everywhere. The kitchen, invisible beneath stacks of dirty plates and decaying pieces of food. The woman downstairs and the aggressive noise from the broom she struck against my floor. I'm not wanted here anymore, with all the noise I tried to create to mask something I desperately tried to forget. I let the phone fall to the floor, and thought about tidying the flat, but instead I lay along the sofa and curled my knees into my chest. I heard the soft churn of the washing machine downstairs and the woman who lived there cough slightly. I wondered if she could hear me crying.*

*I decided to call Mike and give him my month's notice. I told him I was moving away from London when he asked, but he didn't push it further. Maybe he heard in my voice that it's more than that. I fell asleep to the sound of London, impatient car horns and drunk crowds on their way home – the ceaseless noise of the city.*

*I thought about messaging Alice, but every time I typed out a text, I felt so small. Knowing she couldn't have missed me the way I missed her.*

---

*The sun sliced through the curtains and cast a shadow across the lounge. I woke slowly, startled by the figure I saw standing up against the wall. I jolted my head towards the* door and saw just the outline of the coat rack. I yawned, raising my head from a cushion and feeling it stick slightly to my cheek.

I crept to the window and drew back the curtains, letting the light into the room. I looked down and saw the woman in the downstairs flat walking up the front pathway. She hesitated at the gap in the brick wall, pulling up the hood on her coat. She waited patiently for a gap in the traffic of people making their way to work – the early morning rush hour.

I had nowhere to be, I thought, slightly envious as she stepped out onto the pavement. I watched as she walked off down the road in the direction of the tube station. I turned back to my flat and took in the mess. I grabbed a black bin liner and start placing discarded food wrappers inside. I caught myself in the mirror. My scraggly dark auburn hair lay knotted along my shoulders. My cheeks were sunken, with dark circles surrounding pasty skin. I rubbed bleakly at my swollen eyes and bit my thin, dry lips. I dumped the bag and ran myself a bath.

I sat in the bath for hours, scrubbing at my skin, trying to remove the stain of the last six months. I tipped my head back and stared at the loose tile where I hid all the Post-it notes Darren left on my desk for when we would meet. I'd thought they were love letters, I had treated them like they were special pieces of himself that only I had. I reached forward to loosen the tile, but I heard the buzzer thrum throughout the flat. I reluctantly pulled myself from the bath and started to dry myself. The buzzer sounded again, and I quickly draped the towel across the bath and pulled my dressing gown tightly around my waist.

When I walked through to the kitchen, my front door was opening and Mike emerged from the darkness of the hallway. He saw me and took a step back, pulling on the front door, holding a hand up as if to apologise.

'Mike?' I said, as the hallway swallowed him. The door closed and I heard him padding down the stairs towards the main door.

I threw open my door and quickly flicked it on the latch, running down the stairs after him. He was just about to shut the main door, when I yelled his name loudly and he stopped.

'Sorry, I didn't know you were in,' he said, stepping back into the hallway. He closed the main door slowly behind him.

'Did you need something?'

He shifted his head to the side, looking awkwardly back at me, like I had caught him out.

'I thought you'd be gone,' he said, fidgeting with the keys in his hands.

'No, I told you, I'd give you a month's notice.'

He nodded desperately, and pointed towards the downstairs flat.

'The woman who lives there has complained of a leak in the ceiling below your kitchen. It was an emergency, I needed to get in there.'

I frowned. 'She didn't say anything to me.'

He looked up at me. 'Maybe she didn't feel comfortable enough to.'

*I nodded slowly, realising what he meant.*

*'Do you need to look?'*

*'If that's okay?'*

*I nodded, trailing back up the stairs, feeling Mike pace several steps behind me. I pushed open the door and let him into the flat, pointing at the kitchen.*

*'I'm really sorry about the mess. I was in the middle of tidying up. It won't look like this when I leave, I promise,' I said, wincing as Mike trod on a pile of dirty clothes as he made his way to the kitchen. 'Well, I'm just going to be in the bedroom.'*

*I left Mike in the kitchen and heard him opening the cupboard under the sink. I closed the bedroom door gently and started trying to sort through a pile of clothes. There was a gentle knock on the bedroom door, and Mike appeared, pushing the door gently with his fingertips.*

*'It looks okay,' he said, looking around my room.*

*'Okay, well, if I notice anything, I'll let you know.'*

*He nodded, and turned to leave, but stopped with his hand still outstretched and a palm spread across the door frame.*

*'Are you leaving because of him?' he said suddenly.*

*I stared, dumbfounded. 'Who?' I asked, trying to understand him.*

*'The man who was here, who you work with.' He was staring at me, intense brown eyes resting on my face. He looked so sad, defeated, like the question was killing me. I didn't know how to respond, I just stared at him, bewildered.*

*'He doesn't deserve you,' he said, pushing the door wider.*

I tried to speak, but the words tumbled clumsily through my lips and didn't make sense.

'I would treat you like you deserve.'

I wrapped my arms around my waist and took a step back. Catching my heel on the foot of the bed, I fell backwards on the springs and kicked back with my feet.

'I think you should leave,' I said, scrambling bed sheets over my naked legs. 'Now!'

He didn't move.

'Would you let me take care of you like you deserve?' he said, smiling.

I shook my head. 'No, I need you to leave.'

Then he looked at me with a twisted grimace, like a child that had been denied a toy. He took a step closer until he was standing in the doorway. I wanted to scream, but the noise was trapped in my throat.

'I've grown very fond of you, Emily,' he said, taking another step.

I thought back to when I saw him at the bar, the delight on his face when he wanted to win the champagne for me. The card propped up against a bottle outside my flat the next day. Then something worse, Mike letting himself into my flat, my home, so easily. The twist of a key.

## Chapter Forty

I push my tongue through my clenched teeth and will my throat to life. I make a noise I don't recognise and the pain loosens, my vision pricked with small fragments of colour. Mike's voice trickles into my ears, but fades away before I can grip the words. My throat rasps louder, my lips moving, my vision forced open by the sliver of light breaking onto me.

I twist to the side and my cheek brushes against something soft, I swat a hand up to my face and run my fingers alongside, feeling the gentle textures next to me. A motion in front of me, two heavy black boots, heels bouncing inches from my face.

'I didn't mean to,' Mike moans.

I lift my hand slowly and feel a sticky warmth pad my fingers as I clutch at my forehead. I will myself to think straight but my head feels broken, like something has pried it loose and I just need to fit it back into place. I push, hysterically, but moisture just lines my hands and it slips, cascading down my face and hitting the floor. A flash of crimson and the black boots edge further away.

I need to call for Clara or Ian. Mike can't know that they're outside waiting for me. My tongue is swollen and fat and when I try to speak, my teeth dig into the sides and I wince from the pain. My lips are numb against the tip of my tongue as I try desperately to call for my sister.

'She was a slut.'

He hisses the words like they're stuck in his throat and I feel small flecks of spittle land on my face. I need to try but I can't think straight. My head. Something is wrong. I will myself to call for Clara, to try, then there's another thought. The one of you.

My eyes lull back into my skull and I hear Mike sobbing gently.

'Shut up.'

Am I speaking? Have I said something? My throat gurgles but I can't be sure if words are coming out and a sharp metallic residue lingers on my tongue. All I can think of is holding your hand again, resting my head against your chest in our big leather chair, hearing your laugh. I start to cry, and a diluted red liquid skims the tips of my eyelashes. I close my eyes. Mike cries louder. But where is Emily?

'Don't say her name. You don't understand.

His voice is softer, damaged almost, like I've said a

magic word and it's disarmed him. I open my eyes and can almost make out Mike's outline. What did he do?

'I meant as much to Emily as she did to me. She was trying to leave me, like the others, but Emily, she was special, she couldn't leave.'

The others? Other tenants. Through the forming fog I remember. *I had to let it out again because the last girl cut the tenancy short.*

There's a dull thud and the boots shift towards me. I hear my name drowning in static. I feel like I'm underwater, sinking, and you'll catch me and we'll swim away together. *I want to, Ben, I want to see you again.* 'Who's that?' Mike whispers.

Who does he mean? Clara. I strain my swollen eyes and see Mike perched on the end of a chair. He's holding a knife in one hand, grasping it and pointing it my way. I can't see if he has already used it, but I hurt everywhere. I try to reach forward to grab it from him, but it's futile. He moves it slowly away, as if he's fast-forwarding the moment and I'm desperately trying to catch up. The knife points away and threatens something else, an object I can barely make out. It's green, plastic... Emily's handbag. I sob.

His voice lowers and he jolts upright, as if he's woken up from a deep sleep. The knife edges closer to the bag as he repeats the words like a mantra: *slut, bitch.* I think of Emily, how small she must have felt in London in that flat upstairs, how alone. Noise to drown out the loneliness, a thought I once had about her that now feels so misplaced. I feel like I'm staring at her as I watch the knife circle the bag, and I think of all the things I should have said.

*I can't come with you, Ben.* I stare at Emily's small bag. All her secrets, the conversations we never got to have. My name, clearer this time and another thud. Clara. *No, don't*, I gurgle, and spit flies across the rug. Mike bends down, and I feel something slot over my mouth like a bandage.

'Shut up.'

The black boots disappear from sight; sweat and snot congeal around my mouth and crust into my nostrils. I struggle to breathe as the rooms spins. The sound of a door opening and Clara's voice, clear, and authoritative.

'Suzie?' she asks.

*Run, Clara, please go.* I summon up the last energy I have – my love for my sister – and I reach up and dig my fingernails around my lips, scratching at the sodden mask covering my mouth. It eases off gently. Damp and bloodstained, it falls to the floor..

I say her name as loudly as I can, I tell her to run, I cry. I can't be sure if the words ever left my mouth, but there's a sharp noise, like a drill thrumming into my head. Then a loud crash and a coldness hits my back, different footsteps charging away. I bend my neck and see slivers of glass lining the floor and Ian is on top of

Mike, two pairs of boots fighting together, but I don't see Clara. Where is she?

Moisture seals my eyes and lips. There's a weight that presses down and releases as bubbles of spit clot around my lips. 'Clara,' I cry. Then nothing.

## Chapter Forty-One

'Suzie?'

My ears feel swollen and crushed, like pincers have attached themselves to each side. Ben. My head feels whole now, my body alert, my arms swaying gently to the rhythm of a current. I look up and there's a shadow overhead, a boat, balancing gently on the surface. The sun skims across the water, but stops before it gets to me. There are voices, laughing, the sound of chatter and bottles clinking together. *I'm down here*, I call.

But the voices only grow louder, occupied with themselves. I search for you, but see cloudy shades of blue, and distorted branches of weeds trailing from my feet. I stare down at the sea floor, muddled with cerulean coral and stone. *Ben*, I call. And the voices stop. Looking up I see round pink faces staring down at me through ripples of murky water. A hand reaches through, but it is not yours. *No*, I cry. I long for the weeds to coil around my feet and drag me down further. I long to hear your voice, just one last time, to tell me it will be okay.

*It will be*, you say. And I hear you, it skims the water like the pebbles we'd throw on the beach in Hove. This is not where I left you, this is not where you left me. These are memories. This is where I'm trying to get back to. *Come with me*, I say. But the arm is lower now, fingertips brushing against my floating hair. I reach up and take the hand. It feels good to hear your voice again. That you're living in the memories we had, the good ones. I'll live in them too, I promise.

There's a pull, and effortlessly I rise to the top, buoyant and whole.

'Suzie?'

I peel my eyes open and the light pierces the back of my skull.

'Turn it off!' someone snaps.

The light dims and I focus on the hand curled around mine.

'Clara,' I whisper.

Clara's face is bent into an expression I've never seen before, like all her features have sunk slightly on her face.

'Where am I?'

She doesn't smile. 'The hospital.'

'Am I okay?'

This time her eyes shift and her face looks grave.

'You're going to be,' she says slowly. 'Ian's gone to get a doctor. Mum and Dad are on their way.'

'Is my head okay?'

She bites her lip, gripping my hand harder. 'You're going to be okay,' she repeats.

'It's not broken?'

She smiles now, sweetly, her expression happier, and she puts another hand on top of mine. 'They've put you back together again,' she cries, letting the tears run down her face. 'Do you remember what happened?'

I nod. 'Ben.'

She bites her lip. 'You kept saying his name.'

'He…' I look at her. My lips are swollen and skinless; I let my tongue rest on them and look to the side for some water. Clara bends over, grabs a cup, produces a straw and gently rests it in my mouth.

'I was so scared,' she says, guiltily. 'You must have been so scared.' She removes the straw from my mouth and places it gently back on the side table.

'I don't remember how I felt,' I say.

I glance around the hospital room. I'm in a single bed and the glass walls have beige drawn shades. The door is wooden with a slim pane of glass. I can see through it into the corridor.

'Are we still in London?'

Clara reaches forward and strokes my hair.

'We're at the Royal London Hospital.'

The door opens and a breathless Ian enters, almost

dragging a doctor, a hand cuffed around her elbow. The doctor, a young woman, gives Ian a patient smile and shrugs herself free. She catches my eyes and smiles.

'Suzie,' she says, reaching forward to check the monitor. 'You've given us quite a scare,' she says. 'How are you feeling?'

'Okay,' I croak.

'You were in surgery,' Clara sniffles.

The doctor gives Clara another patient smile. 'You had internal bleeding in your skull, and the blood started to clot, but we've successfully drained the clotting and we managed to stabilise you. It's good news,' she says. 'It probably doesn't feel like it now.' She stares down at my face. 'I just need to do a few checks.'

'Can I stay?' Clara begs.

'Of course.' The doctor smiles. 'It won't take long.'

'Can I go home?' I ask.

The doctor flashes Clara a look and is about to speak, but Clara cuts her off. 'Not yet. You need to rest.'

'I don't want to rest, I want to go home.' I try to move, but my limbs feel detached from my body, and a pain shoots up my neck.

'Easy,' the doctor says. 'You'll be a little drowsy as we've had to give you some painkillers.' She looks down at me. 'You're safe,' she says.

I nod, searching for Clara hidden behind the doctor. Ian hovers in the background. I notice blood smeared up his arms and a bruise forming around his right eye. He looks down at the blood uneasily and towards me.

'I have to wait,' he says.

'Suzie, it's okay. The police need to take statements from us, but we didn't want to leave you.'

I lean back into the pillow as the doctor shines a light into my eyes. She retreats and nods at Clara.

'It's looking good. I'll be back in thirty minutes for another check.'

'Thank you,' Clara whispers.

'Are the police here?' I ask.

She nods.

'How you doing, Suzie?' Ian asks, approaching the bed.

I stare at his arms, the blood.

'You're upsetting her. Wait outside.'

Ian stares at me waiting for it to be okay, but I just stare back. Clara's right. Ian nods and walks out, closing the door behind.

'He saved you,' Clara says. 'I can't—' She starts to cry. 'We thought you'd...'

'Mike,' I say. 'The knife?'

She glances back towards the door. 'The blood, it's not yours.' She pauses. 'It's Mike's.' Clara cries harder. 'They want to talk to you.'

'Who?'

'The police.'

There's a rap on the door. Detective Peters appears, looking exhausted and concerned.

'Two minutes,' she says, turning to me. 'I'll be right outside.' She looks at the detective before rising from the chair and leaving us.

He stands awkwardly in the doorway, drops his gaze to the floor and slowly makes his way to the side of my bed.

'I'm so sorry,' he says, lowering himself into a chair.

'Mike?'

He looks up at me, his blue eyes wide and desperate. I see them scan my face, each glance painful for him.

'Is it that bad?' I say, my voice raspy and dry.

He shakes his head and then nods. 'Yeah, it is,' he says.

'I haven't looked yet,' I say.

He doesn't reply.

'Where's Mike?'

'Suzie, he's dead.'

I try to shake my head but a pain spikes across my shoulders and I wince. Dead?

'Ian managed to wrestle the knife out of his hands, but he tried to attack your sister. He wouldn't stop...'

'I want my sister,' I say.

He nods. 'Of course, I just wanted to'—he goes to place a hand on mine, but stops—'make sure you were okay.'

I look towards the door, and see Clara peering

through the pane of glass. I try to nod. She sees, and storms in.

'That's enough,' she says, turning to Detective Peters. 'It's time for you to do your job,' she hisses.

He doesn't react, but just stares at me. He nods, sucking in his lips.

'We'll need to ask some questions, when you're up to it.'

I nod. 'I'm just tired.'

'Yes, of course you are, sorry.'

'Leave,' Clara demands.

She takes his spot in the chair and cups my hand in hers. Detective Peters retreats from the hospital room and leaves me staring after him. I succumb to the weight of my eyes and lie back.

'Are you okay?' I whisper.

'I'm fine,' she says softly.

'He's dead?'

She nods.

I stare longingly at the closed hospital room door and see Detective Peters bent over in a waiting room chair, fingers clasped around tufts of hair. I should have told him it wasn't his fault.

## Chapter Forty-Two

When I wake up, my head is tipped to the side and I'm looking at my mum. Her soft, pale features are framed by her long, fiery hair as she sleeps curled up in a chair next to my bed, her long arms wrapped around her small frame. She's wearing a baggy blue jumper and jeans. Her eyes are stained with mascara and light brown lipstick smudges her cheek. I realise how long it's been since I've seen her; I always denied her requests to visit London, always said I'd come home soon. She looks fragile, thinner, with slim lines circling her mouth. I realise now how much I've missed her, her composure, her optimism. I want to reach out and take her hand and pull her in, but I feel motionless, as if I've been glued to the bed.

I wiggle my tongue, but I can't feel it touch the inside

of my cheeks. The rest of my face feels numb, apart from the gentle brush of eyelashes as I blink.

'Mum,' I attempt, my voice strained.

My mum's eyes flicker open. She has a moment of realisation before she turns to me, blue eyes wide and desperate, searching mine. She leans forward, grabbing my hand.

'Suzie,' she says, resting the other hand on top of my head, something she would always do when I was little. She starts to cry, small droplets landing on my throat. 'Sorry,' she says, smiling. She lets go of my hand and dabs at my throat with the bed sheet.

'Hey, Mum,' I say. I look towards the door.

'Your dad went to get us some coffee. I think he wanted to talk to the police,' she says. 'He'll be back soon, don't worry.'

'Is it that bad?' I ask.

'Nothing that won't fix,' she says, brushing back stray strands of my hair.

'Clara?'

'She's making her statement to the police, with Ian. They'll want to take your statement soon, I imagine.'

'Is Ian okay?'

She leans back. 'He's pretty shaken, but they aren't charging him. It was self-defence and he was protecting you and your sister.'

'I was so close,' I say.

She tilts her head. 'To what?'

'Going home.'

'We'll get you there,' she says.

The door opens and my dad shoulders his way through, carrying two plastic cups of coffee.

'She's awake,' my mum says, rising. 'I'm going to find a doctor, okay? I'll be right back.' She leans forward and kisses the top of my forehead.

'I'm not going anywhere,' I say, trying to smile. My mum winces, then forces a smile. She takes a coffee from my dad and glances at me again before leaving.

'Hey, Dad,' I say as he wanders over to the other side of the bed. Instead of sitting in a chair, he eases himself onto the bed, next to my legs, and lays a hand on my shin.

'Hey, love.' He stares down at me, his eyes scanning my face. 'How you doing?'

'Great,' I say, trying to laugh, but spluttering instead. My chest feels heavy and tight, and I press my hand on it, trying to find a release.

'Easy,' my dad says.

'I'm okay,' I say. 'Will you find me a mirror? I want to see my face.'

He shakes his head slowly. 'I don't think that's a good idea.'

'Please.'

'It'll upset you,' he says. 'No,' he adds forcefully.

My dad takes a long sip of coffee and looks at the door.

'The police want to talk to you. Are you up to that?'

I nod.

'Okay, well, they're going to have the doctor come in and do another check-up before they do.' He stands up. 'Suzie...' he pauses, trying to find the right words, 'what you did for that girl, how far you went to find her—' He nods, his eyes red and swollen, and chokes, shunning the rest.

He raises his hand and signals to the corridor. 'That man in reception, the detective...' He looks at me and parts his mouth to speak, but stops, nodding instead.

The door opens and the doctor enters. She glances at my dad.

'Hey, Suzie.' My mum trails after her, hands clasped tight.

'There's an Inspector Freeman and Detective Peters outside waiting to talk to you. Are you up to that, Suzie?' the doctor says, tending to the machine buckled to me. 'I'm going to come back afterwards and give you more painkillers, but if at any time you're in pain, press this button.' She holds up a control and shows me a small button on top of it. 'Getting you healthy again is the top priority at the moment.'

'Do you want me to stay?' my mum asks.

I try to shake my head, but a pain shoots up my right jaw.

'No,' I say finally.

'Okay, we'll be right outside if you need us.' She

beckons to my dad and takes his hand. I watch them leave. On the other side of the door, Inspector Freeman and Detective Peters hover with notepads in position. They pass my parents, Detective Peters staring down at the floor as he holds the door open for Inspector Freeman.

'Hi, Suzie,' the inspector says, marching across the room. He tugs at one of the chairs and slips it further away from the bed, positioning it at the foot of the bed, so I don't have to angle my head to look at him. Detective Peters stands next to him, a hand gripping the bottom of the bedframe.

'Thank you for agreeing to answer some questions,' Freeman says. 'I'll try and keep this short. I wanted to say, first of all'—he clears his throat—'that we're sorry that this happened.'

Detective Peters's knuckles have turned white from his grip on the bedframe. I try and search his eyes, but he remains passively staring down towards the floor.

'Your sister tells us that you were at Mike's to collect a house key?'

I nod. 'Yeah.' I cough. 'My key.'

'Good, okay, and what happened when you arrived at his place?'

'He opened the door, I asked for the key, he went upstairs to get it.' I try to shake my head. 'No, he didn't go upstairs, sorry. He went to the kitchen, he thought it would be there, but it wasn't.'

'Okay, good, then what happened?'

'When he was looking for the key, I walked into the hallway, and looked through the lounge door, I don't know why.'

I remember the rub of the pamphlet stuck to the bottom of my shoe, the confusion when I pulled it free. Had I thought in that moment that Mike knew something? I can't be sure.

'Mike came back from the kitchen and I moved back, but a bit of his post had stuck to the bottom of my shoe and I saw his name on it, and the name of the bar Emily would go to with work colleagues. That's when he said the key was upstairs. He asked me to shut the door and I didn't think anything of it, but it was the notepad.' *I'm watching you, bitch.* 'I saw a notepad with something written on it and I couldn't place it. When Mike came back his mood was different. Maybe he saw me looking at the notepad, I don't know.' The smell of Mike's stale breath, the pain trembling through my throbbing skull. 'He asked me about Emily.' I look up at them. 'Emily?'

Inspector Freeman looks at Detective Peters and then back to me.

'We need to find out what happened, and we will,' he says reassuringly.

'He was the first person in her flat. He was the first person I called when she disappeared,' I say.

Freeman nods. 'We know.'

'He could have changed something, done something.'

'We know,' Freeman repeats.

'Do you know where she is? Where she might be?'

'We're following up some leads. We've asked his neighbours.' He shakes his head. 'No one has seen Emily in or around his property.'

'What did he do to her?'

Freeman doesn't answer. He closes his notepad. 'We'll keep you updated,' he says. He stands up and leaves, but Detective Peters doesn't follow.

He waits until Inspector Freeman has closed the door and we're alone. 'I want to speak to you,' he says.

Clara bursts through the door, eyeing the detective before making her way to the side of my bed. Detective Peters turns awkwardly. 'Another time,' he says, before leaving.

'He hasn't left the waiting room since he got here,' Clara says.

I watch him through the small window on the hospital door. What did he want to say?

I turn my attention to Clara as she lovingly strokes my arm. I try and remember every interaction I had with Mike, but they just float away from me. I trusted him, didn't I? He had a key to my home, I rang him and complained about Emily and he agreed with me. She isn't being respectful of the tenancy agreement. That's what he'd said. But it was more than that. What else wasn't she being respectful of?

'What did he do to Emily?'

Clara shakes her head sombrely. 'Try not to think about it right now.'

'But it's all I can think about. Did she upset him? Was it an accident? He sounded so angry, he called her a slut. Were there other tenants before her?' I feel bile rise in my throat and tears choke me. 'He said she was a slut. *Was*,' I emphasise, looking at Clara.

'They haven't found her yet,' Clara soothes.

'But what if you hadn't found me?' I say.

Clara flinches. 'Shall I get Mum and Dad?'

'I just want to leave this place. I want to go home and I can't, I'm trapped here. Every time I want to leave, something bad happens, like London is punishing me. I want to go home,' I cry.

'It won't be long.'

I start swatting my arms, trying to pull tubes free. I wriggle my legs against the covers. 'No, I want to go home now, I can't stay here anymore.'

'Please, Suzie,' Clara says, softly placing her arms on mine. 'You need to rest and the sooner you do that the sooner we can go home.'

'No,' I cry. 'It will stop me again,' I say, crying harder. I scream as loudly as my throat will allow me and the door flies open. Footsteps charge across the room and hands coil around me. I cry for it to stop. I see Detective Peters standing in the back of the crowd, and my mum pleading for it to stop, and then my body shrinks and I feel light, before I drop into darkness.

## Chapter Forty-Three

When I wake up the room is deathly quiet and the lights are set to a faint glow. Even as I gaze out through the small glass panel, the corridor looks empty and asleep. I don't see him at first, and it makes me jump. Detective Peters lies slumped in a chair. His large black coat drapes his shoulders, his uniformed legs are propped up and his arms are folded outwards, almost as if he is sculpted to the chair.

His eyes open, like he's aware someone is watching him. His body tenses and his arms propel forward like he's ready – ready for what?

He turns to me expectantly and drops his arms, tiredness ensuing as he realises where he is.

'Where is everyone?' I ask, testing my throat. It feels looser, and the initial burn has subsided.

'I said I'd watch you, that I'd stay.'

'Oh,' I say, surprised.

'Your sister didn't like the idea.'

I want to laugh.

'But she was so tired that her husband managed to convince her to get some sleep.'

'Where are they?'

'A hotel, just down the road. I recommended it. They won't have to spend a fortune.'

I frown. 'Did you not want to get some sleep?'

'Well, it looks like I have been,' he says, stretching his legs. 'I didn't want to leave you alone, after they had to sedate you.'

I close my eyes.

'Are you feeling better?'

'Yes,' I say, looking at him. 'But I've probably cost myself a few more days with that outburst. So stupid, I was just feeling—'

He nods. 'It won't cost you. What you've been through is just...' He looks back at me. 'They'll recommend some people for you to talk to. You'll get referred to counselling, but they won't keep you here, if that's what you're worried about. You're dealing with this better than most people I know, and I've seen some stuff.'

He licks his lips and runs his hands through greasy hair.

'You look awful,' I say.

He laughs now, a mild laugh, but it creeps up to his

eyes as he gazes at me.

'You should go home, shower.'

'I should,' he says. 'But I'm not going to.'

We sit for a moment in silence.

'You shouldn't blame yourself,' I say. 'If that's why you're here.'

'I do, but that's not why I'm here.'

'I don't understand.'

'I lost somebody too,' he says suddenly. 'I know how broken and lost it makes you feel. How you say and do stupid things and everything that happens afterwards just feels like some kind of horrible mistake, even the good things,' he says, tears slipping down his face.

'Who?'

'My wife,' he says, clasping his hands together. 'She was in a car accident.' He shakes his head. 'I wasn't there – she was with friends.'

'I'm so sorry,' I say.

'I just know that loss is the worst kind of pain, and it took me a really long time to stop punishing myself. People saying, "It's not your fault" doesn't even make a mark on how much guilt you feel for something over which you had no control. What if I had been in the car and she had been sitting in a different seat, what if it had been raining and the trip had been cancelled, what if I'd surprised her with our own weekend away… I just know one thing: no one, not a single soul, could ever have talked me out of those feelings. I just needed to ride them, I needed to be consumed by them, endure them, and then one day wake up and feel sad, so painfully sad that I didn't want to live anymore – but not guilty.'

'I would have understood, if you'd told me,' I say.

'I know you would. I know,' he says. 'When I met you and found out about Ben, I panicked. And it all made sense a bit more, how adamant you were about pursuing Emily, mostly by yourself. I panicked,' he repeats.

I nod. 'Maybe you were right too. Look at me.' I smile.

He extends his arm and this time wraps a hand around mine. We sit like that for a while, both lost in our own thoughts.

'Can I get you anything?' he says finally.

I shake my head. 'I'm feeling quite tired.'

'Yes, of course.' He looks down at his watch. 'It's 5am, I'll let you get some more sleep before your family arrive.'

'Do you think they'll discharge me soon?'

'I don't know.'

'I want to go home,' I say. I look at him. 'To Hove.'

'I'll come and see you again later,' he says.

'I'd like that,' I say.

When I fall asleep, I dream about you. The time we went camping in Cornwall, and the rain pummelling the roof as we swigged cheap whisky and laughed. Us relenting the next day and booking into a cheap bed and breakfast, admitting we couldn't quite hack it anymore.

Old, we called ourselves, like we were anywhere near it. We were young, surviving on little sleep and fuelled by passion and thrill. You reached over, your tall frame smothering me, and I loved the weight of it. The weight of you. You anchored me, and now I'm adrift, flotsam in the water, a wreckage.

There's a gentle tug on my arm and I wake up to see my mum's wide eyes staring down at me. Her hair tickles my chin and she smiles, almost mischievously.

'Suzie, you're awake.'

'Yes,' I say, spitting out one of her stray hairs. 'I'm awake.'

She leans back, fidgeting with her fingers. She's sat on the edge of my bed. My dad hovering in the background, holding a coffee cup. He waves awkwardly.

'Hey.'

'How are you feeling?' he asks.

'Better, much better.'

My mum rolls her eyes, then I see her regret it. 'Sorry,' she says.

'You don't believe me?'

'You really scared us last night,' she says, brushing the tips of my hair.

'Emily,' I whisper.

'They'll find her,' my mum soothes.

'When do I get to go home?'

'We spoke to the doctor this morning and they said in a couple of days if you remain stable.'

'So remain stable,' my dad adds.

'They're worried about you, because of last night, but I said, the amount of drugs they've got you on, you can't be expected to think straight. Try to put it out of your mind, focus on getting better.'

'We're so proud of you, for doing everything you could to find that girl.'

'You make it sound like she's dead.'

'We didn't say that, it's just—'

'I know,' I say.

I think about Ian fighting Mike to the ground, the two pairs of boots clashing together, the shattered glass and the struggle that ensued. Clara had screamed, I remember that much, and Ian had saved her the only way he could. But now Mike's dead and I can't understand it. Now there's no one who knows where Emily is.

## Chapter Forty-Four

After two long days spent waiting in the hospital bed, the doctor has finally given the okay for me to leave. My head still aches, but I'm prescribed painkillers to take regularly to ease the pain. The swelling has started to loosen around my jaw, but the bruises around my eyes and neck are more prominent than before. I don't like to look at myself in the mirror. I don't like to remember.

My parents have given me regular updates on the investigation into Mike and Emily, but there's been no progress.

I don't want to leave London with it so unresolved. I've come so far, but it's the way everyone is acting around me, like the efforts have been for nothing. I hate thinking about Mike in those moments I lie alone when visiting hours are over. Replaying all the times I'd spoken to him, alerting him that Emily's door was open, and how he walked around her flat faking concern. I try not to think about what he did to me, but my memory of the event is fuzzy anyway. All I can remember is Clara saying my name, all I can feel is my worry for her.

I know something bad has happened to Emily. I knew it the moment I stepped into her flat. It was the same feeling I had when I woke up the morning after Ben's accident, when I turned over and saw the empty space next to me. How could I even sleep when he hadn't arrived home? He'd stayed out before, at friends', after a heavy night drinking, but never after a fight. You were the emotional one, weren't you? I suppressed everything, always found that easier. I was too logical – until all my logic vanished.

On the day I'm allowed to leave, the doctor comes in carrying a plastic bag full of my things. 'I had to check with the police before we could return these to you,' she says, placing it onto the end of the bed, 'just in case they needed it.'

I look at the scrunched-up bag. The clothes aren't there; they'll be held as evidence, I think. I rifle through it. Taking out my phone, I see the screen is cracked down the middle and I can't turn it on. I must have fallen on it in the commotion with Mike. I place it back down, not wanting to linger on the thought any longer. I see a small flash of red in the bottom of the bag and turn the bag over, shaking it until the object falls loose onto the bed.

It's the key Mike gave me, with nail varnish coating it. I freeze, unable to understand. Red is for the bike shed.

'Is everything okay?' the doctor says, watching me.

'I don't know,' I say.

I try and think back to Mike's hallway, him handing over the key and I stop. I looked down at it, I saw the red, and I looked up at him. I had seen it without really seeing it.

'I need to use a phone.'

---

'Are you sure you want to do this?' Detective Peters asks again as we round the corner into my road. It's weird seeing it again now, like I'd left it so long ago. I'm not sure if I want to do this, but I need to. I nod as we pull up outside my flat. I stare up at the house on the corner, my old home, its white brickwork and overgrown front garden. It looks so full of promise in the lazy afternoon sunlight.

Detective Peters opens the door for me and I see Inspector Freeman pull up behind us.

'She insisted on coming,' Peters says to him, as Inspector Freeman holds out an expectant hand. He acknowledges me as Detective Peters hands him the key and he nods.

'Wait out here,' he demands.

Peters smiles. 'Please,' he adds, before following Inspector Freeman up the path and into the house.

I stand with my arms crossed, trying to see through the closed curtains into my empty flat. I itch, wanting to follow them. I had never given Mike a key to the bike shed. I try to push away the thought of him letting himself into my home, of him peeling the keys off your keychain, the one with the little Lego Indiana Jones that had been returned to me with the rest of your things. How could I not know that it was missing? I hope I'm wrong and when Inspector Freeman yanks open the dusty bike shed all they'll see is your rusty blue bike wedged at the back, covered in spider webs.

I can't wait any longer. I burst through the front door into my empty flat.. I turn to see Detective Peters standing in the narrow doorway leading to the courtyard. He's saying something into a phone, but I can't hear him. I just tread forward until I can see Inspector Freeman above the rows of dead plants outside the kitchen window, the flash of a blue tarpaulin and then Detective Peters's touch on my forearm.

'Emily,' I whisper, as I see a small pale hand fall onto the concrete.

Detective Peters moves his body to block the view, but I can't stop seeing it. Her translucent skin and slim fingers, veins snaking up her limp arm. I want to cup her hand, to comfort her, to tell her I'm sorry.

## Chapter Forty-Five

My dad helped me into the car and gave me a cushion to prop behind my neck. Clara demanded that she ride in the back with me. Ian would drive the van back to Hove with my things.

I felt like I was on the way to a family holiday. I let my neck loll to the side and gaze out of the window, watching London slowly fall away and dissipate into countryside.

I asked my dad to take the country roads home, but he protested at first, saying he didn't want the bends and dips in the road to aggravate my still sore head. I told him it was okay and so we took the long way back to Hove.

Most of the journey was silent, my mum asking if I needed anything every once and a while. Clara fell asleep against the window and I smiled as she twitched at the sunlight hitting the glass through the rows of trees. We stopped after an hour to stretch our legs and I waited in the car whilst my mum fetched coffees and a tea for me. I slurped it lovingly as we hit the home straight.

I started noticing familiarities in the roads, places I recognised when I lived here. Nostalgia swarmed over me and I felt like I was floating through memories that I'd misplaced. Small things. The garage where I'd fill up my car on the way to work. The park where I'd meet friends on sunny afternoons. The old theatre where I'd go to see amateur dramatics on Thursdays.

There are a lot of memories here and most of them are good. Today, even the bad ones seem bright.

'When were you last back here?' my dad asks.

'It must be nearly three years now.'

I'd been so near, but I could never quite get here. Clara stirs next to me and yawns lazily, then, turning to me with sleepy eyes, she grins.

'We must be nearly there.'

'Not much further,' my mum reassures her.

There are so many memories of you lying around, but they're not as painful as I thought they'd be. Instead I smile as we trundle down a narrow road past the local chip shop. I wind down the window and let the buttery aromas circle in the car. I see the bait shop, where you would go early on Saturday mornings. You loved fishing – I laugh as I remember – but you were so bad at it.

'He never caught anything,' I say. 'But he loved the water.'

Clara reaches over and squeezes my hand. 'Maybe that's what surprised me about it, him wanting to move to London. I thought he liked it here.'

The air tastes salty and sweet. I lick my lips and close my eyes, taking a long, deep breath.

'Can we get ice-cream?' I ask.

'Of course,' my mum says. 'We'll get you settled in first, okay?'

I nod.

We pull down my parents' road and my stomach drops, my cheeks flush with pain. I start to cry silently against the back of my hand.

'Are you okay?' my sister asks.

'Yeah, it's just quite overwhelming,' I reply, wiping my cheeks vigorously.

The house sits in a small cul-de-sac just on the outskirts of Hove. It's only a few roads away from the sea and, as Clara helps me out of the car, I hear seagulls squawk high above us and I taste the salty spray carried on the wind. I look up at my old home, a detached Tudor building with exposed black beams, and the small front garden sitting behind a black gate and a red brick wall.

'It's how I remember it,' I say smiling.

My mum leads the way inside. She beckons me in and a soft cinnamon scent wafts through the hallway. I stand for a moment in the doorway and take it in. The walls covered in wooden plaques with quotes written in swirly writing. The kitchen visible through the glass-paned door, the counter covered in celebration tins and wicker bowls filled with fruit.

'We didn't have time to tidy,' my mum says guiltily. 'Judy from next door popped over and put some stuff in the fridge for us, milk and that.'

I wander through the hallway and into the kitchen, tracing my fingertips along the rough oak surface of the large dining table that sits in the middle. The double patio doors open out onto a garden overflowing with shrubbery and plotted plants. My eyes rest on the olive tree obscuring the wooden decking at the back of the garden.

'It's perfect.'

I turn around and my mum produces a gift bag, smiling at me as she hands it over.

'You didn't have to do this.'

'We didn't,' my mum admits, eyeing me coyly.

I peer into the bag and see an envelope sitting on top. I peel it open and read on the front of the card 'Get Well Soon' in sparkly silver letters. I expect it to be from friends in Hove who popped by, but when I open the card I see Noah's name at the bottom before I even read the message. I can feel my mum's hand on my shoulder squeezing gently.

*Dear Suzie,*

*For your collection. Wishing you a speedy recovery.*

*Love, Noah*

*P.S. I've never been to Hove*

I reach into the bag and pull out a book wrapped in soft pink tissue paper. I unwrap it and trace my fingers over the front cover. *The Mysterious Affair at Styles* by Agatha Christie.

'That's her first published book,' my dad says, joining us.

I smile and then repeat it aloud to the room, hearing a small twinge of excitement in my voice.

'He's never been to Hove.'

———————

The next day we take a walk down to the beach. Clara's hand slides into mine and she grips my fingers in hers.

'I have to go back to Brighton tomorrow, for the kids, for Ian,' she says, looking at me guiltily. 'I'll come and visit you again next weekend.'

I nod. 'I'd like to see the kids soon.'

She grins. 'And they'd love to see you. They have a fond memory of you taking them to get chocolate lollipops.'

I smile. 'They weren't supposed to tell you.'

'Ah, well, not much gets past me.'

My mum and dad amble slowly behind us and I can feel them watching Clara and me. It makes me feel little again, feel like running and screaming into the bellowing afternoon sun.

'We should go to the pub tonight, if you're up to it,' Clara says.

I smack my lips. The taste of salt lingers on my tongue and I smile. As we round the corner, the wet coastal breeze licks my face. Clara holds on tighter, as though I might float away like a kite in the gentle wind.

We approach the sea wall and I let go of her hand and place my palms face down on the coarse pebbled surface.

'Do you want to go for a paddle?' Clara asks.

I gaze out across the leaden-blue sea, waves gently lapping the stony beach. A woman is wading in the shallow water, her arms arched over a toddler, grasping his hands as he kicks out as the waves chase him.

'No, I just want to sit.'

My parents catch up to us and my mum slots an arm through mine. 'It's been a while since you saw this beach,' she says.

'It's beautiful, I almost forgot how beautiful.'

They help me over the wall and we lean side by side, looking out onto the sea, It's not far from the place you asked me to marry you. Our love was never quiet, was it? Our love always demanded attention. We were wrapped up in the noise of each other. I look out at the small sail boats bobbing restlessly on the water. I hear the pebbles we once threw break the surface. I see memories, but not just the ones here, the ones wherever we were.

I think about Emily, what she would say if she were here. I imagine me and her, side by side, tucking into a bag of chips, her tanned legs dangling off the sea wall, her red wellies swinging back and forth. We have the conversations we should always have had. She's smiling. For a moment, everything is completely still – everything is silent.

## Acknowledgments

I want to say thank you to my mum for reading everything I've put under her nose since I was little, from my childhood stories about dragons to my edgy teen poetry years. Thank you for teaching me to be resilient and never give up on myself and my dreams.

To my partner for supporting and encouraging me, and for understanding how important it is to me. For bringing me cups of coffee and being a sounding board on long walks – you can have in writing that you're the better cook.

Thank you to my agent, Amanda Preston, for taking a chance on me, guiding me through my publishing journey and helping to shape *The Girl Upstairs*.

To my wonderful publisher and editor, Bethan Morgan, and everyone at OMC for working with me to bring you *The Girl Upstairs*.

To London, you brilliant beast, there really is no place quite like it.

To all the other books and authors out there for inspiring me and giving me the courage to write my own stories.

Most of all, thank you to my readers, for picking up my little book and giving it your time.

**ONE MORE CHAPTER**

YOUR NUMBER ONE STOP
FOR PAGETURNING BOOKS

One More Chapter is an
award-winning global
division of HarperCollins.

Sign up to our newsletter to get our
latest eBook deals and stay up to date
with our weekly Book Club!
<u>Subscribe here.</u>

Meet the team at
<u>www.onemorechapter.com</u>

Follow us!
@<u>OneMoreChapter</u>_
@<u>OneMoreChapter</u>
@<u>onemorechapterhc</u>

Do you write unputdownable fiction?
We love to hear from new voices.
Find out how to submit your novel at
<u>www.onemorechapter.com/submissions</u>